USA TODAY BEST SELLING AUTHOR

KRISTEN PAINTER

BOOK TWO

THE VAMPIRE'S CURSED KISS

THE VAMPIRES'S CURSED KISS
Shadowvale, Book Two

Copyright © 2019 Kristen Painter

This book is a work of fiction. The characters, events, and places portrayed in this book are products of the author's imagination and are either fictitious or are used fictitiously. Any similarity to real person, living or dead, is purely coincidental and not intended by the author.

Published in the United States of America.

Shadowvale isn't your typical small town America. The sun never shines, the gates decide who enters, magic abounds, and every resident bears some kind of curse.

Vampire Constantin Thibodeaux was cured of his sun "allergy" when he moved to Shadowvale. Now he runs the local bookstore, which is really just a sideline to filling his own library. Books, unlike people, are far more forgiving of his prickly nature. But he doesn't care if people don't like him. He is who he is. And he's happy. Well, he's content. Okay, he's…fine.

Sprite and all around party girl Andromeda Merriweather loves her carefree life—or at least she did until her sister cursed her into a magical time out. Thankfully, she's just been set free by a totally hot, but kind of grumpy vampire. Too bad this handsome grouch now holds the key to her freedom, something she'll only get if he agrees to abide by the rules of her curse.

Constantin isn't interested in the terms and conditions Andromeda gives him, until he needs her to be his temporary girlfriend to shut his brother up. Then Constantin agrees. But what happens after a surprisingly fun evening creates brand new problems for both of them. Sure, two opposites can attract, but will that attraction last? Or are they both too cursed to give love a chance?

CHAPTER ONE

The shop's front door opened, and gentle chimes rang through the Gilded Page, alerting Constantin Thibodeaux that someone had entered his bookstore.

He looked out from between the two rows where he was inspecting his inventory. And the shelving skills of his only employee, Fletcher. Whose skills were...fine. But there was always room for improvement.

At least the young vampire was good at getting coffee, something he was doing at the moment. The Black Horse bakery had recently begun serving some of the best Constantin had tasted in a long while, and as a favor to him, they'd started stocking a blend with chicory. Nostalgia wasn't always something he gave in to, but the coffee reminded him of his long-ago life in New Orleans, and he liked that.

He didn't even mind that, unlike everything else in the bakery, the coffee wasn't free. Spending money on coffee wasn't an extravagance. Especially when it was good coffee.

But the chimes hadn't sounded because a customer had come in. It was Arnie, the delivery man. Constantin didn't need to see Arnie to know it was him. He recognized the young man by the particular scent of his blood. Humans were easy to single out that way. At least for most vampires. The Thibodeauxes were no exception.

He came out from the rows to greet the man. "Hello, Arnie."

"Hello, Mr. Thibodeaux." Arnie wheeled the stacked dolly into the shop. "Big shipment today."

"Yes, an estate sale I won in an auction." Constantin had been looking forward to the arrival of this particular allotment since he'd found it for sale online. Winning the auction hadn't taken much—there'd been only a few other bidders, from what he could gather. And none with pockets quite as deep as his. He did a quick count of the boxes. "Is that all of it?"

"No, I've got three more in the truck."

"Excellent." Constantin rubbed his hands together. Although he prided himself on a shop stocked with a good assortment of new books, his true love was the rare and unusual. He had quite a few customers who appreciated the same, but then, Shadowvale was home to a large populace of supernaturals, many with the funds that made such indulgences almost commonplace.

Because of that, his shop did fairly well. Something that pleased him. He liked not relying on family money whenever possible, and he hadn't for many years now.

This lot had been purchased without the chance to inspect it personally, but he trusted the auction house's pictures and descriptions. According to what he'd seen online, there were several books in the assortment that would make the price he'd paid well worth it.

If he decided to sell them.

He sighed. Keeping the best and most interesting for himself was indulgent. He tried to temper that instinct. To keep himself from going down the path that so many of his kind did. His brother was a prime example. Whatever Valentino wanted, he got.

To Constantin, that seemed like a character flaw. His brother didn't agree. But then, Constantin and Valentino hadn't seen eye to eye in many years. They were cordial, but their relationship was a very shallow one, something Constantin was fine with.

Unfortunately, keeping the best books for his personal library also didn't exactly improve the store's bottom line. Fortunately, turning a profit wasn't completely necessary.

Arnie carefully unloaded the boxes, then went out to the truck for the rest. Fletcher passed him as he was headed out. Fletcher had a large coffee in each hand, but he also held a small bag from the bakery.

He set Constantin's cup on the counter. "Here you go."

"Thank you. What else did you get?"

Fletcher glanced at the bag. "Blueberry scone for my break. Fresh out of the oven." He shrugged. "Hard to say no."

Constantin swallowed a comment about impulsive behavior. That would be calling the kettle black when he'd just decided some of the new books would be joining his own library.

Fletcher looked at the boxes. "New shipment, I see. Do you need me to inventory them?"

"No, I'll handle these. The shelves still need to be dusted, and there's a bulb out in the cookbook section." Constantin sipped his coffee. The subtle bitterness of the chicory tasted like home.

Fletcher nodded. "I'm on it." He stuck the bakery bag under the counter, then took the feather duster out and went to work.

Arnie returned with the last of the boxes, and when they were all stacked next to the front counter, Constantin signed the delivery form and wished the man a nice day.

He waited until Arnie was in his truck and driving off before lifting the entire stack of boxes and carrying them into his office. Wouldn't do to show off his vampire strength in front of a nonresident human, even if the town's magic had a way of muting the memories of temporary human visitors, such as delivery people. Somehow, the town allowed them to find Shadowvale, but then removed itself from their minds. Further proof of just how strong the magic was here.

Constantin set the boxes on the floor in front of his desk, then went back for his coffee. He called out to Fletcher, who was on a ladder in the cookbook aisle. "I'll be in my office if you need me."

He answered with a nod. "Yes, Mr. Thibodeaux."

Constantin went back to his office, shut the door,

and inhaled. The smell of old leather and aged paper might not be the most pleasant aroma to some, but to him it was a balm that could right the most chaotic day. He put his coffee on his desk, then began opening the boxes to see what else awaited him beyond the few promised books mentioned in the auction.

He took out a legal pad and inventoried the books one box at a time. In the first, a few philosophy books were mixed in with a handful of bound scientific journals. All very interesting. The high school might benefit from a few of the books. Or perhaps they'd be better off in the library's reference section. Some were definitely sellable.

Besides the folks who lived in Shadowvale, Constantin had amassed a select online clientele over the years, and a few of those names came to mind when he surveyed his new arrivals.

He'd sell a good number of these books. Enough to recoup some of what he'd spent. That would keep Gracie Evermore, his bookkeeper, from cringing too much. Naturally, some of the others would go onto the shop floor to tempt the casual buyer.

Reading was a very popular pastime in Shadowvale, something that made the town that much dearer to him. He'd always held that reading was good for both the body and the soul. If one had a soul.

And while the popularity of reading in Shadowvale was impressive, being able to daywalk without fear of the sun's harmful rays was the best thing about living here. At least for a vampire. Some considered Shadowvale's perpetually overcast skies to be the town's weightiest curse, but for the vampires who called it home, it was the town's greatest asset.

And one of the main reasons the Thibodeauxes had moved here.

Another box held art history books and several coffee-table-type art books. A few of those would go on the shop shelves, but at least one would go into his personal library. As would the three plays by Shakespeare in the next box, except for the copy of *Hamlet*. The one he already had was in better condition.

He kept going, managing to sort out a good handful of books to sell and a couple more that he thought would be of interest to some of his local customers in particular. He wrote their names on slips of paper that he tucked inside the front covers, then those books went on a designated shelf on the office wall.

Those people would be called later and apprised of what he'd found. If they weren't interested, the books would be moved to the shop floor.

Finally, he was down to the last crate. It seemed to hold the oldest books, judging by how carefully they'd been packaged. They were all individually wrapped in brown paper.

Undeniable excitement zipped through him. He was about to dig in, but the disarray of his office caught his eye. He frowned. He preferred order, especially in his personal spaces. So he delayed gratification to gather up the empty, flattened boxes and take them out to the alley behind the shop to the large recycling bin shared by all the stores on that block.

With that done, he returned to his office to unwrap the final books, eager to see if there were any additional treasures among them. One by one, he stacked them on his desk and began to peel the paper off them.

He wasn't disappointed. The first package contained a rare first edition C.S. Lewis that would definitely be going into his personal library. That one had been advertised in the auction. The next few books were valuable, but nothing that interested him. That was fine. He'd have more to sell.

But the last book was so odd that he couldn't help but keep it for himself. He took a seat at his desk and turned the worn hardback over in his hands. The brown cloth cover was tattered, but the title was still readable. He spoke it out loud, just to hear it for himself. *"The Hidden History of Insane Asylums in 19th Century Europe."*

Perhaps a little morbid. But his interest was piqued. History was something a lot of vampires enjoyed reading about, having lived so long and experienced so much of it. Always curious to read another's perspective on something. Not that he'd had any experience with European asylums, but who had in modern times? No one he knew. Thankfully. He was about to crack the book and have a look through it when Fletcher knocked on his door.

"Yes?"

"Lena Scott is here. She said you left a message that her book was in?"

"Ah, yes." He got up from his desk. The book in question, Sir Arthur Conan Doyle's *The Memoirs of Sherlock Holmes*, was on the Purchased shelf. He collected the book and headed out to show it to Miss Scott.

He smiled as he approached her. He wasn't overly fond of witches—he wasn't overly fond of anyone, if he was being honest—but as witches went, she was all right. There was really only one witch he had anything close to affection for. "Miss Scott." He held the book out on his palm, displaying it for her to see. "Your first edition has arrived."

She smiled, eyes lighting up. He supposed she could be considered quite attractive. To someone who was interested, which he wasn't. Not in the slightest. Not in her or any other woman. "It looks wonderful."

"It's a pretty good version considering it was new in 1894." He turned the book so she could inspect the back cover. "These are the original blue cloth boards, and as you can see, the color is still very bright. The gilding has also held up extremely well. The back has taken the bulk of the wear and shows some chipping. Plus, there's a little rubbing on the spine, but that's to be expected in a book of this age."

"Of course. Actually, I expected it to be a lot worse."

He opened the book with great care. "Well, there's some foxing on the pages, too."

She looked at him. "Foxing?"

"The spotting and browning that happens to paper due to age and deterioration. It's pretty much impossible to avoid in old books."

She nodded. "That doesn't bother me. I'm just happy to have such an amazing thing in my possession."

He started to hand the book to her, then stopped. "You're not going to use this in some spell, are you?"

"Why? Would that matter to you?"

"I would just hate to see such a thing destroyed in the name of...witchcraft."

She laughed softly. "You say it like it's a bad thing. It won't be destroyed, I promise."

Which sounded to him like it was definitely going to be used in a spell. But she'd already put a sizable deposit down on the volume. He couldn't very well cancel the sale now, not without creating ill will. "If you promise."

"I do."

With a sigh, he handed the book over. "Fletcher will wrap the book and ring you up. I hope you enjoy it."

"Thank you, I'm sure I will."

Fletcher, who'd been hovering nearby, came to take over the rest of the sale.

Constantin wanted to return to his office and his books, but another customer, Emeranth Greer, walked through the door. Considering who she was, he liked to take care of her himself. In another reality, they might have been related.

She waved at him. "Hi there."

"Miss Greer." He stood by patiently to see if she needed anything. She was the niece of the most powerful witch in town and the only witch he cared for, Amelia Marchand. Amelia and the Thibodeauxes were forever connected by history, which helped him overlook Amelia's being a witch. Her niece was one as well, but so new to the craft that he didn't consider her much of a threat. "Looking for something to read or a gift?"

"Something to read. A few somethings. I'm completely out. Any suggestions?"

"New or classic?"

"I don't care so long as I haven't read it before."

"Biography, thriller, mystery?"

"I really wish you'd carry romance."

He made a face. "I already carry fairy tales."

She shook her head. "You know romance is, like, the most popular genre there is."

"I don't believe in happily ever after." Not after his own life had shown him differently. "Now, what can I point you toward that's worth reading?"

With a tolerant smirk, she sighed. "Whatever you've got that's good. Four or five books should hold me."

He smiled. She was becoming a good, regular customer. It took less than ten minutes to supply her with an armful of books.

Fletcher took care of her at the counter, leaving Constantin to say his goodbyes and at last return to his office.

There was still some organizing to do, though. Calls to make and emails to send to a few customers about some of the new books that had come in, too.

He focused and got his work done, saving the books he wanted to look at more closely as a reward.

He was nearly done when Fletcher knocked again.

Constantin had left the door slightly ajar. Fletcher's knocking had opened it farther. He shelved the book in his hand before giving Fletcher his attention.

"Just wanted to say good night."

Constantin looked at his watch. It was six o'clock already. "Have a good night. See you tomorrow."

"Yes, sir." He left through the back door.

Constantin waited for the snick of the lock, then walked out to the shop floor. It was neat and orderly, just the way he liked it. The shelves were dusted, and the lightbulb had been changed. Constantin nodded approvingly. Fletcher was a hard worker and did whatever he was asked to do. Good qualities, both.

Constantin had hired him because he was a fellow vampire and loved books. But he was also a young vampire, which meant he looked up to Constantin.

That part was less than desirable. Constantin didn't want to be anyone's mentor, but he could see the eagerness in Fletcher's gaze at times. It wore on Constantin a little. Made him occasionally short-tempered.

But Fletcher wasn't a bad employee. Constantin was just a particular man. Some would say he had quirks or eccentricities. Some would say he was prickly. Or difficult. He'd heard all those things whispered about town. Knew they were true, too. But the knowledge of something did not equate to the need for change.

He was nearly two hundred years old. He was who he was, and he was comfortable with that. Perhaps *comfortable* wasn't the right word, but he was settled in his ways.

Ways that didn't make him the most popular vampire in town, but who cared? He had his family, such as they were, and his books. And Chloe.

Not everyone could be the life of the party like his brother, Valentino. Constantin planted his hands on the counter and stared out at the street. Even his brother's name meant *strong*. How could anyone compete with that?

They couldn't, that's how. And Constantin didn't want to.

But deep down inside, Constantin sometimes wondered what it would be like to be a bright, glittering star instead of a serviceable bulb.

His brother owned Club 42, the jazz club in town, and was treated like a local celebrity. In a town like Shadowvale, that was a remarkable feat. There was no shortage of interesting people in this hamlet.

But Valentino was one of those people who drew others to him like a moth to flame. He had all the charm and charisma and glamour that a vampire was supposed to have. The man probably hadn't picked up a book in a hundred years. Or more. And yet everyone wanted to be his friend.

Constantin's shoulders tensed. He forced himself to relax. So what if Valentino was everything Constantin wasn't? Why should that matter? It didn't.

Except for when Constantin felt those despicable, unexplainable pangs of jealousy.

Why did he feel that way? He didn't want Valentino's life. He really didn't. It was chaotic and messy and spur-of-the-moment living. All things Constantin loathed.

Order, self-control, moderation. Those were qualities of a life well-lived.

But there was something about Valentino's life that Constantin wanted to experience just once. The perfect casualness of it, maybe. No, that wasn't quite right. It was the underlying current of energy that made his older brother seem kissed by providence.

Things—good things—just fell into Valentino's lap. He didn't *try* to accomplish anything. It just happened.

Constantin, on the other hand, had to work at life. He wasn't complaining. His life was good. He was an immortal vampire, after all. And he enjoyed what he did very much.

But Valentino had it all. A thriving business, a horde of friends, more women than he could count.

Constantin snorted out a laugh. Who was he kidding? That sounded dreadful.

Mostly. No, it was dreadful. Well, some of it was.

Books were all he needed. His smile faded as he walked back to his office. Maybe not all, but books didn't judge or lie or require anything more than a little of his time.

His gaze returned to the books that had just arrived.

He picked up the one about insane asylums and carried it back to the front counter, then he settled onto the tall leather barstool behind the register so he could keep an eye on the shop. He'd be open until nine to catch the evening crowd, then head home for a late supper and possibly a movie.

Chloe would curl up next to him, no doubt. That was all the company, female or otherwise, that he generally required.

He put the book in his lap. Perhaps he'd forgo the movie for more reading, depending on how interesting this book turned out to be.

Another glance toward the street told him he wasn't likely to have any customers for a while. It was the dinner hour. Fine with him. An empty shop was a chance to read.

He opened the book, curious to see if it could hold his interest. The spine creaked with age, and the pages were far more foxed than the Sherlock Holmes book. Then a large plume of violet smoke burst forth from the pages.

Constantin jumped out of his seat, throwing the book onto the counter. "What in the blazes?"

The smoke funneled through the store and began to take form on the other side of the counter.

Constantin stared at it, trying to make sense of what he was seeing.

A form. A female one.

A short, curvy woman with a mass of honey-blond curls and as best as he could tell, bright violet eyes. She was dressed in ripped jeans, a tank top sporting a picture of a cat in sunglasses, and a worn leather jacket.

She didn't seem to have noticed him yet, as she'd come into being facing the side of the shop and not the counter.

She patted herself down. "I'm out. I'm finally out. Halle-freaking-lujah." She turned and saw him. "Hey."

"Hello," he answered. For all the questions swirling through his head, he couldn't find the words to voice any of them.

"You opened the book, huh?"

"I did." Her accent was faintly British, and she looked to be in her late twenties or early thirties. That wasn't much to go on. "Who are you?"

"Thank you for that." She raised her hands in triumph. "I can't believe I'm finally out. Oh man, that was brutal." She looked around. "Where am I?"

"The Gilded Page," he answered, hoping she'd soon provide him with some answers of her own.

"What's that?"

"My bookstore."

"Huh. Out of a book into a bookstore." She shook her head. "Man, I can't believe she really did it."

"Who did what?"

The woman tucked a loose tendril of curls behind her ear. "What year is it?"

"Can you please tell me who you are? And why you were in that book?" Magic abounded in Shadowvale, and strange things happened all the time. That didn't mean he wasn't entitled to answers. He sighed. "It's 2019."

Her mouth fell open. "Are you kidding me?"

"No." Great Scott, she was terrible at answering questions.

"A whole freaking year. That little—"

"*Where* did you come from? And who are you?"

She narrowed her eyes at him. "Are you daft? Or did you really not see me come out of that book?"

He straightened, frowning. "I am *not* daft. I saw smoke come out of the book. Clearly, that smoke was you. But one doesn't start out in a book, in my experience. Unless the jinn have given up on bottles and lamps. And you don't look like any jinn I've ever seen."

Her brows lifted, pinching together. "Oh good, I ended up with a Rhodes Scholar." She sighed. "Yeah, I was in the book, but I didn't start out there."

He briefly squeezed the bridge of his nose. "Whatever your situation, I am not the reason for your predicament. Neither you nor your attitude are required here, so feel free to leave."

"I don't have an attitude." She crossed her arms, causing the leather jacket to squeak slightly. "And I can't."

"Can't what?"

"Leave."

"Why not?"

She dropped her arms to her sides, looking rather forlorn. "You opened the book. I'm sorry to say you're stuck with me."

He stared at her. "What? I don't want you. I-I-I don't even know who you are!"

She shrugged. "Don't blame me, blame my sister. She's the one who cursed me into that book to begin with."

CHAPTER TWO

"One thing at a time," the man said. "Who are you?"

"Andromeda Merriweather." She made herself smile. She needed this guy to like her. A lot. So she had to be on her best behavior. Which meant she needed to chill the snappy comebacks. That wasn't going to be easy, but at least she knew that much about herself. If only she could curb her impulsive side. "But everyone calls me Andi."

"Why were you in the book?"

"Because my sister cursed me into it." For reasons that Andi wasn't about to go into. Not with the man who held the key to her freedom. Fortunately, he was cute, in that brainy professor kind of way. That would make this a little easier.

He didn't seem particularly moved by what she'd shared. "I take it my opening the book released you, but I don't understand why you can't leave."

"My sister is a bit of a...practical joker, I guess you could say. She built some stipulations into the curse that bind me to the book."

"A practical joker?"

"Yes. For example…" Andi tried to get a better look at the book on the counter. "What's the title of the book I was in? Something with crazy people, am I right? Because it was bananapants in there, let me tell you."

One of the muscles in his jaw jumped. It was a very attractive jaw, square and stern and bitable. Not that Andi was remotely interested in this guy for anything more than what it'd take to get her freedom back. He seemed a little uptight. Which was so not her type. Cassi would love this guy, though. Too bad for her.

He closed the book and showed her. "*The Hidden History of Insane Asylums in 19th Century Europe.*"

"Just a little light reading, then. Oh, that is so like Cassi." Andi nearly growled at her sister's nonsense. "I'm sure she thought that was hilarious." And not a book anyone was likely to open in a long time. Except for this guy, who obviously thought it sounded interesting. What did that say about him, exactly? Not much. Unless being the conductor of the Snoozetown Express was something to be proud of.

"Cassi is your sister, I take it?"

"Yes. My older sister. Older and grouchier. You'd probably love her." She looked around. She was in a bookstore, that much they'd established. And a very nice one, by all appearances. "Great store. Do you own this place?"

"Thank you, I do."

She glanced at him. "Who are you, by the way?"

"Constantin Thibodeaux."

She smiled broadly. "Nice to meet you, Constantin. Vampire, right?"

"Yes."

"The fangs kind of give it away." She laced her hands together in front of her. "I'm a sprite. In case you were wondering."

He peered at her. "Don't sprites have wings?"

"Of course. Can't you see mine?" She glanced over her shoulder. There was nothing there. Panic ripped through her. She turned pointlessly, trying to see better. "Are you freaking kidding me? She took my wings?"

She reached for the chain around her neck and the vial that it held, the vial she stored her wings in when she needed to pass as human. It was gone. Andi's ire leveled up.

"Can you get back to the part about why you can't leave?"

"No, I can't," she snapped. "My wings are gone. *Gone.* Along with the magical vial I keep them in. Do you understand what that means? No, of course not, because you're a vampire. Well, my wings are everything. The source of my magic. My mode of transportation." She was trembling with anger and disbelief, all while a knot twisted up her insides. Her wings were everything. "I can't believe she would do that to me. And all because of—"

She stopped before she let too much out. Certain details were better kept close to the vest at the moment. She wrapped her arms around herself as her anger turned to self-pity. Her sister had screwed her royally. First the book, now this. Cassi was clearly a lot madder than Andi had expected her to be. Madder than she'd ever been before, and that was saying something.

"I'm sorry about your wings."

She looked up, surprised to see genuine concern in his eyes. He'd seemed rather cold until this moment. But maybe that had just been shock. Wasn't every day a woman popped out of a book. She sniffed. "Thanks."

"You're welcome. Are you going to be okay?"

"I have no idea. Nothing like this has ever happened to me before." More concern from Mr. Ice In His Veins. Well, it was better than her blood. Which caused a new alarm to go off inside her. She stepped back. "Hey, you're not going to, like, try to have me for dinner or anything, are you?"

One of his brows cocked up. "Calm down, sprite. In this town, the needs of my kind are met by a regular delivery service."

She took a breath. Crisis averted. "Good to know. So what town is this?"

"Shadowvale."

"Never heard of it."

"I wouldn't expect you to have. It's purposefully hidden to protect its citizens." He narrowed his eyes. "Again, you're free to leave, but I should tell you that this isn't a town like most."

"That's great, but like I said, I can't leave. I'm

stuck with you. You're stuck with me. However you want to put it, we're in this together. At least until I can get my freedom, once and for all."

He put his hands on the counter between them. "Explain."

"As I've told you, my sister cursed me into that book, but the curse doesn't end there. Unless..." Andi had to do some quick thinking. If she told him what Cassi had told her about what it would take to get free, this guy would turn tail and run. What guy wouldn't? "Okay, here's the thing. If I don't get the man who released me from the book to kiss me three times, I'll be sent back into the book for eternity."

At least the part about being stuck in the book for eternity was true. Cassi must really have been beyond furious to put such a stipulation in the curse.

"And what if the book had been opened by a woman?"

"Not a possibility. My sister specified that in the curse."

Constantin frowned, then snorted. "I'm not kissing you. I don't even know you."

She maintained her cool. "Fair enough, but I'm not asking for a box from Tiffany's and a white picket fence here. Just three kisses."

"Just three kisses. So one, two, three, and you're free? That seems awfully easy." His mouth bent with practiced skepticism. "Did my brother put you up to this? Is this some kind of game he's playing?"

"I have no idea who your brother is, and no, it's not *just* three kisses." She needed time with him, or this was never going to work. "It's three kisses, but they can't be one right after the other. One every forty-eight hours. And you have to give them to me. I can't kiss you. So you have to want to kiss me. Got it?"

She wanted to pat herself on the back. That was brilliant. A kiss every two days would give her six days with him. That was plenty of time to work her magical charm on him. Even without wings. Which she was going to kill her sister for when she saw her next. If her wings didn't come back when she earned her freedom, that was. If they did come back, all would be well.

Okay, not *well*. But Andi would be in a much better place with wings than without.

He was staring at her. Thinking, maybe. But the quiet combined with the hard glower was unnerving.

She held on to her smile as best she could. "Any other questions?"

"No. Not interested."

She gaped at him. "You opened the book. You don't have a choice. I don't have a choice."

"I'm sorry for you, but I'm not interested."

She'd have to sweet-talk him. "Connie, look—"

"My name is Constantin."

"Right, sorry, Constantin." Note to self, touchy vampire was touchy. "If you don't help me, I'm going to end up stuck in that book for eternity. You, of all immortal beings, should understand the gravity of that." She moved closer, looking desperate without much effort. "Please. That book is terrifying. I don't belong in a book like that. I don't belong in any book, but certainly not that one."

He glanced at the book. "No, I suppose not."

"Just help me. Six days, three kisses, and I'm out of your hair." His dark brown hair, which looked unfairly thick and gleamed with the kind of high-lights most women paid a fortune to achieve.

He frowned. "No. I understand your predicament, but there's got to be another way to get you free of the book. Listen, there's a bed-and-breakfast down by the park. You should be able to get a room there. Then you can come back to the shop in the morning, and I'll call some of the witches in town, see if they know how to—"

"Yeah, that's not going to work. The bed-and-breakfast part anyway." She laughed. He really didn't get it. "When I said I can't leave you, I really meant it. I'm stuck to you until I'm free. Stuck as in genuinely attached. Like, I don't think I can get farther than a hundred feet from you. So it really behooves you to help me since we're in this together."

A slight look of terror brightened his eyes. "That can't possibly be true. What kind of monster would build a curse like that?"

"Remember the part where I mentioned my sister?"

He growled softly. "I refuse to be saddled with you. With this. It's nonsense."

Saddled? What was she, a horse? She bit her

tongue and stayed on track. "It's also too late. You opened the book. The die, as they say, is cast."

He pointed at her. "Go to the front of the store and stand by the door."

She humored him. Some people had to see things to believe them. Although a vampire should know better, but maybe this guy was just a natural-born skeptic. Some intellectuals were like that, and he definitely struck her as an intellectual. She walked away from him, then waved from the shop's entrance. "Good enough?"

"Yes." He sidled toward the back of the shop, keeping an eye on her.

When he got a few feet from the rear entrance, she felt a tug as if an imaginary rope had been lassoed around her midsection and given a good pull. She let out a yelp as she was yanked toward him.

His eyes widened. "You're doing that."

She sighed. "I promise you, I'm not."

His jaw tightened. "What if you go back into the book and wait for someone else to open it?"

"It's cute you think I have any control over this."

"I don't want this." Frustration made his words a low growl.

A little heartsick as the reality of her condition set in, she stared at the carpet, her voice nearly a whisper as she said, "Neither do I."

A moment of silence passed before he spoke again. "No, I suppose you don't."

The unexpected sympathy made her look up. His brow was furrowed in what appeared to be sincere concern. She felt for him. Thanks to Cassi, he was as much a victim in this mess as Andi was. More the victim, probably. Well, not more. But equal, for sure. His life had just been upended. And she was at least out of the book now. "I'm sorry you're stuck with me."

He shrugged as he walked toward her. "It's not your fault."

If he only knew. "Thanks. I don't want to disrupt your life."

"I believe that ship has sailed." He sighed. "To think my love of books has betrayed me in such an underhanded way. But I suppose there's nothing to be done now but move forward toward a solution."

She smiled, happy that he seemed to be settling into the idea that she was going to be around for a bit. "If it makes you feel any better, I'm generally considered the life of the party wherever I go."

His expression became oddly strained. "I do my best to avoid parties."

"Oh." So he was an introvert. She could deal with that. "Well, I'll try to stay out of your way. As best I can."

"Good." He frowned. "I didn't mean that the way it came out." Then he muttered something she didn't quite catch. "I am not generally considered the life of the party wherever I go, which is why I rarely go anywhere."

She leaned on the counter, facing him. "I kind of picked up on that." Then she shrugged. "It's okay. We are who we are, right?"

"I suppose so."

Chimes rang out through the store. She took that to mean the front door had opened. She turned to see who'd come in. No one she knew, obviously, but he was effortlessly handsome in the kind of way men were when they knew how attractive they were. She greeted the man with a smile that was pleasant, but nothing that said she was bowled over by his handsomeness. "Hi there, looking for a book?"

"Andromeda," Constantin rushed in a harsh whisper. "I'll handle this."

But the customer's face lit up with a bright grin, and he made a beeline for her. "Hello there." Then he looked at Constantin. "I didn't know you'd hired more help." His attention returned to Andi with a slow, inventory-taking gaze. "And such *nice-looking* help."

Oh brother. She barely refrained from rolling her eyes at his attempted charm. "Does that mean you are looking for a book? Because this place is loaded with them, so you're in the right spot." Not that he struck her as a reader.

He laughed. "No, I'm just here to see my brother."

Constantin walked up to join her. "Valentino isn't much of a reader."

She'd pegged him correctly, then.

But she hadn't pegged the tension between the two men, which was instantly apparent. Then Andi rethought that. In truth, Constantin was the only one who'd tensed up. His brother seemed oblivious to how he was being received. In fact, he was giving off a vibe that said he pretty much thought everyone loved him.

Maybe that was true of most people, but Constantin wasn't one of them. Interesting. Andi could relate to sibling issues.

Valentino kept on smiling, although his expression turned a little sardonic. "I read."

Constantin shot back, "I'm talking about more than financial statements."

Valentino's wry expression never faltered. He was unashamed of his literary lacking. "But those are at least interesting."

Constantin's mouth hardened into a thin line. "What did you stop by for?"

"To see if you wanted to come by the club tonight. Since Cousin Isabelle's laryngitis has returned, this was the perfect opportunity to bring in a special guest." He leaned forward. "A *very* special guest."

Constantin sighed like he was bored beyond belief. "Just come out with it."

Valentino held his silence a moment longer, maybe for dramatic effect. "Miranda Moore is here, and she'll be singing around eleven."

Constantin's expression changed for a microsecond. From bored to tortured, then straight to utter indifference that was clearly a lie. Whoever this Miranda person was, she meant something to him. "Good for her. You could have texted."

Valentino shook his head. "This felt like one of those messages that needed to be delivered in person." He winked at Andi. "Plus, I got to meet your lovely new assistant."

"She's not my assistant," Constantin said as he slid over to Andi and put his arm around her. "She's my girlfriend."

CHAPTER THREE

Constantin had no idea why the words that had just come out of his mouth had even formed. They were nonsense. What was he doing? Where was his brain? Andromeda wasn't his girlfriend. She was his burden.

Valentino's jaw dropped in unreserved surprise, and Constantin knew *that* was exactly why he'd made the claim.

For once, he'd wanted to shut his brother up. Or in this case, leave him speechless.

And it had worked.

So far. Andromeda had yet to say anything, and with one word, she could make a fool of him with the truth.

Then her arm slipped around Constantin's waist, and she looked up at him with a smile that said she knew what he was doing and he was about to owe her big-time. He was okay with that.

Her gaze stayed on him a moment longer, then she turned to speak to Valentino. "We were just going to have a nice quiet dinner at home, but we could drop by the club for a bit if you like."

Constantin shook his head. He didn't like. Not where Miranda Moore was concerned. "It's been a long day. I'm not sure I'm up for it."

Valentino regained his voice with a snort. "We're vampires, brother. Finding the energy for an evening out is for humans."

"It's about the mental energy, not the physical. Crowds drain me."

Valentino's brows lifted. "Look, if being around Miranda again intimidates you—"

"No one intimidates me."

"Then I'll see you there." He glanced at Andromeda. "Both of you." With a little nod, he turned and left, his annoying smile back in place.

As soon as the shop door closed behind him, Constantin took his arm from Andromeda's shoulders and pinched the bridge of his nose as he closed his eyes for a moment. "I shouldn't have said you were my girlfriend, but thank you for not exposing my lie to my brother."

He felt her hand on his arm. A gesture of comfort? Sympathy? He was so unused to being touched, he wasn't sure.

"When it comes to troublesome siblings, I completely understand."

He looked at her and smiled, a rare thing for a man who found his joy in books and his companion, Chloe. "I suppose you do. Thank you all the same."

"We're in this together, right?"

"Right." Such as it was. He really hadn't been given a choice. But he understood she could have called him a liar in front of Valentino and hadn't. He owed her. Whatever that was going to mean. He supposed he ought to stop thinking of her as his burden, too.

She crossed her arms. "Who's this Miranda Moore person?"

He took a breath. He hadn't given space to those memories in a long time. Of course, Valentino was to blame. He'd brought the woman up. Hell, he'd probably brought her to town just to aggravate Constantin. "She's someone from my past."

"I got that much. Girlfriend?"

"More than that, I'm afraid." He stared into the shop, seeing none of it. "Fiancée, unfortunately."

"Did you break it off with her?"

He shook his head, this time grimacing at the scene playing out in his head. "I wish. But no. She left me. The morning of the ceremony."

Andromeda hissed through her teeth. "Ouch."

"Yes, indeed. So you can see why I don't want to go to the club this evening."

"Are you crazy? That's exactly why you want to go to the club!"

"It is?"

"Sure." She planted her hands on her hips as she cocked one to the side and gave him a big, sultry smile. "Besides the fact that your brother practically dared you not to go, you've got a girlfriend, remember? Proof you're not just pining away for your ex. Proof that you've gotten on with your life. That you've forgotten all about her."

He gave that a long moment of thought. "It would be nice to show her that she didn't destroy me." Although that was another lie.

Andromeda's hands dropped from her hips. "There's just one thing."

"What's that?"

"I'm not really club-ready at the moment." She glanced down at herself. "This is literally all I have to my name. I didn't exactly get to pack a bag before Cassi did her thing. I don't even have a toothbrush."

"That can be rectified. Many of the shops along Main Street stay open late to accommodate the supernaturals who prefer evening hours. Just get what you like and tell them to charge it to me." Whatever she spent, it would be a small price to pay for the comeuppance that Valentino—and Miranda—was about to receive.

"So just go out and shop?"

"Yes. Within reason, of course, but get what you need."

"Great. Do you want to leave now?"

"I don't want to leave at—oh. I have to go with you, don't I?"

She nodded. "Yep. That whole tethered-by-the-curse thing."

He sighed. "That means I have to close the shop."

"Sorry." She laughed weakly. "I seem to be apologizing to you a lot."

37

That gave him pause. She wasn't the first to say that to him. "People do that around me. Why is that, do you think?"

She tilted her head in thought. "I suppose it's because you seem upset a lot. Apologizing is kind of a natural reaction to that kind of mood. No one wants to be the reason someone else is angry."

"I'm not angry. Not exactly."

"But you're not bubbling over with joie de vivre either. It's obvious you're bothered. By me, by the burden I've put on you, by your evening being disturbed, by your brother stopping in, by this woman coming to town—"

"Point taken." He frowned at having his prickliness laid out in front of him so blatantly. "But I already told you I'm not an easy person to be around."

She didn't say anything, just watched him. Like she was taking notes.

He tried not to let *that* bother him, too. "I need to get a few things from my office, then we can go do some shopping. We should have some dinner, too. Then get you settled at the house."

"Sounds good to me." She climbed onto the stool behind the counter, crossing one shapely leg over the other.

He started to walk to his office, trying not to think about her in his house. A stranger in his personal space. He shuddered at the thought.

"You should put this somewhere secure. Lock it up, maybe."

He stopped, looking back to see her holding the book she'd come out of. "Is the store's safe good enough?"

"I'd think so."

He retrieved the book and took it with him. Once in his office, he spun the dial to open the wall safe, tucked the book in, and locked it again. He took his wallet and keys from the top drawer of his desk, then locked his office.

He made sure the back door was locked as well, then returned to the counter. She was looking through the latest issue of *Fine Books & Collections*.

She glanced over the top at him. "You really like books, huh?"

"They're my life." The words suddenly had a sad ring to them, something he'd never heard before. "What I mean is, they're a big part of my life."

She closed the magazine and slipped out of the chair to stand in front of him. "I get it. You like them better than people. And they are your business. Hey, I love reading, so I think it's cool."

He nodded. "Right. Good." But he wasn't thinking about books anymore. He was thinking about her. About how close she was. And how nice she smelled.

And the surprising bonus that she was a reader.

She gazed up at him. Her eyes reminded him of the marbled endpapers inside his favorite collection of Longfellow poems—swirls of violet speckled with gold. She smiled. "It's okay, you know. I bet there are a lot of people who'd prefer a book to me."

Her words caught him off guard, and he laughed—really laughed, like he hadn't in a long time.

Her eyes crinkled as her smile grew. "You're probably going to be one of those."

He shook his head as he regained his composure. "I don't think that's going to be the case."

Somehow, those words didn't feel like a lie, or even a pleasantry said just to soothe her feelings.

She sucked her bottom lip between her teeth for a second, like she was waiting on something. "You could kiss me if you want to."

His breath stuck in his throat. More words he hadn't expected. He swallowed. "Right. Because of the curse."

She nodded. "Right." She put her hand on his chest. "You have to want to, though. You can't do it just to get it over with."

"Makes sense." Her touch ignited dormant feelings in him. Something dark and unexpected. A longing. No. A hunger. But not the kind of hunger he was used to. This came from a place much deeper.

"So...do you?"

"Do I want to kiss you?"

She nodded, her body somehow closer to his than it had been just a second ago.

"Yes, I do." He pulled her into his arms.

And the shop door opened.

He released her with the quicker-than-a-blink speed only a vampire could manage. When he stopped moving, he was in front of the customer. "Good evening, Mrs. Gallagher. What can I help you with?"

The old woman, a banshee whose brilliant red hair had long gone gray, didn't come into town often. But when she did, she always stopped at the Gilded Page. She spoke softly, in the perfected whisper her kind used when in town. "What have you got that I might like? I'm bored."

A bored banshee, no matter how old, was never a good thing. Nala Gallagher wasn't prone to bouts of wailing, but then, he wouldn't put it past her if she had too much free time on her hands. "I had a few new philosophy books come in. From an estate lot. Haven't even had a chance to put them out yet. And there are new selections in almost every area of the store."

She nodded as she looked around. "I'll browse, but bring me the philosophy books, too."

"I'll have them at the counter for you."

By the time Mrs. Gallagher was done, she'd put a good dent in his stock and nearly filled two shopping bags. He was happy about that.

But not happy about the interrupted kiss, which was all he'd been able to think about since the woman had come in.

He walked Mrs. Gallagher to the door, wished her a good night, then locked it behind her and flipped the sign to say Closed. For good measure, he turned off the shop's lights, leaving only the front windows illuminated.

Andromeda had a little half smile on her face as he walked back to the counter. "So about that kiss."

But Constantin didn't use words to reply. Instead, he pulled her into his arms and let his mouth do the talking.

CHAPTER FOUR

Andi barely had time to let out a gasp of shock as Constantin pulled her close and covered her mouth with his. She'd expected to be kissed, she just hadn't expected him to be so...forward about it. In the moment that he'd reached for her, he'd looked like a man possessed.

There was no asking for permission, no double-checking to see if she was ready, just him and her and the soul-scorching heat of the moment. She was surprised he was capable of such action—and such passion.

She was also not one bit mad about his sudden decision to take what he wanted. Not when what he wanted was her.

Every nerve ending in her went electric with the thrill of being in his arms. His kiss was hungry and needy and not at all the kind of sober kiss she'd thought she'd get from him. She fought to maintain her balance against the surge of pleasure rising through her.

At last, she let it take her, leaning against him and forgetting that the kiss was something she was supposed to need to earn her freedom. Forgetting everything, really, while she was pressed against his muscled frame. And for a few very long, indulgent seconds, she was just a woman being kissed by a very desirable man.

Then he ended the kiss and released her, the muscles in his jaw contracting with an emotion she couldn't quite name. He shook his head. He seemed upset for some reason. "That was more than you required, wasn't it? My apologies."

Was he bothered by his loss of control?

"Don't apologize. That was perfect." In so many ways. Sweet sparkly starlight. Her whole body felt light and floaty and warmer than it had in a long time. For a man who preferred books, he was really good at kissing.

His brows bent. "It was?"

"Yes. The best kiss I've had in…well, a long while."

He looked skeptical. "You've been in that book for nearly a year. I suppose any kiss might seem good."

"Sure, but that doesn't mean I've lost my ability to judge what good kissing is. And that was good kissing." Had he enjoyed it? Hard to tell. He seemed to be more focused on analyzing what had just happened, rather than lost in the pleasure of it all, which was how she felt.

His eyes narrowed to slits. "And if the kiss was bad, you would tell me that, too?"

She paused. The memory of his mouth against hers lingered so strongly she could still feel it, but the blissful aura was fading with this conversation. "I wouldn't deliberately hurt your feelings, but if you were honest in your efforts, then what more could I ask for?" She blinked up at him. "Why? Do you think I'm just stroking your ego?"

He shrugged and looked away, but not before she caught a glimpse of past hurt in his eyes. "It behooves you to make me happy, doesn't it?"

She laid her hand on his arm, hoping she could get through the pain of his memories. "I'm not playing you, if that's what you're thinking. I get that keeping you happy makes my life easier. After all, I need you to go along with all this, or I'm in a lot of trouble. But that's not what I'm doing." She gave his arm a squeeze. "I like you. Even if you are prickly."

He shot her a look, but said nothing for a moment. Then he glanced at the door again. "We should get your shopping done."

"Okay. Thanks, by the way."

"For what?"

"For being cool about all this."

"You can't help what's been done to you. I can't help being the one who freed you. There's not much point in ruining either of our lives for longer than necessary."

Not quite the response she'd hoped for, but

they'd only known each other for an hour. There was still plenty of time for him to fall madly in love with her.

She hoped.

*

What was he doing kissing her like that? Letting his basest urges overrule his brain? There was no trying to kid himself that it was what the curse required. He'd kissed her for far longer than necessary.

Maybe it was the memories of Miranda that had been stirred up. Maybe kissing Andromeda was his attempt to soothe that pain. Because he certainly wasn't trying to lose his head and his heart again.

Not after Miranda. Not after that humiliation.

And while he liked Andromeda, that was as far as this—whatever *this* was—would go.

Fortunately, he didn't have to kiss her again for two days.

At least they were out and about now, and she'd be distracted with shopping. He could have some time to cool off this way. Time to straighten himself out and make sure that kind of display didn't happen again.

They entered the first boutique, Parks & Main, and while Andromeda got to browsing, he chose to sit in the leather love seat near the back of the store. He didn't need to be involved in her purchases. He was just here so she could be, too.

And to pay.

He frowned. That was what women did. They made you pay.

Not that the current situation was Andromeda's fault, but the fact remained that he was footing this bill.

Lydia Parks helped Andromeda take about half of the store into the dressing room, then came to check on him. "Hello, Constantin. I must say, I didn't expect to see you in here this evening."

Or ever, her eyes seemed to add.

He nodded. "Hello, Lydia." He glanced at the dressing room. "My friend needed some things, so…" He finished with a shrug, hoping Lydia would leave it there.

"Your friend, hmm?" She smiled. Probably hoping he'd elaborate.

He didn't. Just nodded and picked up a magazine. After a moment, Lydia walked away. She knew his mother and sisters because they shopped here, so there was no way the news of his visit with Andromeda wasn't going to be spread. But he'd just explain to the female side of his family what had happened and —

He went very still. He couldn't just explain, though, could he? He'd already told Valentino that Andromeda was his girlfriend. How could he now tell his mother and sisters differently? One of them, his mother most likely, would tell his father, and the truth would inevitably get back to Valentino. Even if it was just a slip of the tongue.

There was no way around it. He'd have to tell his entire family that Andromeda was his girlfriend, or face the relentless ridicule that Valentino would put him through for lying.

He groaned softly. His sisters were going to get excited and instantly try to make Andromeda feel welcome. It was one of the more wonderful things about them, but in this case, it would serve only to complicate the situation, and his life, when Andromeda's curse was broken and she was able to leave.

Unfortunately, none of this could be avoided, because tomorrow night he'd be expected to appear (as all his siblings were) at the family dinner.

Which meant, thanks to the curse's tether, he would be forced to take Andromeda. She'd be dragged along whether she wanted to go or not. And there was no canceling, unless a drastic circumstance arose. And he couldn't think of one drastic enough to qualify.

Of course, if the tether wasn't functioning for some magical reason, he'd have to take her anyway. If he didn't, the assumption would be that they had already broken up. That would mean questions and insinuations about his ability to hold on to a partner. Or how he wasn't over Miranda yet.

But taking her meant they'd *both* be peppered with endless rounds of questions.

Which was worse? Hard to say. They had six days together at a minimum. After that, he would have to come up with a reason for her disappearance. So what then? A manufactured breakup story?

He closed his eyes. This whole thing was a gigantic mess. And all because he'd told a lie to protect his pride.

"What do you think?"

He opened his eyes and found Andromeda standing before him in a small dress of merlot-colored velvet and a pair of strappy black satin heels. The dress fit her perfectly, and the thin straps showed off what beautiful shoulders she had. And what remarkable cleavage. None of which had been all that evident in her T-shirt and leather jacket.

He blinked, trying to remember what he was supposed to be doing.

"Con?" She peered down at him. "Yes or no? Or don't you have an opinion?"

He nodded, so full of opinion that he didn't bother to correct her use of a nickname for him. "Is that for tonight? Actually, it doesn't matter what it's for, you should get it."

"It is for tonight." She grinned. "So you like it, huh?"

"That's an understatement. It looks like it was made for you."

"The shoes, too?"

He glanced at them again. Her toes were painted a deep, sparkling burgundy. It must be her favorite color. "The shoes, too."

"They're kind of expensive."

He shrugged. "It's only money." Something that suddenly didn't matter as much to him as it usually did.

"Okay, if you say so." Still smiling, she strode back to the dressing room. He watched her go with great admiration. Too much admiration, perhaps.

Was he in trouble?

She was beautiful. She had an incredible figure. She'd made him laugh more than once. The scent of her was the slightest bit intoxicating. And kissing her was…more pleasure than he'd experienced in a long time.

Then there was the fact that he was a man who'd purposefully not had a relationship since his last one had ended so disastrously.

He wasn't lonely, exactly. He'd genuinely come to enjoy time alone. But the thought of being forced into spending time with Andromeda seemed less and less like punishment with every passing moment.

That was fine. It would make the days pass with much greater ease. But there was a fine line between *like* and *love*. It wasn't one he wanted to cross again. Not at the risk of having to rebuild himself.

Because despite what he told people, Miranda had destroyed him. And that wasn't something that was ever going to happen again.

Andromeda came out of the dressing room, the strappy black heels dangling from her fingers, the velvet dress over her arm. "All set."

He stood and joined her. "That's it? I thought you'd need more than—"

Lydia came over to take the items. "I'll put these at the register so you can look around some more."

Andromeda smiled and said, "Thanks."

When Lydia left, Andromeda lowered her voice a little. "I do need more, and I know you said it's only money, but this place is expensive. Really expensive."

"It can't be that bad. My mother and sisters shop here." He reached for the nearest item, a red sweater with bands of black sequins at the wrists, and checked the price tag. It was almost three hundred dollars. His brows lifted as he dropped the tag. "Then again, what do I know about their clothing budgets?"

He'd brought Andromeda here only because it was the one shop he was sure would have nice women's clothing. How nice, he hadn't realized. But really, it *was* only money. "I don't care about the cost of things. Get what you need."

She frowned. "Not at these prices. There has to be another store in town we could try. Plus, this stuff is nice, but it's not exactly all my taste."

It probably wasn't her style. Parks & Main wasn't known for leather jackets and ripped jeans. And he doubted they'd ever even consider selling tank tops with cats on them. "Okay. I know of another place."

"Good. Let's go there next."

And so they did, after he paid the bill at Parks & Main.

He stopped outside another shop. "Is this okay?"

She looked up at the sign. "Because it's secondhand? Yeah, I'm fine with that. I love thrift shops. My leather jacket came from one."

"Really?" In truth, he'd expected her to balk. But he was coming to realize that his assumptions about her were often wrong.

"Yep. But I'm not buying my underwear here."

He snorted, hands up. "I won't argue with that."

He held the door for her, and in they went to Stella's Bargain Bin. He'd never been in the place, and he was a hundred percent sure his mother and sisters hadn't either.

Andromeda let out a little coo of appreciation. He liked that. She could have put up a fuss and refused anything that wasn't brand-new, but she hadn't. Better yet, she seemed genuinely excited to check the shop out.

And while he'd never been inside, he knew Stella, the owner and store's namesake. She was a regular customer of his. A good one, too, even if she was also constantly prodding him to stock romance novels. So while the woman behind the counter looked a lot like Stella, almost identical really, she wasn't. The scent of her blood was not the same. Very close, but a few subtle notes were different. Also, the last time Stella had been in the Gilded Page, her hair was fire-engine red. This woman's was blue. He nodded at her. "Evening."

"Evening."

"You're not Stella, are you?"

She gave him a sharp look, then it quickly turned into one of amusement. "You're a quick one, aren't you? No, I'm not Stella. I'm Della, her twin sister."

"Nice to meet you, Della. I didn't know Stella had a twin."

"I don't suppose anyone did. I just moved here a month back. Long story, big divorce, bad feelings, but all done with now." She gave her deep-blue coif a few pats as if checking to see that every hair was still shellacked into place. "Anyway, I told her I'd pick up the night shift, make myself useful. You know."

"Of course." He introduced himself and Andromeda, as was only polite. "I'm Constantin Thibodeaux, and this is my friend Andromeda Merriweather. I own the nonmagical bookstore in town. The Gilded Page. Your sister is a frequent customer. But that's beside the point. The reason we're here is Andromeda is in need of some clothes. Whatever she likes, just so that she's happy."

"Got it." Della popped off her stool with surprising quickness. "Hi there, Andromeda."

Andromeda lifted her hand in a little wave. "Hi. You can call me Andi."

"What are you looking for?"

Andromeda glanced down at her current outfit. "Some T-shirts, another pair of jeans, maybe. A robe, maybe? A few things to get me through the week. I didn't really have a chance to pack, and this trip was pretty unexpected, so…"

"Say no more." Della smiled and rubbed her hands together. "Let's do some shopping."

CHAPTER FIVE

Della seemed to find things on the racks that Andi had somehow missed. Racks she'd just looked through suddenly produced covetable items that were just her size and taste. In about twenty minutes, Andi had a pile of things (including new underwear, which the shop miraculously stocked) that weren't just cool and hip, but priced exactly right.

Which was to say cheap.

Sure, the other shop had been high-end fabulous (although also a tiny bit boring), but she didn't want Con spending buckets of money on her when she was going to disappear as soon as she had her freedom back. That would just add insult to injury. Both of which she wanted to avoid.

She double-checked that she had everything from the dressing room that she wanted: a pair of dark skinny jeans that could be rolled up or not, some black leggings with rivets down the sides, a couple of T-shirts, a funky appliqued cardigan, an oversize sweater that hung off one shoulder, the cutest leopard-print ankle boots, a denim miniskirt, and a vintage purple robe that seemed right out of a classic old Hollywood movie.

She planted the stack of goods on the counter. "I love this place."

"Thanks, honey." Della smiled and started ringing things up.

Andi checked out the jewelry in the display case and the little stand of earrings sitting on top. She found a thick rhinestone stretch bracelet and a pair of earrings that seemed made to match. She held them up to Con, who was sitting by the door in a chair that looked more like a throne. "To go with tonight's outfit?"

He put down the paper he was leafing through to have a look. "Sure. Whatever you want."

That kiss had done wonders. Naturally for her—because who didn't feel better after a kiss that curled your toes?—but for him, too. He was a lot less uptight all of a sudden. Which didn't mean he was suddenly happy and smiley and super relaxed. He was still uptight. Just not in such a noticeable way. He hadn't even corrected her when she'd called him Con.

She was glad about his mood shift. They had a lot of time to spend together, and it would be considerably easier if he wasn't grumpy about her presence twenty-four seven.

She added the jewelry to the pile, then looked at him again. He'd put the paper down and was sitting very still with a contemplative look on his face, fingers steepled in front of him. Thinking about what? She wondered. His ex?

Poor guy. It seemed to Andi that this Miranda person had really done a job on him. Being left at the altar would do that, Andi supposed. For hurting Con the way Miranda had, Andi despised her.

She almost laughed at that thought. How had she gotten so protective of this random vampire? She felt almost bonded to him, but she supposed that was a natural reaction, considering he held her freedom in his hands.

Well, in his heart, really.

She sighed. How was she supposed to get a man who'd been so badly burned by love to love her in six days? She'd initially thought it was going to be easy, but now she wasn't so sure. She'd know more tonight, after she saw how he reacted to seeing his ex in person.

For his sake, she hoped he was just angry at her and not still hung up on the woman.

"That'll be twenty-three fifty."

Andi looked at Della. "Did you get the jewelry?"

"Yep."

"And the shoes?"

Della nodded, making her giant hoop earrings swing. "Sure did."

"Then you must have forgotten the jeans."

"Honey, I got it all."

"That can't be right. That's not enough." When had she ever argued to pay more? Of course, it wasn't her money, but still.

Della shrugged. "T-shirts are buy-one-get-two-free, jeans are half price if you're buying shoes, and jewelry is seventy-five percent off if it sparkles. There's a reason my sister named this place the Bargain Bin."

That was some kind of crazy math. "If you're sure."

"I'm sure. Stella went over it all three times to make sure I was sure." She rolled her eyes. "Sisters, am I right?"

"You can say that again."

With a laugh, Della pulled a big shopping bag from under the counter and started putting Andi's purchases in it.

Andi waved at Con. "I'm all rung up."

With a nod, he got out of the throne chair and came to the counter, producing a money clip with bills, just as he had in the last store. "How much?"

"Twenty-three fifty."

His eyes narrowed. "Did you only buy one thing?"

"No, I bought a bunch of stuff."

He peeled a fifty off the top. "That can't be right."

"That's what I said, but Della said there's a big sale on."

He laid the fifty on the counter. "All right then. Maybe you should have gotten more."

"I can always come back."

Della got his change, handed it to him, and then made sure Andi had her bag. "You two have a good night now. And come back and do some more shopping real soon."

"Thank you," Andi said. "You were a great help."

Con held the door for her, and they went out into the evening air. It was a beautiful night with an incredible starry sky overhead. He took her shopping bag from her, leaving her hands empty, so she stuck her arm through his.

She smiled up at him. "Thanks for the clothes. I really appreciate it."

"You're welcome. It wasn't much."

"The first store was."

"True." He glanced at her arm linked with his, then looked at her. "We'll go to the drugstore next. You should be able to get whatever toiletries you need there."

"Sounds good. Is that within walking distance, too?"

"Anything is walkable, but in this case, we'll go back and get the car."

"Okay."

They walked in silence for a while, which Andi was fine with. Gave her a chance to take in the town. It was pretty. Lots of big trees draped in Spanish moss and the mist that settled over everything gave the place the cozy feel of a small European village.

Sort of.

"Where am I, exactly?"

"Shadowvale."

"Right. But where is that?"

"In the Carolinas. In the United States." He shot her a look. "Where did you say you came from?"

"Paris. My sister works there, so we've been there

for a few years. We were in Rome before that. And Edinburgh prior to that."

"I see. You move a lot, then."

It wasn't a question, but she answered it anyway. "A fair amount. Wherever her job takes her. She's an event planner and really good at it. Like, big-league good."

"And you live with her?"

"No, not with her. But near her. I like to travel, so it works out."

"Do you think you'll ever settle down in one place?"

"Maybe someday. If I find the right place. The right guy." She gave him a little half smile, but he was staring at the sidewalk ahead, looking rather glum.

She couldn't figure him out. "What about you? Do you like to travel?"

"I have. Not so much anymore. It's hard for a vampire. Takes more planning."

"Oh, right. The whole sun thing."

"Which is why so many of us live here."

She wasn't sure what he meant. "Why?"

"Because the sun never shines in Shadowvale."

She stopped abruptly. "It's night all the time here?"

He shook his head. "No. But the days are all overcast. The sun can't penetrate. Or at least not enough to be a danger to us. It gets light, of course, but there's no such thing as a sunny day in Shadowvale. Unless you go above the twilight line."

"Which is?"

"A certain point on the surrounding mountains where the clouds end. I understand there's a specific spot up there, Nightingale Park, where people go to sun themselves and have picnics and such. I've never been. Obviously."

"Obviously." Her brows rose. "This place is a lot more interesting than I thought."

"There's deep magic here. Strong meridian lines. And the powerful work of a very gifted witch."

"Is that the witch you were going to call about my curse?"

He looked at her. "No. But I suppose she would be the right choice. We are well acquainted."

Her brows lifted. "Another ex?"

He laughed softly. "No, not that kind of well acquainted. I guess you could say my family has a long history with her. She might help us with this."

"That would be great." They were back at the bookstore now.

Con took his keys from his pocket and let them into the shop. "My car is in the back alley."

"Right behind you." She followed him through the shop into the alley.

She'd expected some kind of expensive European sedan. Something sleek and spendy, but safe and ultimately a little boring.

Instead, there was a gleaming black Chevy Tahoe. Not cheap, by any means, but a lot more rugged than anything she'd guessed he'd drive.

She had to ask. "An SUV, huh?"

He locked the back door of the shop, then clicked his key fob to open the vehicle. "Yes. I need the room."

"For?"

He gave her a look like the answer was obvious. "Books."

"Really? You carry around that many books?" She got into the passenger seat while he put her bags in the back.

"On occasion. I periodically go through my inventory and donate some of it to the library and schools. Or sometimes I have to make a large delivery to a customer."

She smiled at him. "That's very cool of you."

He climbed behind the wheel. "Books make life so much better. Everyone should have access to them."

"I agree, and I love to read, but I haven't had much chance lately."

He froze, then turned toward her. "That's too bad. Escaping into a book is one of the greatest pleasures in life."

She could also think of a few equally great pleasures, but she kept those to herself. "Right, but escaping into a book is pretty hard to do when you're already stuck in a book. Literally. No pun intended."

He laughed. "That's a valid reason to be behind on your reading. Listen, you're welcome to look through the shop and help yourself to whatever looks interesting."

"That's very kind of you. Thanks. I'll pretty much take any new releases in romance from the past year."

"I don't carry romance."

She frowned at him. "What? It's, like, the most popular thing people read."

"Happy ever after is a lie." His smile faded, putting an end to that conversation.

But she was never one to let things lie. "Um, it's fiction, though, so..."

He started the car, but didn't say anything more on the subject. She sighed and watched the town go by, getting her bearings as best she could. In minutes, they were at the drugstore.

She went to work, filling a basket with cosmetics, toiletries, and one paperback romance novel. Because that's just who she was.

He didn't comment on it when they were checking out, but he had to have seen it. Stubborn, stubborn vampire.

They were back in the car and headed to his home a few minutes later.

Even in the darkness, she could tell the landscape was changing. A lot. "Where are we going now?"

"My home."

"I know, but where is it in town? This looks very different than where we just were. Very...swampy."

"I live in Bayou Orleans. Most of my family does, except for my sister Juliette, who lives in an apartment in town."

"This place has a bayou?"

"Several of them. But Bayou Orleans is the biggest."

"Aren't bayous like swamps? And don't swamps have alligators?"

"Yes and yes. In fact, Bayou Orleans has a somewhat famous gator named Brutus, due to his size."

"I'm okay not meeting him." She watched the scenery for a moment. "How large is Shadowvale exactly?"

"As large as it needs to be."

She glanced at him. "That's not really an answer, you know."

He shrugged. "It's the only answer I can give you. The town seems to resist surveying."

"The *town* resists it?"

He nodded as he turned off the main road and onto Orleans Road.

They passed several homes on stilts, each more beautiful than the last. He pointed out his parents' house as they drove on.

Then a house rose out of the mist ahead of them, a beautiful place of dove gray with a red door and charcoal roof. It sat on stilts like the rest with a gorgeous wraparound porch and three dormers on the roof above. Fat pots of ferns hung between the posts on the porch. It was not only beautiful, but welcoming.

Not at all the kind of place she'd pictured him in.

"I'm impressed." Maybe more so, considering her last residence was a fourth-floor cold-water walk-up in a less-than-desirable part of Paris. She'd shared the two-bedroom flat out of economic necessity. Chuck had probably gotten a new roommate by now. Not that she could blame him. "You live here alone?"

"Yes." He hesitated. "Well, not entirely alone. There's Chloe."

He parked the truck and got out before she could ask who Chloe was. Girlfriend? Roommate? Housekeeper? Ghost? Anything was possible.

She got out, still pondering the Chloe thing, but also wondering how a prickly vampire ended up with a place that looked like it could grace the cover of a fancy-house magazine. Maybe Chloe had decorated it. That was the name of a woman who'd probably love decorating with someone else's money.

He opened the back of the SUV, got her shopping bags out, and headed for the house, leaving her to catch up. Maybe he didn't want to tell her who Chloe was. Or maybe he didn't want Andi to ask.

Like either of those was going to stop her.

She jogged after him, joining him in a few seconds. "Who's Chloe?"

He took the steps by two. "My cat. And be careful when you open the door. She's been known to run out. I think she fancies herself a bit of an escape artist, although she's never gone farther than the porch. Regardless, I don't want to risk it. Not living out here."

She stopped halfway up and stared after him. "You have a cat?"

"Is that so odd?" He unlocked the front door and held it open for her.

"No, I guess not, but I wasn't expecting—" His house was even prettier on the inside, but the thing that caught her eye was the large ball of white fluff sitting at the edge of the foyer. "I take it that's Chloe."

At the sound of her name, she meowed.

Con walked in and set the shopping bags down. "Yes, that's my girl."

Andi shut the door, not willing to risk the cat getting out.

He knelt and softly clapped his hands together. "Come here, Chloe. Come on, baby."

The cat sauntered over to him for pets and scratches, then let Con pick her up. She curled into his arms like it was her favorite spot in the world. Maybe it was. Andi had been in those arms, and it was a pretty comfortable place.

Andi shook her head. "You look like a Bond villain."

Con smiled and scratched beneath Chloe's chin. Her eyes were shut, and she was purring loudly. Lucky beast. "I found Chloe next to the dumpster in the alley behind the store. She was so tiny she fit in the palm of my hand. Maybe four, five weeks old. I thought she was gray until her first bath. She was sick with fleas and ringworm, had an eye infection, just a mess."

"Wow."

He kissed Chloe on the head. "No one expected her to make it. But she did. And now she lives like a queen, don't you, baby? Queen of this house anyway."

Andi's heart almost burst. Not in a million years would she have labeled Con an animal lover or rescuer, but to see him with Chloe was like looking at a different person. "You did a good thing for her. You saved her life."

Chloe glanced at Andi by tipping her head back over Con's arm, her eyes full of love for the man who held her. Andi got it. Totally.

"It was mutual, really. All right, sweetness, let me get settled." He set Chloe down and picked up the shopping bags again. "Come on, I'll show you the guest room."

She wanted to ask more about what he'd meant by the life-saving being mutual, but she had an idea it had something to do with Miranda again. At least that's what she guessed, since his face had taken on that same tormented look as it had in the shop when he'd talked about his ex.

Andi was really curious to see what this femme fatale looked like.

CHAPTER SIX

Constantin hoped the guest room was to Andromeda's liking. His sisters had helped him decorate the room after they'd insisted it needed a woman's touch. He doubted that, but liked that they'd wanted to help him. They'd already helped him with the rest of the house, so what was one more room?

Even with all his appreciation for their work, he'd had to rein them in, letting Juliette paint only one wall with the mural she'd insisted upon.

He opened the door and stepped back so Andromeda could enter.

"This is really nice. I'd say pretty, but there's a masculine touch in here, too."

"My sisters helped me decorate it. But I had the final say on everything."

She nodded as she looked around. "I can see you in here for sure."

He tried to see the room through her eyes, the taupe walls (the one behind the bed painted with delicate trees sprouting early-spring leaves and the very occasional pale pink blossom), the accents of ivory and copper, and the dark wood furniture. "Too masculine?"

"No, not at all. Anyone would be comfortable in here." She ran her hand over the bed's quilted silk coverlet, surprised he cared what she thought, but touched that he did. "I think it's the nicest room I've ever stayed in."

"Good."

"Is Pussy Galore allowed in here?"

"Who?"

She laughed. "Chloe."

"Oh. That's another Bond reference, isn't it?"

"Yes, and the last one, I promise."

He nodded. "She's allowed anywhere. But if you'd rather she not visit, just keep the door shut."

"No, I don't mind." Andromeda tipped her head and put her hand to her stomach. "I hate to ask, but could I have something to eat? I'm kind of starving. But, you know, not for, like…blood. Actual food. You have that, right?"

He sighed and shook his head. "I'm rubbish at having guests. I imagine you are very hungry. And yes, I have actual food. Vampires eat. What would you like?"

"I'd take a PB&J at this point."

He stared at her blankly.

"Peanut butter and jelly sandwich."

"I don't think I have that." He thought for a moment. "I can do ham and cheese on a baguette. Some grapes, maybe. There are cornichons, I know that."

"Sounds like heaven. And you don't need to make it, just point me in the direction of the kitchen."

"I can do that."

He showed her to the kitchen, a sleek, modern space that he thought still had a warmth to it, thanks to the dark wood and whorled granite.

She shook her head.

"What?" he asked.

"It's beautiful, but I'm guessing this space doesn't get used much, does it?"

"Actually, it does. I live by myself, and being a vampire means I don't eat as much as a human would, but I do cook occasionally."

"Then you keep an impeccably clean house."

"I have a little help."

"Cleaning service?"

"Housekeeper, twice a week."

"Must be nice." She opened his stainless-steel refrigerator. "Huh. Actual food. All laid out with military precision, but food nonetheless." She eyed the shelf of plasma. "Well, mostly food."

"Told you." He was happy to see she hadn't reacted with squeamishness to that particular shelf. He couldn't change who he was or where his primary source of nutrition came from.

"Yes, you did." Refrigerator door still open, she looked at him. "Where would the cheese and ham be?"

"Second middle drawer."

While she got that out, he went to fetch a baguette from the bread box. Fresh bread, especially baguettes and croissants, was something he couldn't do without. His French heritage, by way of Louisiana, wouldn't allow it. When he'd been human, bread had been life. Now it was blood, but bread was a close second.

He took out a serrated knife and sliced the loaf in half, then lengthwise.

She was laying things out on the counter. Ham, the sliced Gruyère cheese, the homemade pickles, mayonnaise, the good grainy mustard. He approved of her choices, but then, they had all come from his larder.

She twisted the lid off the mayonnaise as she looked at him. "Am I making two?"

"Sure. I could eat. Especially since we're going out in a bit."

"Good. Then I don't have to eat alone."

She hummed to herself as she worked, a soft, happy tune he didn't quite recognize.

He laid out plates and poured two glasses of water. Then Chloe came in and meowed at him. He bent toward her. "You want some dinner?"

She meowed again.

Andromeda laughed. "She's talkative, huh?"

"She is. I don't mind." He got Chloe's dish, washed it, then filled it with a new can of food and set it on her mat. He did the same with her water bowl. Behind him, Andromeda was rummaging around and working away.

It was nice, all the activity in his house. There wasn't much of that usually, and the change was a lot more pleasant than he'd anticipated.

He went back to the counter as Andromeda was laying the sandwiches on the plates. She then brought them to the other side of the counter where three stainless-steel and wood stools sat at a perfect distance from the granite's edge. She put a plate in front of the middle and right stools before taking the middle for herself.

He sat on the one to the right. "Sandwiches look good."

"It doesn't take a culinary degree to get them right." Then she made a funny little face. "But thank you."

"You're welcome." He tucked into his food as she did the same.

One bite later, he lifted the bread. "Did you combine the mayo and mustard?"

"I did. And I sprinkled a little dill on there."

"I was about to ask what those flecks of green were."

She held her sandwich before her. "Is it okay?"

"It's great." He was about to take another bite, then hesitated. "You like food?"

"I do. I mean, who doesn't? I like to try new and interesting things. Broadens the horizons and all that."

"It does, I agree. Maybe tomorrow night we could have dinner at the Table." Although something poked at him, like that might not be a good night. But what? He couldn't remember. Andi was too distracting.

"Is that a restaurant in town?"

He nodded. "Very interesting food."

"So, like a date, then?"

"I...yes, well, you are supposed to be my girlfriend." His quick-thinking explanation hadn't actually factored into his idea about going out.

"True. Can I wear the same dress?"

That gave him pause. "You could, but most women wouldn't, would they?"

"Not two nights in a row, no." Her nose wrinkled. "Sorry."

"You'll have to go shopping again."

"You realize that means you have to go with me *again*."

"I know." He shrugged one shoulder. "Wasn't so bad."

"Resounding praise for my shopping abilities. I'll take it." She laughed, then bit into her sandwich again.

He was already looking forward to it, which was the oddest feeling.

When they finished, he offered to clean up so she could get ready. She jumped at the chance for a hot shower and disappeared toward the guest room. When he heard the door shut, more because of his excellent hearing than the proximity of the space, he crouched down to talk to Chloe, who was cleaning herself with the fastidiousness of her feline kind.

"What do you think of her, Chloe?"

The cat paused while licking her paw to look at him, then returned to her bath.

He nodded. "I like her, too. But that's weird,

right? She came out of a book. It isn't like we're together now because of any mutual attraction. It's just the magic of the situation. We're being forced together. And yet I think she likes me, too. At least a little."

Chloe switched to the other paw.

He stood up. "It's only for six days. We can handle a guest for that long."

Chloe sneezed, then got up and walked away.

Whatever that was supposed to mean.

He finished cleaning up the kitchen, then went to his bedroom and got ready. Hot shower, fresh shave, a little more attention to his hair than usual, which reminded him he needed a trim, then to his closet to pick out a suit. He chose one he'd never worn before, one his sisters had gotten him for his birthday a few months ago.

It was a nice suit, that much had been clear by Valentino's reaction to it, but not Constantin's style at all. The fabric was a medium deep blue with a slight sheen to it. Very hipster, he thought. But maybe just the thing for his brother's club.

He paired it with a crisp white shirt, black alligator belt and shoes, the last two being Christmas gifts from his sisters as well. They were definitely trying to push him in a certain direction sartorially, and he trusted them, so this must be a good look.

But a glance in the mirror made him question his choices. He didn't look like himself, exactly, so he wasn't sure if this ensemble was the way to go or not. The last thing he needed was to come off like he was trying too hard. Not on the night he was going to see Miranda again.

He'd let Andromeda decide. If she liked it, he'd keep the suit on. If she laughed, he was putting on his favorite charcoal Brooks Brothers.

He went back to the kitchen and poured himself a small glass of plasma to take the edge off.

Andromeda showed up as he was rinsing the glass out.

She was in the dress, heels, and jewelry purchased earlier, but she'd done darker eye makeup and twisted the top section of her hair off her neck. The rest lay in soft honey waves that framed her face, but he had a hard time looking beyond the stunning display of her throat and shoulders.

She did a quick twirl. "Good?"

He nodded, a little breathless. If his heart could race, he had no doubt it would. The sight of this beautiful woman in his kitchen was creating urges in him. Urges that caused his fangs to extend.

His eyes must have the shine of hunger, too. But she didn't seem frightened. "You look incredible."

Her coy smile was matched with a little point of her finger. "I take it fangs out is a good sign?"

He got control of himself, swallowing the bloodlust that had risen up in him and willing his teeth to recede to a more suitable length. "Yes. My apologies."

"Don't apologize for who you are. Or for showing a woman you like what you see." She came closer. "At least not to this woman."

"I'll remember that." He'd also never forget how incredibly sexy this woman was. He spread his arms. "My turn. Your honest opinion of this suit?" He had no doubts she'd tell him exactly what she thought.

"I think it's hot. And not what I expected you to be in, but I love it. You look..." She stepped back, raking her gaze over him. "Like a million dollars. Modern and sharp. Like a man with a firm handle on his life." She raised her eyes to his. "Like a man who gets what he wants."

He dropped his arms. "Did I not look that way before?"

"If I'm honest..." She cringed a little. "Not exactly. Before, you looked like a man who sort of let life flow over you because you didn't care. Now you look like the kind of guy that life takes orders from."

He frowned. "Thank you for your honest assessment."

She came toward him and put her hand on his chest. "There was nothing wrong with how you looked before."

He turned away. "Not if being run over is a good look."

Her hand came up to his cheek, bringing his face back toward her. "Con, listen, you're a very attractive man. If you're not showing that to the world because of some past hurt, then you've got to get over that. You deserve to like what you see in the mirror. And you should. I do."

"Of course you like what you see in the mirror. Look at you, you're gorgeous."

She laughed softly. "I meant I like what I see when I look at you."

He finally made eye contact with her. "You do?"

She nodded, leaned up, and pressed her mouth to his for a brief moment, but the firmness of the kiss was full of affirmation. The kind Constantin didn't get much of in his life.

It was intoxicating.

He was tempted to kiss her back, but she broke away almost as soon as the kiss began.

Her smile placated him. "I do. Now let's go show this ex of yours just what she's missing out on."

CHAPTER SEVEN

The real truth was, Andi didn't like how good-looking Con was. On one level, she totally did. But on another, she didn't. When she'd walked into his kitchen, she'd almost taken a step back because of how handsome he looked in that suit. Instead, she'd caught herself and turned it into a spin at the last moment, mostly because her stomach was doing the same thing.

He was achingly handsome. And that was bad. Very bad. She had a weakness for gorgeous men. Who didn't? But that gorgeousness made her do stupid things and caused bad ideas to seem like great ones. Like that all-too-brief kiss in the kitchen.

Most of her adult life, she'd never really given two thoughts to her actions. Until now, because her actions mattered. Especially if there was a chance one of them could prevent her from shedding this curse.

Cassi could probably write books about the bad decisions Andi had made when it came to men. Maybe she'd already written one. It had been nearly a year.

Andi was glad she and Constantin were going out. It would be a nice distraction. Still, she sighed as she watched the bayou disappear through the car window.

"Something wrong?" Con asked.

"Just how good-looking you are." She winked at him, hoping that would distract him from the bare truth of her words.

He smirked. "Okay, enough laying on the flattery. I get what you're trying to do, and I appreciate it, but I'm not that delicate. I'm not going to fall apart just because I'm in the same room with Miranda."

Good. He thought building up his ego was all she was doing. If only her stomach would get that message and settle down, too. It was full of caffeinated butterflies right now, and they were eager for her to get close to him again. As in lips-on-lips close.

That did sound fun, didn't it?

No. Well, yes. But she couldn't push this guy. Sure, she'd kissed him in the kitchen, but that had been all about reassurance. She wanted to kiss him in a way that was much more recreational.

And while some men would definitely welcome that, Andi got the sense that Con would think she was trying to pull something. Especially if she kissed him like that before the curse dictated it. He was a cautious guy. Probably because he'd been so burned before. She had to cool it. At least until he gave her an indication that heating up was all good.

She needed something new to think about. "Your brother owns this club, huh?"

"He does."

"He must love music."

"We come from Louisiana, so music is in our blood a little, but more than the music, I think he likes the show of it all. Being a club owner, I mean."

She understood how fun attention could be. "Makes him a popular guy, I'd imagine."

"It does. He's well-loved in this town."

There was a thin layer of resentment in Con's voice. "And you're not?"

He shrugged. "Not like Valentino. He's the charmed one. The prince of Shadowvale's nightlife."

"But you provide a lot of entertainment to the people of this town, too."

"I suppose." He shook his head. "But it's not the same thing. Nor is the town's response. My brother provides not only entertainment, but a place to socialize. I can't hope to do that with books."

Andi thought about that. Con could start some book clubs that met at his store. Maybe bring in authors to speak or do signings. Host readings. Do a kids night. Events weren't that hard to come up with, so there were things he could do that would tip the social scale, but she didn't think he'd appreciate her suggestions. Not when they'd imply that she thought he was lacking. "Okay, so he's loved for what he does because it's different from what you do. I bet it seems to you that he's getting all these accolades without really doing much to earn them. Things just come to him that way, don't they?"

He gave Andi some side-eye. "You've met him once. How do you know all that?"

"I can generally figure people out." Especially when they were a lot like her. She fidgeted a little uncomfortably, hoping Con didn't realize that. "You're not the only one with siblings, remember?"

Except her relationship with Cassi was the opposite of Con's with his brother. Andi knew Cassi resented her and felt the same way about her that Con felt about Valentino. Their roles were reversed. Valentino, like Andi, lived in a different world than Con. A charmed world where everything had a way of working itself out.

Cassi had said as much right before trapping Andi in the book. She'd said that Andi didn't know what real life was like, because things just fell into her lap. That Andi needed to grow up and understand the meaning of responsibility. That Cassi couldn't understand why people loved Andi so much when she did nothing to earn that love.

But the one that had hurt the most was when Cassi had blamed Andi for the way men reacted to her.

Andi couldn't help that. Maybe she was a little too flirty at times, but that was who she was when it came to men. Friendly. Chatty. Outgoing. Not reserved like Cassiopeia. So of course men liked Andi. There was a lot to like.

Andi had told Cassi something along those terms a few days before the fateful night, and she was pretty sure that's what had prompted Cassi to buy the spell that had trapped Andi in the book.

Sprites didn't have that kind of magic, so Cassi had to have gotten the spell from someone who did. A witch, most likely. A witch who ought to have her magic license revoked, frankly.

"Andromeda?"

She snapped out of her thoughts, realizing the car was already parked. "Yes?"

"We're here. Are you okay?"

She nodded. "Sorry. Just thinking about…things." She dragged a smile onto her face. "Let's get this party started."

His eyes widened a bit. "I don't think—"

"It's just an expression. I'm not going to do anything crazy."

That seemed to be the right thing to say. "Okay. Good."

She put her hand on his arm. "I won't embarrass you. I promise."

He nodded. "I appreciate that. Thank you."

But she knew he'd been thinking that. Because why wouldn't he? She embarrassed her sister all the time, according to Cassi. Why not Con, too? He didn't know her reputation, but she hadn't done anything to hide who she was. Not much anyway.

Tonight, she would be different. More like Cassi. To some extent. She didn't want to bore herself to sleep either.

He got out and came around to her side to open her door, then offered his arm. She took it, and they walked toward the club. This was a different part of town than Main Street, where Con's shop was.

There were little lights strung throughout the trees, giving the street a very romantic vibe. Lots of little restaurants with outdoor seating and more interesting shops were here. A record store that sold old vinyl, a custom-perfume boutique, a cobbler who not only repaired shoes, but made them to order. She counted two art galleries and three antique shops.

The faint smell of patchouli and smoke from food grilling drifted past. "What part of town is this?"

"Fiddler Street. It's a bit more artsy than Main."

"I see that. Pretty cool."

He frowned. "If you like that sort of thing."

She glanced at him. "You don't?"

"It's all right."

She chuckled. "You really are uptight, you know that?"

He stopped walking. "I am not. I just like things a certain way. And I've already told you that." Then he sighed. "I can't help who I am. I am very old. And that makes it hard to change who I am."

"No doubt. I get it. You probably don't want to change either."

He looked away for a moment, then finally made eye contact again. "Do you really think I'm uptight?"

"Yes. And I say that as someone well aware of her own faults. Doesn't mean you're not a good guy. Just that you could let go a little."

His mouth firmed into a hard, thin line. "That's...kind of you. I guess."

She ran a finger down the front of his suit. "You didn't pick this suit out yourself, did you?"

"No. My sisters bought it for me. Same with the belt and shoes."

"Not your taste, are they? Too flashy, like the suit?"

He nodded. "Exactly."

"But you look like a million bucks in this outfit." Maybe more. Just looking at him made her stomach get all flippy. "It's just that calling this kind of attention to yourself makes you uncomfortable. Am I right?"

"Yes."

"Why is that, do you think?" Why she'd suddenly chosen this moment to analyze him, she had no idea, but he seemed to be okay with it.

"Because I will always be compared to my brother." He turned away, putting himself in shadow. "And found lacking."

Was that how Cassi felt about her? Andi's heart unexpectedly ached at the thought.

A second later, a sound of disgust slipped out of him. "I don't want it to be that way."

Time for a little hard truth. The kind Cassi was so fond of giving her. "My gran always said if you're eating a crap burger, it's probably because you ordered it."

He moved to look at her, putting himself back in the light again. "What the devil is that supposed to mean?"

She cringed a little, worried about how he'd react to the explanation, but not about to back down from the truth. "You did this to yourself. You let yourself think you are less than, so now other people think you are."

Anger flashed in his eyes, then he looked down. Almost like he was ashamed. "That might be so, but I don't know how to change that."

"Instead of blaming yourself for the past, focus on the present. Maybe start by doing the opposite of what you usually do. If something bothers you, let it slide off your back. If you want to leave, stay. See what I'm saying?" It was advice, she abruptly realized, she needed to take herself.

"Easily said, not as easily done. But you probably wouldn't know that because lack of confidence isn't something you suffer from."

"No, it's not." She put her hand on her head for a moment. Confidence was something she probably had too much of. A hard truth. And something worth confessing, because he needed to know she had flaws. A dangerous path to take. She prayed it didn't backfire. "Listen, I'm going to tell you something about me that isn't exactly complimentary."

He looked skeptical. "I'm listening."

She took a breath. She was about to admit something she'd never admitted. Not out loud anyway. "I'm full of myself. I think I'm fantastic. And that I have a great body, a cute face, that I'm smart, witty, and fun. I figure if people don't like me, there must be something wrong with them. Not me. Get it?"

For a brief moment, he didn't respond at all. Then he abruptly burst out laughing. "Yes, I get it."

She crossed her arms, abruptly feeling a little sickened by her own reality. "I didn't expect my heartfelt confession would result in you laughing at me."

"Not in a bad way, I promise. More at your audacity. Because you're so honest about it. You're so...comfortable with who you are. You own it. I wish I could have a quarter of your confidence." He looked down the street. Toward his brother's club. There was an odd mix of steely determination and longing in his gaze. "But I don't know how."

She wanted with all of her heart to help him. It was a strange feeling. She wasn't used to helping others. Another sad truth she needed to change. Well, why not start with Con? "What if you...faked it?"

His face was incredulous. "Faked being confident?"

"Sure. Pretend...I don't know...pretend you're me. But, like, without the boobs and stuff."

He snorted. "I don't think I can do that."

"Look, your brother thinks you and I are a couple, right?"

"Right."

"So what kind of man do you think I'd be attracted to?"

He frowned. "One just like my brother."

"But I'm with *you*. So you must be the kind of man I really like. That has to give you some confidence, doesn't it?" She put her hands on her hips. "I get that it's pretty egotistical of me to say having me as your girlfriend should be that much of a boost, but hello, that's who I am."

"You are fantastic, you know that?" He was smiling now. That made her happy, too.

"My sister would tell you different."

"What does she know?"

Only that Andi had ruined her life. Andi managed a smile anyway. "Exactly. So let's go in there and show him the new, improved you."

"Right." Con faced the club, extending his elbow so Andi could loop her arm through his again.

They started walking.

She leaned in a little. "You want me to lay on the doting-girlfriend stuff? Really sell it?"

"Yes. I'm not sure what all that entails, but yes." He blew out a breath. "I want the impossible. I want my brother to be jealous of me."

She laughed and patted his arm with her free hand. "My darling Constantin, that's not even remotely impossible. You just watch and see."

CHAPTER EIGHT

There was a lightness in Constantin's step he'd never experienced before. Was that what confidence felt like? Did Valentino feel like this every day? If so, Andromeda was right. Having her on his arm *was* a boost.

That was possibly the most superficial, shallow thought he'd ever had, but he was leaning into it. Hard. And since he needed any kind of lift he could get tonight, he almost didn't care that it was shallow and superficial.

Because while he was ready to make this evening a brand-new experience, he was also, deep in his gut, feeling like an absolute impostor.

Andromeda was *not* his girlfriend. All it would take was for someone to figure that out, and the gig, as they said, would be up.

But no one would find out. How could they? No one knew the truth but the two of them, and Andromeda was possibly more into this prevarication than he was. But this was Shadowvale. A town filled with people cursed with all sorts of bothersome abilities. If one of them were to see through this charade...

He growled in frustration at himself. Already, his confidence was slipping. He had to stop these head games, or this night was going to be a disaster. The kind of disaster Valentino would never let him forget. He slowed a little. Maybe they should turn around now and go home while he still had his dignity.

His feet kept moving, though. Somewhere within him lived the desire to see this through.

They were a block from the door when Andromeda put the brakes on.

He stopped beside her. "Everything all right?"

"Kiss for good luck," she whispered.

That was just what he needed. He bent to meet her, allowing himself to believe the fantasy that this crazy-beautiful creature really was his. And she was—for six days.

Six days.

When she'd first mentioned that, it sounded like an eternity.

Now it seemed like the blink of an eye.

She leaned in farther. Deepened the kiss. He put his arms around her, sinking into the warmth of her mouth and body and letting each nuanced sensation descend into his bones. The softness of her mouth, the sweetness of her perfume, the little sounds of pleasure she made, the rhythm of her pulse, the velvet of her dress under his hands. All of it. He wanted to imprint this moment—and her—on his memory.

For when those six days were up.

When he finally drew back, she looked flushed and breathless. It amused him that she was so deeply committed to pretending that she'd even faked such a response. That deserved a compliment. "You're very good at this."

She grinned. "So are you."

He had no choice but to smile back. So help him, he liked her. Just being around her was an ego boost, even if her part was a big put-on. Right now, he didn't care. Right now, he wanted to be the man she thought he was capable of being.

Especially in light of who was inside Club 42. And he wasn't thinking about Valentino.

They headed for the club's front door and the large man standing out front. He reached to unhook the rope, but his hand stayed put on the brass end of the thick red velvet. "Evening, folks. Twenty-dollar cover charge. Ladies free."

"Outrageous," Constantin muttered as he reached for his money clip. The bouncer had the low brow, square jaw, and thick chest of a holler troll. He had the requisite piney, earthy scent as well. "No wonder my brother's raking it in."

The man leaned toward them. "You Mr. Thibodeaux's brother?"

"Yes." Constantin flashed his ID before yanking a twenty free of the clip.

The bouncer finished unhooking the rope and, with a big smile, moved it out of the way. "Y'all go right on in and have a good time."

Constantin put his ID away, but stuck the bill into the man's hand. "Thank you. Have a good night."

The man glanced at the money and smiled. "Thank *you*, Mr. Thibodeaux."

As they went through the door, Andromeda nodded appreciatively. "That was very nice of you."

"You told me to do the opposite of what I'd usually do. My first instinct was to put the money away, so I gave it to him instead."

"Good thinking. I guarantee he'll remember you next time you come here."

"*If* there's a next time."

She nudged him with her elbow. "Think positive, will you?"

"Right. Yes." He'd been to the club before, but not in a very long time. It looked pretty much the way he remembered it.

Brick side walls, brass sconces with glass shades above each intimate, half-circle booth. Posters of great jazz and blues musicians in between the lights. Down the middle of the floor, round tables with chairs in very simple dark wood.

Lazily spinning fans overhead kept the smoke from accumulating. The fans helped mitigate the smell of booze, too, letting the perfume from the gardenias in the bud vases on each table sweeten the air. Con knew their sister Daniella grew those specifically for Valentino in one of her greenhouses. Next to the vases were thick glass votive holders, the tiny candle flames flickering away inside.

More sounds reached them as they walked deeper

into the club. The clink of glasses, the hum of quiet conversations, and over it all, the music coming from the far stage. In this case, a quartet putting a bluesy twist on some old standards.

They could have been in some locals-only joint in New Orleans. It was a vibe Valentino loved. Constantin could understand that. The familiarities of home were always a comfort, and the Thibodeaux family as a whole hadn't strayed far.

After all, they still lived in a bayou.

"This place is about as cool as it gets, huh?" Andromeda looked around. "I suppose we should find a table."

"I've got this." He approached the hostess stand. "Any chance there's a booth reserved for Constantin Thibodeaux?"

Andromeda joined him as the hostess scanned the names scrawled in the book before her. "I don't see one, sorry. Is that you?"

"It is. I'm Valentino's brother." Constantin produced another twenty. "Can you find us one? Not too close to the stage and on the far wall."

The woman smiled as she accepted the tip. "Of course, sir. If you'd like, I can let Mr. Thibodeaux know you're here."

"No need to tell him. He'll figure it out. He's a bright boy."

"As you wish, Mr. Thibodeaux. Right this way."

She led them to a booth that fit his exact description, scooping up the reserved sign and depositing it on the next booth over. "I'm Brin, if you need anything else. Your server will be Zane. Have a wonderful evening."

They slid around the table and onto the half-moon banquette, one on each side, meeting in the middle. He nodded at the hostess. "Thank you, Brin. You've been a big help."

She smiled again and left them.

Andromeda moved a little closer. "Put your arm around me. We're supposed to be an item. You have to act like it."

"Right." He looped his arm around her. It was surprisingly comfortable. Ages had passed since he'd been out with a woman who wasn't one of his sisters. This was, without question, a very different kind of experience. Much more to his liking, frankly. Even if it was a ruse.

Andromeda reached up to twine her fingers with his hand where it draped the top of her shoulder, then looked up at him. "That was pretty impressive, sliding her a little money for the table. Nicely done."

"Thanks." Her praise filled him with a warm feeling that he instantly knew he could get addicted to. "I just did what you said. The opposite of my usual. I can't believe how well it works. Apparently, I've been doing things wrong most of my life."

"No, you haven't. It's just that most people don't understand how going a little outside their comfort zone can work wonders."

"Is that what you do? Go outside your comfort zone?"

She laughed softly. "Not really. I live in my

comfort zone, which is outside of everyone else's. But I'm a rare bird that way."

"Yes, you are." Impulsively, which was definitely not in his comfort zone, he leaned in and kissed her temple.

She slipped her arm from between them to rest her hand on his thigh.

Her touch was light as air, but sparks of desire shot through him all the same, tensing his muscles and heating him the way nothing else could. He stretched slightly so that his thigh touched hers.

"Don't you two look cozy." It was only the sound of Valentino's voice that brought him back to reality. His brother stood at their table. Valentino shook his head. "I can't believe it. You came."

Constantin stopped thinking about Andromeda long enough to greet his brother. "Hello to you, too, Valentino. Yes, we came. Thanks for reserving us a booth."

Valentino sighed. "I would have if I'd thought you'd actually show."

Constantin lifted one hand. "You're looking at us."

"Yes, I am. And I'm glad you're here. Miranda will be thrilled."

Somehow, Constantin doubted that.

Valentino smiled at Andromeda. "You look lovely, Andi. Thank you for dragging my brother out."

She laughed a little. "It's the other way around. He dragged me out." She shot Constantin a smoky gaze. "I would have been very content to spend the night in."

New flames ignited inside Constantin. How did she do that with a few words and a glance? He took a breath, hoping to cool himself off enough to respond properly, but when he looked at his brother, Constantin knew he wasn't the only one affected by Andromeda's charms.

Valentino looked positively shocked.

Constantin barely refrained from barking out a laugh.

Their server showed up. "Evening, folks. I'm Zane, and I'll be taking care of you tonight. What can I get you?"

Valentino waved a hand. "Whatever they want is on the house."

Zane nodded. "Yes, sir."

"I'd love a glass of champagne," Andromeda said. "Thank you, Valentino. That's very kind."

"Call me Val. Please." He put his hand to his chest. "And it's my pleasure."

Constantin thought it was more about his brother showing off. "I'll have a brandy."

Zane nodded. "Very good. I'll be right back with those."

Valentino gave Constantin a closer look. "Miranda is backstage, but I'm sure she wouldn't mind if you popped in to say hi."

Constantin matched his brother's penetrating gaze. "She might not, but that wouldn't be very kind to Andromeda, would it?"

For the briefest of moments, surprise overtook Valentino's cool demeanor. Then he smiled. "No, I suppose not." He stood there without saying another word for a spell, then brightened his smile a little. "I should go check on the rest of the club. I hope you enjoy the show."

Then he disappeared into the growing crowd.

Andromeda squeezed Constantin's thigh. "I don't think he knows what to do with the new Constantin."

"Good," Constantin said. "Because I like this new me."

"Having fun, then?"

He didn't even have to think about his answer. "More than I ever thought possible."

CHAPTER NINE

Andi was happy for a host of reasons. The club was fun, they were getting free drinks, Con was really loosening up, but most of all, he seemed the happiest he'd been since she'd arrived.

That was great, and not just because it boded well for her and her situation.

His consideration of her feelings when Valentino had tempted him to visit Miranda backstage had been unexpected—and had given her the sweetest thrill, even if it was all for show on his part. Maybe it wasn't, though. Maybe he would have been that way without their sidewalk conversation. That was more likely, considering his general bent toward respectability.

Constantin, for all his proclaimed shortcomings, had known that very few women would appreciate their boyfriends going to an ex's dressing room alone. And he had treated Andi with respect and courtesy. Even calling his brother out for suggesting it.

To say she'd been flattered by Con's consideration of her was an understatement. Most, if not all, of the men she'd spent time with probably would have been back in that dressing room as quick as you could blink.

What did that say about her choice of men? Not a lot. It said even less about how she allowed herself to be treated.

What did it say about Con? Did it mean he was getting better at playing pretend, or that he was thinking of Andi as a girlfriend? Hard to tell. Either way, it was a step in the direction Andi needed him to go.

But all that consideration was making her like him, too. She was back to wishing he wasn't so nice to look at. Because spending time with a gorgeous man who was also sort of a jerk meant never getting her heart involved.

She'd thought that's who she'd ended up with.

Now that wasn't the case at all. For whatever reason, Con was becoming the gorgeous man who was also a prince on the inside. Maybe a reluctant prince, but his past made that understandable.

Had she caused this change with her sidewalk pep talk? Had she unleashed something in him with the confidence boost of being able to pretend in front of his brother? Or was this who he'd been all along, and he'd just been afraid to show it because of past hurts?

She had a feeling it was the latter and not at all due to her. Which was good. She didn't want to be responsible for such a turnaround.

But not being responsible didn't change the fact

that she was starting to like him in a way she hadn't counted on.

Zane returned with their drinks—a bottle of good champagne, along with two glasses and an ice bucket on a stand, which he set up next to their table, and a large brandy in a snifter for Con.

A second server followed with platters of assorted cheeses, crackers, cold shrimp, a bowl of caviar with some accompaniments, and fruit.

When they were all done setting things up and had left Con and Andi alone again, she raised her brows at Con. "Look at your brother trying to impress you."

Con laughed. "Pretty sure you're the one he's trying to impress, but I don't care. If it makes you happy, then I like it, too."

"Snazzy finger food, good champagne, and the most eligible bachelor in the room at my side? I'm very happy."

"I wouldn't go so far as to say I'm the most eligible—"

"Hush now. Don't argue with your girlfriend."

With a soft chuckle, he lifted his snifter. "Then let me toast to the most beautiful woman here." His expression turned more serious, but no less warm. "Thank you for helping me with all this. I know your current situation isn't ideal, but we're going to get you through it."

"Thank you." And just like that, they'd become a team. She picked up her champagne flute and clinked it gently against his glass. She smiled as she sipped the golden bubbles, but inside she was cracking into pieces.

Being a team was great, but he was falling for her. And fast. She could sense it. That wasn't supposed to happen. It *needed* to happen to break the curse, but it came with a horrible side effect. If he fell in love with her, he'd expect her to stay.

And as soon as the curse was broken, she was headed back to Paris and her sister. She had to. Sure, she'd thank Con for everything he'd done for her, but she was definitely leaving. For one thing, if her wings didn't return with the curse being lifted, she had to get them back. But she also had to explain to her sister what had really happened.

Cassi deserved to know the truth. Even if it was going to hurt.

The quartet onstage took a break, and Valentino walked on, preening in the spotlight. "Ladies and gentlemen, welcome to Club 42."

She'd been so distracted with Con and her thoughts that she hadn't noticed how packed the room had become. Definitely the place to be in Shadowvale tonight.

Valentino continued, "As you know, I've brought in a very special guest this evening. A singer whose incredible beauty is only surpassed by the angelic qualities of her voice. She's serenaded supernaturals and humans alike. Kings and queens, heads of state, dignitaries, and celebrities, but tonight she graces us with her voice." He put his hand on his heart as though he was deeply touched.

An appropriate murmur of appreciation went through the crowd.

Andi rolled her eyes. That was quite a buildup.

"Please welcome the incomparable Miranda Moore." He gestured to the right of the stage as he exited left.

The spotlight narrowed. And Miranda walked out.

Her black dress, which was tight enough that it might have been mistaken for body paint, was covered in sequins that made her glitter like a diamond bracelet. Her makeup—a sleek cat eye and a red lip—was magazine flawless.

She was curvy, a textbook hourglass, and just tall enough not to be considered short. She oozed feminine charm and sex appeal. If Marilyn Monroe had been a brunette, she would have been Miranda Moore.

Hmm. The stage must be a nod to the late blonde superstar, meant to conjure up her appealing image.

Then Miranda opened her mouth, fangs fully on display, and the clearest, sweetest sound came forth as she began to sing.

She was perfection, in vampire form, from the top of her impeccably coiffed head to the bottom of her undoubtedly manicured toes.

Andi hated her.

*

Constantin's gut felt like it had just taken the full-force blow of a cannonball. Miranda was unchanged from the last time he'd seen her, but somehow he'd forgotten just how beautiful she was.

Maybe that had been time being kind to him by allowing the sharp details of her perfection to blur. But there was nothing kind or blurred about the ache in his heart.

He didn't love her anymore, he was sure of that. But the pain he was feeling told him he still felt something. A longing for what might have been, maybe? Or a reminder that this was the woman who'd heartlessly changed her mind about marrying him?

Either way, he no longer wanted to be in the club. All the fun he and Andromeda had been having vaporized like a drop of water on a hot griddle.

Andromeda's hand tightened on his thigh, bringing his attention back to the woman at his side. "Hey," she said softly. "Don't let her own you."

He frowned and shook his head, unable to find the words to express what was going on inside.

Andromeda turned to put herself into his line of sight a little more, which also blocked some of his ability to see Miranda, but he still couldn't take his eyes off the stage. "Do you still love her?"

Finally, he looked at Andromeda. Really looked at her. She was just as beautiful as Miranda, but in a much more natural way. Miranda's beauty was manufactured and required a lot of upkeep, something he knew from his years with her. She also had the unnatural benefit of being a vampire. Her beauty had a razor-sharp edge to it.

Andromeda's beauty was a carefree thing. Wild and easy, and it seemed very much who she was every day. Without trying.

Her brows lifted a little. "Well, do you?"

"No."

"Then what's upsetting you? Your eyes are shooting sparks, and if your fangs get any longer, I might have to sit somewhere else."

He bent his head and closed his eyes for a moment as he pulled himself back from the brink of his emotions, tried to regain some control. When he raised his head, he asked, "Better?"

"Much." She sighed. "If this is too much for you, we should go."

"That's exactly what I want to do."

"Then let's—"

"But that's what the old me wants to do." He fought the urge to storm out. But that would cause a scene. And Miranda would know she'd won, in some way. "So we stay."

Respect and perhaps a little sympathy gleamed in her gaze. He was okay with that. Sympathy was something he usually got only from his mother and sisters. "You're sure?"

"I am. If we leave, she'll see us go and..." He glanced at the stage, where Miranda was sashaying from one end to the other, belting out the kind of sweet words that made her betrayal that much more bitter.

"And she'll know she got to you," Andromeda finished.

He nodded slowly. "Yes. And that would be worse than what I'm enduring."

"I agree. And I think staying is the way to go. Now she'll see how happy and content you are with another woman. I'm proud of you. I know it's tough." Andromeda smiled as she picked up her champagne for another sip.

"It is. But I need to focus on the outcome I'm after." He joined her, lifting his brandy and drinking. The liquid burned a pleasant trail down his throat, soothing some of the pain Miranda had caused. But that wasn't true. The brandy had done nothing. It was Andromeda who'd done the soothing.

And she was far more intoxicating.

She snuggled closer to him. He buried his nose in the top of her curls, inhaling the delicious scent of her. That was what a lover would do, wasn't it?

Zane returned to check on them. "How are you two doing? What else can I get for you?"

Constantin looked at Andromeda. "Do you need anything, my love?"

Her grin was instant and knowing. Her eyes stayed on him as she answered, "I have everything I need."

"Great," Zane said. "Just let me know if you do."

Miranda's song ended, and the crowd greeted her with applause. Constantin and Andromeda joined in, but not with any great enthusiasm.

She sang two more songs, during which Andromeda got even closer and was especially attentive. She fed him some grapes, made him refill her champagne flute, then made him taste the cheese she liked best, nudged him twice to point out someone interesting in the crowd, which was then followed by a snarky little comment that inevitably made him laugh.

All while touching him in some way.

He understood what she was doing, or at least he thought he did. Either way, she made an excellent distraction, and as Miranda's first set drew to a close, the initial gut-punch he'd felt had diminished to a minor stomachache.

Valentino's arrival at their table was no surprise, other than Constantin had thought he would have come by sooner. "How are you two enjoying your evening?"

"Good," Constantin replied. No need to be gushy.

That wasn't a satisfactory answer for Valentino, naturally. "Miranda sounds great tonight, don't you think?"

Constantin nodded, fighting the urge to disparage her and knowing that was what the old him would do.

Thankfully, Andromeda stepped up. "The acoustics in your club would make a screech owl sound operatic. Miranda should give a big thank-you to whoever designed this place."

Constantin almost snorted. Valentino had designed the club, so there was no way he'd contradict Andromeda, but that wasn't doing Miranda any favors either. Watching him squirm was something brand-new and wholly captivating.

Valentino finally gave her a curt smile. "Well, thank you."

Then he turned and walked away.

Constantin released the sharp laugh he'd been holding back. "*He* designed this place."

"I figured that," Andromeda said. "He seems like just enough of a control freak to have a hand in everything."

Constantin let out a long, contented sigh. "I adore you."

She raised her eyes to him, and her expression looked oddly hopeful. "You do?"

He nodded. "You've made this night not only bearable but enjoyable. And you stopped me from making a fool of myself by walking out."

She shrugged, her expression still bright and buoyant. "I'm really happy that I could do that for you." She paused, glancing away for a moment. "After all, you're the man who's going to give me my freedom. I need to keep you happy."

CHAPTER TEN

She shouldn't have said that, but the words had slipped out before she could stop them. She was always most truthful when she was particularly moved, and Con had certainly moved her with his heartfelt words.

He kept smiling. "I don't think you have to worry about that."

She almost exhaled in relief that he hadn't read more into it.

He was such a good guy. So honest and straight up, despite how he'd been hurt. Or maybe that had pushed him to become this way.

She wasn't sure if that was the only reason he was the way he was, but she liked him regardless. She liked all of him, actually. Even his prickly side. Which wasn't showing itself quite as much since they'd had the chat on the sidewalk.

Liking him still remained a dangerous proposition for her, but something new had become abundantly clear. There was no way for her to get out of this situation without him getting hurt, and that bothered her more than it ever had before in her life.

She'd left a lot of guys. Broken a lot of hearts. And never given any of them this kind of thought or consideration.

She'd always figured those guys had broken a lot of hearts themselves before they'd gotten to her, so a dose of their own medicine wasn't such a bad thing.

Maybe even a life lesson they'd learn from.

But Con was the broken one in this situation. And she couldn't bear to put him through that again. If he was indeed falling for her.

Maybe it was time to let her real light shine. Her self-absorbed, the world-revolves-around-me light. But if she did that, and she wasn't even sure she could be that way with him, she ran the risk of him not falling in love with her and not saving her from getting stuck in that wretched book for the rest of her years.

There was no easy path here. Which was probably the exact kind of challenge Cassi had hoped for.

But then Andi remembered something he'd said. "Con?"

He set his brandy down. "Yes?"

"You said something in the shop about talking to one of the witches in town to see if they could help with my curse. Do you think you could still do that?"

"Of course. I'd be happy to. In fact, I could slip out and make that call right now."

"Really?"

He smiled. "It would be my pleasure."

"Thank you."

"Be right back."

She grabbed his hand as he started to slide out of the booth. "Hey."

He stopped. "What?"

"A good boyfriend wouldn't just leave."

A look of honest confusion masked his face. "He wouldn't?"

She pursed her lips, shook her head, and said, "Uh-uh," as best she could without unpuckering.

He laughed. "I am so out of practice." He leaned toward her and gave her the kiss she was after. "Now I'm going to make that call."

She nodded. "Perfect. But don't go too far or you'll tug me after you."

"Right." He glanced toward the door. "I'll just be outside the front door. That should be in range."

"Okay."

She watched him until he disappeared into the crowd, which didn't take long. Then she sighed at her dilemma. She was royally screwed. This really felt like it was all part of Cassi's plan.

Andi shook her head. Poor Cassi. She really deserved an explanation.

Andi sipped her champagne as she thought about her sister. She really hoped Cassi had moved on. Or gotten over it. And, above all, forgiven Andi. But that probably wasn't going to happen without an apology. Something Andi couldn't deliver until she was free of her curse.

It was going to be the first thing she did right after that, for sure. She refilled her glass halfway. If Cassi felt as bad as Con did, then Andi understood why her sister had responded with the curse.

It was kind of surprising she hadn't done it sooner.

The weight of being watched brought Andi back to reality. Miranda stood at the table's edge, looking down at her.

Miranda rested her hands on her hips, her expression coy. "Good evening. I thought I'd find Connie here, but I see he's left already. Was the show too much for him? It was awfully brave of him to come."

Brave? Oh, this woman needed to be slapped. In fact, Andi wanted to leap across the table, grab Miranda by the throat and give her a good bite. Sprites were kind of known for that, sporting a wicked set of pointy chompers in full sprite form, but Andi wasn't sure she could go into combat mode without her wings.

She wasn't willing to attempt it either, just in case it went dreadfully wrong. She might try a little sprite dust, though. A sprinkling of that magical glitter could help turn the tide in one's favor, making whoever inhaled it very biddable.

She wiggled her fingers at Miranda, ready to command her to go away.

Nothing happened. She clenched her teeth in sheer anger. No wings, no magic dust. Fabulous.

Instead of freaking out further, she took a calming

breath, which only partially worked, and answered the woman. "He's making a phone call. The show was fine. We got a little distracted with each other, so I'm not sure we gave it our full attention, but it's really just background music anyway, right?"

Miranda's coy expression faltered. "My show is not background. It's the reason people came out tonight." Her fake smile returned. "It's the reason *you* came out tonight."

"Actually, we're here because I was bored and wanted to get out of the house. And Val invited us, so it seemed like the polite thing to do." Andi made a big show of yawning. "We've done the polite thing, though, so now we'll be heading out."

She grinned with all the lascivious pleasure she could manage. "There are a lot of interesting things to do with Con at home."

Miranda's eyes took on the same hard gleam that Con's had earlier. "If you're trying to spin me up—"

"I'm not trying. But you do look pretty spun up. I guess you never really got over him, huh?" Andi slipped out of the booth to stand toe to toe with the vampiress. Thank the stars she'd found a pair of heels to go with this dress. Miranda was still a good head taller.

Andi lifted her chin and faced the woman down. "I get it. I do. He's kind, sweet, generous, crazy-handsome, and knows just how to make a woman smile. Of course you're not over him! But he's mine now, so it's time for you to move on."

With that, Andi turned and bumped straight into

Con. His eyes shared Miranda's predatory gleam. How long had he been standing there?

His gaze softened a little as he touched Andi's cheek. "Are you all right, my love?"

She nodded. "Just coming to find you. I'm ready to go."

"Whatever you want." He gave Miranda a cursory glance, then put his arm around Andi and turned them toward the exit.

Andi was trembling with adrenaline from the confrontation. Con had to feel her shaking, but he said nothing.

Until they were back on the sidewalk. They broke apart, and that's when she realized he was seething. His eyes were still bright with anger, his fangs extended, and his body seemed like a coiled wire ready to snap. "I am very sorry you had to deal with her. She had no right provoking you. I should have expected it, though. I was a fool to leave you alone."

"I'm...fine. All charged up with confrontational energy, but I'm okay, I promise." She blew out a breath before looking at him again. "Are you okay?"

The hard edge to his gaze was lessening even as she looked at him. "Yes, of course. I wasn't upset about seeing Miranda. I was upset that she was bothering you. I was...worried about you." Then he shook his head. "But you did fine."

So he had heard. At least some of it.

Fangs now receded, he snorted. "Actually, you did more than fine. You held your own against a very powerful vampire. That was impressive, Andromeda. Truly impressive."

"How much did you hear?"

"All of it. I saw her approach the table as I was coming through the crowd. I would have been there sooner, but our server stopped me to see if I needed something. And then, to be honest, I was a little too captivated by your handling of her to step in immediately."

"You could hear our conversation in all that noise?"

He tapped his ear. "Vampire senses are pretty acute."

"Oh, right."

He took her hand. "You put on a better show than she did onstage."

"What I said about you, that wasn't a show. I know you told me you don't like people and you're prickly and difficult and all that, but you've been nothing but kind and sweet and generous to me. You sell yourself short, Con."

He made a little face.

"Sorry, I keep forgetting you don't like nicknames."

He shrugged. "It's not so bad when you say it."

"But you don't like Connie because that's what she used to call you, right?"

He nodded, looking disgusted. "It sounded like such a diminishment when she said it."

"I won't call you that. Ever. But I do like calling you Con."

One side of his mouth quirked up. "Okay. You can."

"And please, call me Andi. Only my sister calls me by my full name, and it means she's mad at me. Which is pretty much all the time."

He laughed. "Andi it is, then."

She laced her fingers through his. "Cool."

He looked down at her hand in his. "You're still trembling."

"Sugar deficiency."

He grinned. "Is that what it is?"

"I'm serious. Sprites are part of the fairy family, and we need a lot of sugar. We have very high metabolisms. And getting all worked up like that means we burn through our reserves pretty quickly."

Concern replaced the amusement in his eyes. "Are you okay? Do you need me to carry you?"

She almost laughed at how adorable he was. Being carried by him sounded lovely, but she didn't want him to think she was that incapacitated. "No, I just need some sweets."

"Ice cream?"

"With some toppings? That should do it." She felt like there was something else she should be asking him about, but whatever it was had slipped her mind in the excitement of the Miranda confrontation.

He offered her his arm. "I know a place."

CHAPTER ELEVEN

Thankfully, Shadowvale had at least one twenty-four-hour ice cream shop. Of course, there was the Sunshine Diner, too, but Constantin wasn't sure it had more than chocolate and vanilla. And he'd have to wait out front while Andi went in alone, since the diner's UV lights weren't vampire-compatible.

As he parked in front of the ice cream shop, Andi peered through the car window at the place.

"Are you sure this is good?" she asked.

He turned the car off. "I don't eat much ice cream, but it's generally considered the place to go for the stuff. My sisters love it."

She looked at him. "The Creamatorium?"

He bent his head to peek at the sign, which showed a banana split inside a coffin-shaped container. "The name and sign are a little morbid, I'll give you that, but it's all in good fun, I promise. We can go somewhere else if you want."

She unbuckled her seat belt. "No, let's try it. I need sugar. I'm sure they can manage that. I just hope the flavors aren't too weird. I see any eye-of-newt swirl, and I'm out."

He snorted. "I'm with you on that one."

They went inside, and just as they started to review the selections, Constantin's phone vibrated. He took it out of his pocket and checked the screen. Valentino. "Andi, I need to take this. I'll be right back."

"Sure. I need time to read through all of this anyway."

He stepped outside. "Yes?"

"You left rather abruptly." Valentino sounded upset and hurt. That was unusual.

"Miranda went out of her way to make Andi uncomfortable."

"She wouldn't do something like—"

"If you're calling me a liar, then I suggest you check your security cams. I know you have them. You can see for yourself that Miranda approached Andi at our table while I was outside making a call. Thankfully, Andi has enough backbone to stand up for herself." One of many things Constantin really liked about her.

Valentino went silent for a moment. "I'm sorry Miranda did that. I really had no idea she'd be so petty."

"Really?"

"Really. Despite what you think, I didn't invite her to poke at you. When Isabelle's laryngitis flared up, I was desperate for a replacement. And Miranda owed me. But I regret bringing her in now. I'm sorry."

Constantin almost pulled the phone away from his ear to be sure he was still talking to his brother. He couldn't remember a time when Valentino had said the word *sorry* to him in a genuine way. Hearing it twice was staggering. "Thank you. But what did you think would happen when you invited me to see the woman who broke my heart?"

Those were words Constantin had never said to his brother, and Valentino was slow to respond. Maybe shocked by them. Or by Constantin admitting something so personal.

"I just thought you'd like to see her after so long. You claimed her leaving you didn't affect you, so I figured it was no big deal. I didn't realize..." He sighed. "Did you have a good time at all?"

Constantin's mind flashed to Andi tucked against his side, her hand on his thigh, her warmth radiating through him. "Yes. We did. Thank you for the drinks and the food."

"You're welcome." Another pause, this time not as long. "I guess I'll see you two at family dinner tomorrow night?"

How had Constantin forgotten that? He'd already promised Andi dinner at the Table. He'd tell Andi that they'd go out to dinner by themselves another time and hope she was okay with that. Unless there was a way out of it... "Are you bringing Miranda?"

"No."

"Then yes, you will see us."

"Good. Give Andi my regards. I'd better get back to work."

He hung up before Constantin could say goodbye, but that was just Valentino's way. With a smile, Constantin tucked the phone away and rejoined Andi, who was still staring up at the menu board.

The tip of her tongue was running over her teeth, and her nose was slightly wrinkled in indecision. She was quite possibly the most adorable creature he'd ever known.

He sidled up to her, not wanting to break her concentration. "Did you decide on a flavor yet?"

"I think so." She looked at him. "Everything okay?"

"Valentino says hello." Constantin shrugged. "He just wanted to know why we'd left so soon."

"You told him?"

"I did. And he apologized for Miranda's behavior. Also, with everything going on, I forgot tomorrow night is my family's weekly dinner at my parents' house. I hope that's all right. I promise we'll go to the Table another night."

"Family dinner?" She got a sudden, strange look. "Is your whole family vampires?"

"Yes. And dinner isn't us devouring some hapless soul, so calm down."

"Just checking." Her expression remained slightly skeptical. "But you know I have to go with you, right? Because of the whole curse thing."

"I know. I wasn't implying that I intended to leave you at home."

"Okay." Her smile was back, big and bright.

"Thank you. Now that that's settled, let's focus on getting you some sugar. What looks good?"

She turned her attention back to the menu. "I think I'm getting that Chocolate Coronary sundae."

"Sounds like a sugar bomb."

"I know, right?" She grinned. "What about you?"

He looked at the board. "I'm not really an ice cream person, but I think I'll try a scoop of that Caramel Cayenne Casualty."

She made a face at him. "You like spicy things?"

"It's my Louisiana heritage."

They ordered, then found a table while they waited for their ice cream to be served up. Didn't take long for it to arrive, despite the small crowd.

Andi dug in immediately and kept going for a few spoonfuls, her only sounds those of sheer happiness.

He laughed softly. "I take it the sundae meets your approval."

She nodded, a smudge of chocolate at the corner of her mouth. "It's the best."

"Feeling better, then?"

"Completely." She held out her spoon to him, dripping with ice cream, hot fudge, and a heavy dollop of whipped cream speckled with chocolate shavings. "Try it."

He couldn't say no to her. He took the bite. His fangs ached at the sweetness, but it was good. "Wow. That's a lot of chocolate."

"I know." She grinned as she scooped up another mouthful. "Isn't it amazing? How's yours?"

Was she angling for a bite? He wasn't sure. When his sisters wanted a taste of his food, they just took it. "Sweet, but spicy."

She lifted one shoulder, a look of pure sass on her face. "It's like me in an ice cream."

The thought took away the chill the frozen dessert had created in him and replaced it with the heat that Andi seemed to stir up on a regular basis. His eyes were probably reacting to the rush of desire, so he quickly pushed his bowl toward her. "Try it."

She dug her spoon in and had a taste. He could practically see her roll the creamy confection over her tongue, analyzing it. "Wow, that's pretty good. And I usually shy away from spicy stuff. But the heat and sweet together is nice."

She pushed the bowl back to him. "Nice choice. Not one I would have gone for either." She pointed her spoon at him while she talked. "You know, I really need to break out of my ruts."

Why that amused him, he wasn't sure. "Are you in a lot of them, then?"

She shrugged and went back to her sundae. "Yeah, I think so. I mean, who isn't, right? We all like what we like, and sticking with the tried and true is just easier most times." She downed another massive spoonful of ice cream, giving him a deep appreciation for her appetite. "Look at you, for instance."

He put both hands on the table. "What about me?"

She kept talking while she ate. "You're not at all the kind of guy I'd normally go for, but now that I'm getting to know you, I can see how wrong my initial assumptions about you were. You're totally my kind of guy."

His heart expanded, breaking the shackles he'd put in place after Miranda to keep himself from loving again. He was her kind of guy. A few simple, one-syllable words, and he was smitten. What was wrong with him? Or better yet, what was so right about Andi?

Well…everything.

He gathered himself together. "I will endeavor to continue being your kind of guy, but I warn you, you've only just met me. I promise I am everything I told you I was. You'll see."

The light in her eyes said she wasn't taking him seriously. "Is that a threat?"

Before he could answer, she leaned in, still utterly amused. "Out of all the stuff you told me, you know what you failed to mention?"

"What's that?"

She dug her spoon into his ice cream, stealing another bite. "What a good kisser you are."

More heat. Throughout every part of his body. And the urge to drag her across the table and into his lap was only barely contained.

She licked the spoon clean. Which didn't help his current state *at all*. She used it to point at him. "Your eyes are doing that thing again."

He didn't even bother trying to calm himself down. "You do that to me."

"Is it a good thing? Or a bad thing?"

"That depends on your perspective, I guess. But if you really were my girlfriend, you'd think it was a good thing."

Her smile went a little shy, and for a moment, she didn't say anything. At last, she spoke, her gaze on the remains of her sundae. "Is your family going to like me?"

"I...don't know. My sisters will. And I think Valentino does already. But my parents can be a little more critical." Then he decided to test her, just to see if he was reading her right. "But really, you don't have to worry about that. This is just for five more days."

Her smile faded. And that small change in her expression caused a shower of sparks inside him. That had to mean she was unhappy about ending things between them. Which meant there was a real possibility that things wouldn't end at all.

"Right," she whispered so softly only his vampire hearing caught it. "Just five more days."

❧

Why hadn't she said two weeks? Or a month? Or a year, even? Andi knew why. Because at first glance, she'd wanted away from this guy as fast as possible. Granted, there was a seven-day timer on Cassi's curse, too.

But now...now she wanted to curl up next to him and do nothing. She wanted to go to the movies with him, and sit in a coffee shop and people-watch with him, and slow dance, and stay up late, and laugh at inside jokes, and do all the things that couples did.

Because she was falling for him. But if he was thinking about the deadline, then she was on this ride by herself. Which told her she really had to work harder.

The family dinner was the perfect opportunity. She'd get his family to love her, then he'd love her, too.

She hoped. Or she was doomed.

All he had to do was say those three little words, and she'd be free. That had to still be possible.

Staring at her empty sundae glass like she'd just been kicked certainly wasn't attractive. She put a smile on her face and raised her eyes to his again. "Do I need another fancy outfit? Or is dinner casual?"

"Pretty casual. But if you want to shop some more, that's fine with me."

"I should bring something." She tapped her fingers on the table, thinking.

"You don't need to. My mother and sisters do all the cooking. There will be plenty of food, I promise."

"Well, I should at least get a bottle of wine tomorrow. That would be okay?"

He smirked. "You mean with my money?"

She put her hand on her forehead. "I totally forgot I have no cash. I'm sorry."

"Don't apologize, but that reminds me. We're going to see Amelia Marchand in the morning. She's the witch I told you about."

Andi clapped her hands together. "The phone call! In all the Miranda nonsense, I totally forgot to ask you about that."

"Well, it's all set. She said to bring the book, and she'll see what she can do. No promises, of course, but she's very powerful."

Andi took Con's hand. "You're my knight in shining armor, you know that?"

He lifted her hand to his mouth and kissed her knuckles, giving her hope again. "Just doing what I can to help. I know things would be easier if we weren't attached by this invisible thread."

So he wanted them apart? Honestly, she'd never found a guy so hard to read. But she held on to her smile and nodded, hoping she didn't look as miserable as she felt inside.

CHAPTER TWELVE

Morning came dull and gray, and it felt like an unnaturally early hour. Andi checked the bedside clock. It was seven a.m. Unnaturally early, for sure. When had she ever been up that early on purpose? She rubbed her eyes. Nothing about the room looked familiar.

She stared at her strange surroundings for a long moment before remembering where she was. Con's guest room, which he'd assured her was close enough to his room that neither one of them would accidentally drag the other out of bed due to the curse.

Right. The curse. Which they were going to see some witch about today. That meant Andi had to get moving.

She rolled to the side, put her feet on the floor, and inhaled, hoping for the scent of coffee. Smelling it put her in a good mood instantly. She tied on her new vintage robe and shuffled barefoot to the kitchen.

Con was at the stove in silk pajama bottoms and a

white undershirt. His hair was rumpled, and a dusting of dark stubble covered the lower half of his face. He looked incredibly at ease and very sexy. And not just because he was standing over a waffle maker.

He looked up as she came in. "Morning."

"Morning." She ran a hand through her hair, thinking she should have done that before she'd left the guest room. Especially since Con looked like an ad for some very expensive men's cologne, and she probably looked like, well, she didn't want to think about that horror at the moment. Chloe was at her bowl, eating, which was the perfect distraction. "Hey there, kitty cat."

Chloe didn't respond, but Con did. "She's not really a morning cat."

Andi nodded in complete sympathy. "Who is?"

He pointed toward the far counter. "There's coffee. Cups in the cabinet above."

"Thank you. Cream and sugar?"

"Cream in the fridge, sugar in the same cabinet as the cups, spoons in the drawer below."

She got the cream on the way to the coffee and went to work fixing a big cup. "Do you make waffles every morning?"

He laughed. "No. I don't ever really make waffles unless my sisters are coming over for something, and that hasn't happened in a while."

Coffee prepped, she turned to face him, holding her cup in both hands. "So you're making them for me?"

He nodded. "I am. I probably should have asked if you like them first, but waffles seemed like a safe bet. Plus, I have a jar of my mother's triple-berry compote to go on top of them, so—"

"You had me at waffles." She sipped the coffee. It wasn't the coffee she was used to, but it was good. Different. "What kind of coffee is this?"

"You're tasting chicory. That's how we drink it. I can get some without today."

"No, I like it. It's different than what I'm used to, but I'm getting out of my ruts, remember?"

He flipped the waffle maker. "That's right. I'm glad the coffee is okay, then. How'd you sleep?"

"Like a rock that was super tired. But then, that was my first night out of that crazy book. Sleeping in there wasn't great." It was more of an exercise in survival, really.

"I bet."

"What was it like in there?"

"Dark. Scary. Like one of those Halloween scare houses, but...real." She shuddered. "I don't really want to think about it."

"I understand."

She drank more of her coffee and started to feel the life come back into her. Chloe finished eating and rubbed against Andi's bare legs on her way past. Andi smiled as she reached down to give the cat a little scratch on the back.

Andi wasn't sure when she'd had such a domestic morning before. It was nice. Cozy. Not a word she'd ever thought she'd use to describe breakfast with a vampire, but there it was. "What time are we meeting with the witch?"

"Nine. Then I need to get the shop open."

And since they were stuck together, she'd be going with him. She didn't mind. She liked being with Con, but she also didn't want to get in the way of his livelihood. "I'd better get in the shower as soon as I eat, then."

He opened the waffle maker, took the waffle out with a fork, and plated it. "Here you go."

He put the plate and fork on the counter, then got a glass crock out of the microwave, stuck a spoon in it, and set it next to the plate. "Breakfast is served."

She took a seat in front of the waffle. "Smells great." She glanced at him. "Aren't you eating?"

"I, uh, drank my breakfast earlier. I thought maybe I should get that out of the way."

She grinned. "As much as I want to say I wouldn't have minded, it might have been a bit much first thing in the morning."

He went to refill his coffee cup. "That's what I was thinking."

She spooned the compote on top of her waffle and cut a big bite. It was delicious. Crispy, a little chewy, laced with vanilla and the berries. She couldn't stop the moan of happiness that came out of her. "Wow. So good. Well done."

She immediately went in for a second forkful.

He sat next to her, smiling and clearly pleased with himself. "Thank you."

"I'd like to apologize for my lack of manners right

now, because I'm about to inhale this waffle."

He drank his coffee, still grinning as if bad manners were a great compliment. Maybe they were. She couldn't take her eyes off him.

"What?" he asked.

"I was just thinking about how you've started smiling a lot more."

He gave that a second of thought. "I have a reason to now."

"You mean…me?"

He nodded. "You make me forget all the reasons I had to be in a bad mood."

She continued stuffing waffle in her face. "I like that."

"So do I."

She finished her food at about the same time as he finished his coffee. She hopped up and took her plate and silverware to the sink.

He shook his head. "I'll clean up. You go get ready."

"Don't you need to shower, too?"

"I do, but I'm guessing it takes you longer to do your hair and whatever else women do. I have sisters, remember? Which reminds me, there's a hair dryer under the sink."

"Okay, cool." He wasn't wrong. "What time do we need to leave?"

"By eight thirty."

"No problem. Meet you back here. Thanks for breakfast, by the way. It was great."

"You're welcome."

She practically scampered off to the guest room now that she was full of sugar and caffeine. Plus, after all that time in the book, she was never going to take a hot shower for granted again.

But she didn't let herself linger too long. She had hair and makeup to do and an outfit to pick out. Not that she had a lot to choose from, but she still wanted to look nice. Being around Con was great, but not being tethered to him would be nice, too. Ditching the curse altogether would be even better. Andi needed this witch to want to help them.

After she finished squeezing the water out of her hair so her curls could air-dry as much as possible, she dug her purchases out of the shopping bag they were still in. She'd been too tired last night to put them away. Hopefully, they weren't too wrinkled.

As she pulled the clothes out, she realized something extra had been added to the bag. Another small brown bag was tucked inside. She opened it, dumping the contents on the bed. More jewelry. A cute pair of silver hoops and three beaded stretch bracelets in colors that matched the clothing she'd bought.

There was a note, too.

A couple extra pieces on the house. Enjoy!

Wow. What a thoughtful and nice thing to do. Because Andi hadn't gotten any daytime jewelry, just the sparkly stuff for the evening. What a great way to ensure repeat business, because she was definitely getting Con to take her back to Stella's Bargain Bin for her family dinner outfit.

For this morning's meeting, however, she went with the dark jeans, a black T-shirt, the funky appliqued cardigan, and the leopard shorty boots. It was totally her style, but not too crazy, she hoped, for the witch.

Hey, witches were a little left of center, right? This outfit shouldn't raise any eyebrows.

Another twenty minutes and she was made up, her curls were sufficiently dry and tamed, and she was dressed. She headed back to the kitchen to wait on Con.

There was no waiting. He was already there, sitting at the counter drinking another cup of coffee with Chloe at his feet.

His brows shot up. "You're ready early."

"Am I?"

"I figured another ten to fifteen minutes, easy." He stood.

She shrugged. "Picking out my clothes didn't take long."

He laughed. "I don't suppose it did. That reminds me. You'll need something for tonight."

She stretched her arms out. "I could wear this, but I'm thinking it's too casual. I'd rather have something a little dressier. I want your family to like me."

"They will. Your outfit doesn't matter." He hesitated. "Okay, it might matter a little to my mother. Don't worry, Fletcher can watch the shop if we need to visit Stella's again."

"That would be great." A new thought occurred to her, about what his family would think when she left, but she kept that to herself.

"You want another cup of coffee before we go? We have time."

She shook her head. "I'm already jittery enough."

"Then we can go. I just need to open one of the back windows for Chloe. She likes to sit at the screen and watch birds. Then I'll take the scenic route to Amelia's, but I don't think she'll mind if we're early."

Andi rubbed her hands together. Getting this help could change everything.

CHAPTER THIRTEEN

Constantin left the bayou and took the roundabout route through town to show Andi more of Shadowvale. The town was nicely lit in the evenings, but seeing something by daylight, such as it was in Shadowvale, was still different.

She watched out the window with great interest. "I know you said the sun never shines here, but that didn't really sink in until now. It's bright enough, for sure, but there's definitely not a hint of sun."

"Like I said, it shines above the twilight line, but that's not a place any sane vampire would go."

"I'm sure." She tilted her head to see the sky better. "But always overcast below that, huh?"

"Always. You get used to it."

"I'm sure. But at first, that might be a little... depressing."

"Not for a vampire. Not when the alternative is death-by-sunlight or being trapped indoors all day."

She snorted. "Well, when you put it that way."

"There are places in town you can go for artificial sunlight."

"Really? That might do the trick."

She was talking like she was considering staying in town after her curse was lifted. Was that because of her feelings for him? Constantin figured it had to be. Why else would she stay here? She obviously had a life somewhere else.

She sat back and faced forward again. "So what's this Amelia like?"

How did one describe Amelia Marchand? "She's...a very interesting character. Old, but she doesn't look it because of her magic and the magic of this town. Both of which are very strong. She's crucial to Shadowvale's existence. She's the reason many of us are here. Especially my family."

"Oh?"

He nodded. "My great-uncle, Pasqual, essentially did to her what Miranda did to me."

In his peripheral vision, he could see Andi's mouth come open. "And you guys live here? And she doesn't make life miserable for your family?"

"Not at all. She's the reason we're here."

"I need to know more of this story."

"She was so deeply in love with Pasqual that she wanted to give him the best gift she could think of. A place where he could daywalk, but without fear of the sun. So she created this town for Pasqual. From what I understand, the sacrifice—and the magic— involved was tremendous."

"I can imagine. Why would your uncle walk away from such a gift? And a woman who clearly loved him more than herself."

"No one really knows. But as you can imagine, when he left she was beyond heartbroken."

Andi stared at her hands neatly folded in her lap. "I'm not sure I can imagine that, actually."

"I assure you, it was devastating." He knew from personal experience all too well what that pain felt like. "Amelia wasn't just hurt, she was also incredibly lonely, too."

"All alone in a town? That would be a little eerie."

"There were a few other families in town, but nothing like the population we have today. Anyway, because of that loneliness—and, I suppose, the desire for some kind of connection that was as close to family as she could hope for—she reached out to my parents and invited them to move here."

"And they did? I mean, obviously, but that had to be weird. Strained, at least."

"I don't know if it was or not, my parents don't talk about it much. But the timing was right. Accusations of being a vampire had been made against my mother—her already suspicious seamstress found a vial of blood in the pocket of a dress that needed alterations—and things were pretty hot for them. So moving made a lot of sense. Especially to a place as safe and hidden as Shadowvale."

She peered at him. "You make it sound like you didn't come with them."

"I didn't. Neither did Valentino. Only my sisters still lived with them at the time. But after a few years of them being here, we came, too. My cousin Isabelle joined us about a year later. Life in Shadowvale for a vampire is unlike life anywhere else."

"I bet it is. The no-sunlight thing has to be life-changing."

"More than that. We don't have to hide who we are. We aren't feared. And our particular nutritional needs are taken care of with a regular delivery service. It's the best of being a vampire combined with the best of being human."

"That is pretty nice. But there are a lot of other kinds of supernaturals that live here, too, right?"

"All kinds. And there are humans that live here, too. But everyone comes here for one reason. Because of their own personal curse. Shadowvale is a safe haven for everyone who's different. No one has to live in fear of being an outsider here. Being different is pretty much expected."

"That's kind of amazing." She squinted a little. "And the witch we're going to see started this whole town?"

"Yes."

Andi shook her head and let out a little whistle. "She must be loaded."

"She is, but the town essentially pays for itself through the gem mines that inhabit the mountains surrounding Shadowvale."

Andi's eyebrows rose. "Gem mines? For real?"

He nodded. "It's a big business. It's the main business. There's a whole team of lapidaries that—"

"Lap-a-whats?"

"Gem cutters. There's a whole team of them that

work on the best and biggest stones that are unearthed. But a lot of the smaller ones are sold as rough, too."

"Wow." She let out a little laugh. "Do Snow White and the Seven Dwarfs live here, too?"

"Yes. Well, sort of."

Her gaze narrowed. "Now you're just messing with me."

He snorted. "No, I'm not, I swear. But she prefers to be called Bianca Wynters."

"That's wild. For real?"

"I promise. She runs the Red Apple Bed and Breakfast that faces the big park in the middle of the residential district. Although it's not so much a B&B as it is a boardinghouse."

"If you tell me there are seven rooms—"

"No, there are eight." He paused for effect. "She lives in one, after all."

Andi's gaze was stuck to him. She inched forward until her seat belt strained. "Do miners live there?"

"They do."

"And are they dwarfs?"

"They are. But you know they're not really that small, right? Short, yes, but solid like linebackers. Hardy stock, those guys. And hard workers, too."

She sat back, waving her hand. "I know all about dwarfs. I dated one years ago. Good guy. Never liked it when I ate apples."

"They're a superstitious bunch, aren't they?"

"They are." She laughed. "How do you know all this?"

"Bianca's a vampire. You get to know your own kind after a while." He shrugged. "In a town like this, you get to know almost everyone. I even know the alpha of the werewolf pack, Rico Martinez. Met him when he came into my shop to order a book on rugby."

"Werewolves and vampires getting along... I had no idea this town was so wild!"

"Never a dull moment in Shadowvale." He turned onto Hollows Lane.

Andi went quiet for a few moments. "There are some impressive houses here. Not that yours isn't. Your place is great. But these are kind of..."

"Grand?" He nodded. "Amelia set the tone for that with her home, I'm sure. Hard to build something on the same street as hers without trying to live up to a little of that."

"Big house, huh?"

"Very. The grounds around it are quite something, too."

"And she lives there alone?"

"She did for almost her entire life here, but recently her niece moved to town and now lives there as well."

"That's nice that she has company now."

"Oh, she had company. She has a staff. But Emeranth is family, so that's different. Having her around has helped Amelia a lot."

Andi went silent and stared at her hands again, making Constantin wonder if she was thinking about her sister. For as poorly as he and Valentino got on, neither had ever done anything as harsh as cursing the other into a book.

He pulled into Amelia's driveway, glad for the new distraction. "We're here."

Her head lifted, and she sucked in a soft breath. "You weren't kidding about this house. Amazing."

"Wait until you see the inside."

He parked near the front door, then got out as Andi hopped out, too.

Beckett, Amelia's majordomo, opened one of the doors. "Mr. Thibodeaux. Good morning."

"Good morning, Beckett. This is my friend, Andromeda Merriweather. I spoke to Amelia about her."

Beckett smiled at Andi. "Miss Merriweather, welcome to Indigo House. I'm the majordomo here."

"Thank you. Nice to meet you." Andi clasped her hands in front of her and smiled back without her usual enthusiasm. Was she nervous? Maybe. Probably smart, considering who Amelia was.

"We're a little early," Constantin said.

"It's fine," Beckett assured him. "Amelia's already in the sitting room. Follow me."

Andi gave Constantin a look that confirmed her nerves.

Without hesitation, he reached out and took her hand.

She seemed surprised by that for a moment, then smiled gratefully.

Then the house distracted her with its luxurious interior. As they followed Beckett, Andi's head turned like it was on a swivel. Constantin had no doubts she'd have a lot to say about it later.

At the doors to the sitting room, Beckett stopped and announced them. "Your guests are here, Amelia. Mr. Thibodeaux and Miss Merriweather."

Amelia stood. "Come in, Constantin."

"Thank you for seeing us, Amelia."

She gestured to the couch across from her chair, which was pulled close to the crackling fire in the fireplace. "For you? Of course."

He put his hand on Andi's elbow. "This is my friend, Andromeda. As I told you on the phone, she's the one I released from the book."

Amelia didn't extend her hand to greet Andi, but she nodded with great concern. "I'm so glad Constantin was able to free you."

"So am I," Andi answered. "Pleasure to meet you, Ms. Marchand."

"Amelia will do. Please, sit."

Constantin let Andi go ahead of him, then they both took a seat on the couch.

Beckett gave a short bow. "Unless there will be anything else?"

Amelia glanced at them. "Would you care for something to drink? Coffee? Tea?"

"No, thank you. I'm fine," Andi said.

"So am I," Constantin added. "We don't want to take up any more of your time than necessary."

Amelia gestured at Beckett. "That will be all."

He left, and Amelia settled herself a little deeper into her chair. "This spell, who cast it?"

Constantin let Andi speak.

She cleared her throat. "My sister did. But we're sprites, so we don't have that kind of magic. I'm sure she bought the spell from a witch, but I don't know who."

Amelia nodded. "I see. That witch should be ashamed of herself. At best, a spell like that is gray magic. At worst, it's a virtual death sentence, making it black magic. How long were you bound?"

Andi twisted her hands together. "I was in the book for almost a year. And it wasn't a very nice book."

Amelia's brows lifted, and she looked at Constantin.

"*The Hidden History of Insane Asylums in 19th Century Europe,*" he supplied.

"I see," Amelia said. "That does sound dreadful. What are the terms of the curse? The limitations? Tell me what you know."

"First of all," Andi started, "my wings are gone. I don't know if my sister did that separately, or if it's part of the curse, but without them I have very little power or magic. I'm not even sure I can take on my full sprite form. Secondly, Con and I are tethered. We can't be more than a hundred feet from each other, tops."

Amelia nodded like she was taking mental notes. "And to break the spell?"

Con chimed in since he knew this one. "Three genuine kisses, forty-eight hours apart."

Amelia's gaze narrowed. "Interesting." She looked pointedly at Andi. "Anything else?"

Andi shook her head, saying nothing.

Amelia sighed. "If you were still in the book, I could probably do more, but since you've been released, the spell is well underway. It's a much more difficult proposition."

Andi's hands stopped fidgeting. "But can you do anything?"

"I don't know." Amelia paused. "It's like stopping a rolling car. At five miles an hour, you could just stand in front of it and bring it to a stop with neither you nor the car any worse for wear. But try that at sixty miles an hour, and it's not the car that's going to get hurt. While you were in the book, the curse was going at five miles an hour. Now that you're out, it's moving at a good clip. Understand?"

Andi let out a long breath and nodded. "Yes. And if there's any chance you might be hurt, then I don't want you to even think about it."

Amelia offered them a gentle smile. "There might be something else I can do."

CHAPTER FOURTEEN

Andi felt as torn and twisted up as an old rag. She couldn't tell Amelia the truth about the curse, not with Con sitting right next to her. But maybe it didn't matter anyway, since as the woman had pointed out, the curse was already well underway and nearly impossible to stop. Still, she had to act like anything that could be done was good news.

So she smiled hopefully. "What do you think you can do?"

Amelia tilted her head, her eyes bright. "I believe I can break the tether."

Andi hung on to her smile. "That would be... great."

Except it wouldn't be. Not really. Her proximity to Con was an important part of the process in getting him to fall for her. Without that magical tether, he could put her in a hotel. And out of sight was out of mind.

Then his big hand closed over her knee. "That *would* be great." He smiled at her. "You could go shopping on your own. Explore the town. You wouldn't be stuck in the shop with me, bored silly."

"I wouldn't be bored, but it would be nice." She tried to be positive. "I could run down to one of the restaurants nearby and get us lunch."

He gave her knee a reassuring squeeze that didn't jive with the look in his eyes. "You could get a room in town, too, if you wanted to."

She didn't have to try to look earnest, because her words were coming from her heart. "I don't want to. I'd much rather stay with you. If that's okay."

"Of course it's okay."

She exhaled. He was such a kind man. Kinder than she deserved. But maybe...she could be better. Maybe she could become the sort of woman that he already thought she was. People could change, couldn't they? "Thank you."

Amelia shifted in her chair. "Then are you interested in attempting the separation?"

Still feeling some reluctance, Andi nodded. "Yes."

Amelia stood. "It'll take me a few moments to create the counterspell. And I'll need a lock of hair from both of you."

Con got to his feet. "Take what you need."

Andi nodded as she rose. "Yes, whatever you need."

Amelia lifted the thin chain around her neck, pulling it free of her brilliantly colored caftan. At the end of the chain was a small pair of petite gold scissors. "I had a feeling I'd need these today."

She snipped a few strands of hair from both of them. "I'll be back with the counterspell shortly."

"Thank you," Con said.

As Amelia left, he looked at Andi. "Are you okay? You seem unsure of all this."

She looked toward the door, but Amelia was gone. "I know this counterspell is to help us, but I get a little uneasy layering magic upon magic. It's tricky business, from what I understand. It doesn't help that I feel so vulnerable without my wings."

He put his arm around her shoulders. "I can imagine. But Amelia is very skilled. It's going to be fine. And then you'll have at least a small amount of freedom back."

She nodded and smiled for his sake. "I know you're right."

As if sensing her need for a distraction, he took her hand and pulled her toward the windows. "You should see Amelia's garden. It's really something. Especially considering one of the garden's residents."

"What kind of resident?" Andi figured he meant a bird or some unnaturally large frog, so she humored him, standing in front of the window to see what all the fuss was about. The gardens beyond the house were beautiful. "How do all those plants grow and flowers bloom without sunlight?"

"The ground here is laced with magic. It seeps out of the meridian lines that run beneath the town. It's the reason this whole place works the way it does." He had the funniest look on his face. "That pond is really something, isn't it?"

She looked at the pond again, thinking she'd

missed something. "It's very pretty. It looks like every other garden pond I've ever—" Something moved behind the pond. Something enormous and furry and striped.

She went very still, eyes focused for all she was worth. "Is that...a tiger?"

Con's soft laugh answered her. "His name is Thoreau. He's been a guest at Indigo House for almost as long as Amelia's lived here."

Andi was very glad to be behind the window. "I know witches like cats, but that's pushing the envelope."

"He's no real threat. At least, he's never mauled anyone that I know of."

Andi slanted her eyes at him. "That's so reassuring."

The soft clearing of a throat turned them around. Beckett stood there. "Just thought I'd see if you were doing all right or would like a drink?"

Con looked at her. "You want anything?"

"Actually, I would. A glass of water would be great."

Beckett nodded. "And for you, Mr. Thibodeaux?"

"Coffee. Splash of cream, no sugar."

"Very good."

He left them alone again.

Andi glanced out the window, but the tiger was gone. Moved on to a different part of the garden, she guessed. Good thing they were inside, but she was going to look twice when they went back to the car.

Beckett returned shortly with their drinks, and

just as they were finishing them, Amelia rejoined them.

She held two small vials of gray water.

Andi really hoped they didn't have to drink those.

Amelia held the vials out to them. "Drink these."

So much for that.

They each took one, waiting for further instruction.

Amelia's brow wrinkled. "Well, go on. Down the hatch. If you're waiting for something more magical than that, you're not going to get it. Also, don't expect it to taste good."

Andi eyed the vial. "I'm not."

Amelia laughed. "Good magic always comes with a price. Drink up. The potency diminishes with each passing second."

Con took the top off his, lifting it toward Andi. "Cheers."

She did the same. "Cheers."

Then they tipped the vials back and drank.

Andi sucked hers down in one gulp, which was smart, because as soon as the taste hit her tongue, she wanted to spit the stuff out. She didn't, but gagged a little as she tried to breathe. "What is in that? Fish? Garbage?"

Con grimaced. "My apologies, Amelia, but that's the worst thing I've ever tasted. And I've had troll blood."

Still smiling, she shook her head. "I warned you."

Andi stared at the now empty vial before setting it aside. "Is that it? Are we untethered?"

Amelia nodded. "You should be. But let's test it. Constantin, why don't you go out to your car and stay there for a few minutes just so we can be sure? That should be distance enough."

"All right." He set the vial on the coffee table and looked at Andi. "Call me if you need me to come back in sooner."

"Will do," she answered.

He left, and as soon as the sound of the front door closing reached them, Amelia stepped closer to Andi. "You lied to me about the curse. Or at least you omitted something. What didn't you tell me?"

Andi managed not to retreat. "I couldn't, not in front of Con."

"What was it? Out with it."

Andi's hands clenched. "He's got to fall in love with me. The kisses every forty-eight hours are just to buy me time to make that happen."

"You can't make a man fall in love with you."

"Yes, I can. I've done it many times before."

Amelia's mouth thinned. "You're confusing lust and love."

There was no point in arguing with the witch, and Andi didn't want to anyway. Not after the woman had helped them. Or had she? "Was the counterspell really a counterspell or not?"

Amelia nodded. "It was. I'm a woman of my word." A low noise came from her throat. "You're going to break Constantin's heart. I'm not sure he can take that. Not after what the first one did to him."

"I know all about Miranda. And if it's only lust he's feeling toward me, then he'll get over it, won't he?"

"And if it's love?"

Andi swallowed as the sinking feeling in her belly grew. It had to be love for her to be free. "I don't want to hurt him. I like him a lot. More than I have a right to, I suppose. But I can't stay here after the curse is lifted. I have to get my wings back, and I'm pretty sure that's going to take a lot of groveling at my sister's feet."

"You could tell him the truth."

Andi frowned. "Right. Because nothing makes a person fall in love like being told they need to fall in love."

"Then tell him you have to leave once you're free, but you'll be back."

"To live here? In the same place for the rest of my life?" Andi had thought about it, sure, but saying it out loud made it seem so permanent. "I don't think I can promise that. I don't want to tell him something I can't stick to."

Her answers did nothing to erase the displeasure in Amelia's eyes. "Listen to me, girl. If you break that man, I will make sure the gates of this town are closed to you for good. Do you understand me? Because I can do that."

Andi nodded slowly, a twinge of fear zipping through her. "I swear, it's not my intention to—"

"Then make sure he knows what your intentions are."

"I will. I'll tell him tonight. Not the falling-in-love part, but about the leaving part. And possibly coming back. At least to visit." But not until after the dinner at his parents'. There was only so much drama she could handle at a time. But Amelia was right. Con deserved to know. Especially since it seemed like things were developing between them.

"Good," Amelia said. "Be sure you do."

"Well? It worked, right?" Con appeared in the sitting room doorway.

Andi smiled and took a breath. "Not a single tug."

"Excellent. I went all the way down to the end of the driveway, too." He looked at Amelia. "I owe you. Thank you."

"You're welcome. You owe me nothing." She looked at Andi, who was already making her way toward Con. "Take care, sprite."

Andi nodded, the warning in the witch's words clear. "I will. I promise."

CHAPTER FIFTEEN

Constantin turned out of Amelia's driveway and headed for his shop. "What did she mean by 'take care'?"

Andi, who hadn't said a word since they'd left, just shrugged. "Just to...take care? I guess? I don't know. Witches are like that. All mysterious and cryptic."

Constantin nodded. "True."

But he knew Amelia enough to know the tone of her voice, and her words to Andi had sounded like a warning. He didn't want to press Andi for more, though. If she didn't want to talk about it, then he'd let it be.

Besides, Amelia would tell him if he asked.

Andi stayed quiet until they were back in his shop. "What can I do to help you open? I've worked retail before."

"Turn all the lights on. Walk through the rows and make sure everything's in order. I'll set the register up and start the music."

"Okay." She went off to do as he'd asked.

He watched her for a moment, his mind still on Amelia's words, but then he made himself let that go. He had to. Dwelling would do him no good.

Andi finished up and came back to the counter a minute or two after he'd finished his own opening tasks. "Straightened a few things, but everything looked pretty good. You might need a little restocking in the mystery section. Oh, and the romance section seems to be missing."

He shook his head. "So noted. Thank you."

She tapped her fingers on the counter's edge. "There must be more I can do. Dust or vacuum?"

"You could do those things if you want, but Fletcher dusted yesterday, so we should be good. Cleaning supplies are in the bathroom, but really, don't worry about it. If you want to do something, you could keep an eye on the counter while I get some work done in my office." He still had calls to make about the books that had come in yesterday.

"I'd be happy to, but maybe first..." She bit her bottom lip.

"Yes?" He almost laughed. It wasn't difficult to figure out she wanted something.

"I could go get us some coffees? I think I used up all my caffeine energy at Amelia's."

"Sure, I could have another one, too. Black Horse Bakery is right up the street. They have coffee." He took his money clip out. The coffees were cheap, and she wouldn't need money for any of the baked goods, but she ought to have some spending cash on her all the same.

"Should I get anything else? Like something to bring to dinner tonight?"

He thought about that. "My mother does love their pineapple upside-down cake."

"I'll get one, then."

He loosened a small stack of bills from the clip and held them out to her. "Here."

She took the money, but made no move to put it in her pocket. "How expensive is this cake?"

He thought about telling her all the baked goods were free, but figured that would be more fun for her to find out on her own. "The extra is for when you go shopping later. You need something to wear tonight, right?"

"Right." Reluctantly, she tucked the money away. "I'm going to pay you back, you know."

"You don't need to. Nor do I expect it."

"Well, that's really nice of you, but I am." She backed toward the door. "Splash of cream, no sugar, right?"

He smiled. She was a quick study. "Right. Tell them it's for me. They have a chicory blend I like."

She left, and his thoughts wandered back to Amelia's, but not because of her parting words to Andi. This time, he was thinking about the mix of emotions he'd felt about Amelia separating them.

It was a step back toward a normal life. Toward not having to lie about having a girlfriend.

Back to having no girlfriend. Not even one who was pretend.

He sighed. There was no question that she had to

accompany him to his family dinner this evening, but that was his own doing. His family was going to think she was his girlfriend. Valentino already did.

So how was Constantin going to explain things when she left? Because he had no doubt she would leave at some point. She had her own life to get back to. Could he convince her to return? Or better yet, to return permanently?

Because if he couldn't, his family would once again think him incapable of maintaining a relationship. He wasn't sure he could take the pitying looks from his sisters. Thankfully, Andi was no Miranda.

Still, they needed some kind of exit strategy. A story that would cover her leaving. And a story that would explain her not returning, if that was going to be the case.

The thought of that hurt. She would come back, wouldn't she?

After tonight's dinner, maybe they could talk and figure it all out. They'd have to at least concoct a story to explain her exit. He did not want to be the subject of an entire town's pity.

He also wanted to tell Andi how he was feeling. How could he not? They were going to discuss the future. She needed to know what was going on inside him. That scared him like nothing else. Feelings and emotions were such raw things. And she could very easily reject him, just as Miranda had.

He didn't think she would. At least not as harshly as Miranda had. But if he didn't tell Andi the truth, how else would she know? He wasn't good at showing such things. Miranda had made it clear that that was one of his faults.

So he was going to try harder with Andi. Even if that meant putting himself out there in a way that could result in him being hurt again.

But she might also think he was rushing things. They'd known each other little more than a day.

He ran a hand through his hair. Maybe he was going too fast. Maybe he was overreacting, reading too much into the situation, because a woman was showing him attention.

After all, Andi needed him happy. She needed to fulfill the demands of the curse. Her life as a free sprite depended on it.

Could she be playing him for her own ends?

He desperately didn't want to think that. And yet...memories of Miranda loomed over him like a dark, unshakable shadow.

He and Andi had to talk tonight. And they would. But first, he'd see what his family thought of her. His sisters especially. They were good judges of character. They'd been leery of Miranda from day one.

Until they weighed in, he'd try to keep himself in check. As much as a man could when he was already falling in love with a woman he'd just met.

The lightness in Andi's heart could mean only one horrible, terrible thing: She was crazy about Con.

So crazy that she had started thinking she'd ask him to go with her when she went back to apologize to Cassi.

She'd have to explain things to him ahead of time, give him the real details, and hope that he'd understand, but she thought he would. At least she thought the new Con would.

She hoped he wouldn't react badly, but when it came to emotions, he seemed capable of keeping them in check. Which made him a little hard to gauge, but she imagined Miranda was partially responsible for that.

Regardless, Andi felt sure he'd see that what she'd done hadn't been designed to hurt him or play some kind of game, but to save herself from a bleak eternity. He couldn't fault her for self-preservation, could he?

She walked through the door of Black Horse Bakery with coffee and cake on her mind, but that all disappeared as the delicious aromas hit her. Sugar was abundant in this place, and she had a momentary lapse of purpose as she inhaled.

Underlying it all was another scent. Coffee. That pulled her back to the task at hand. She walked up to the coffee bar. Con's order was easy, but she wasn't sure what she was getting for herself yet.

"Hi there, what can I get you?"

Andi smiled at the woman behind the counter. "I'm thinking a mocha latte. With extra whip. And I need a tall black coffee with a splash of cream to go."

"No problem. I'll have that right up." The woman

paused, to-go cup in her hand. "Would that tall black with the splash be for Constantin, by any chance?"

"It is, yes." Andi smiled. "That's his usual, I guess, huh? I was supposed to tell you it was for him."

The woman nodded. "The chicory blend. We get it in for him special. Do you work for him? I don't recognize you. Not to be nosy, but new people stick out in this town."

How to answer? "I'm helping out a little. I'm just here temporarily. Long story. Big curse. It's a whole thing." Andi waved her hands and smiled, trying to make light of it all.

The woman snorted. "Curses aren't anything unusual in this town."

"So I've heard."

"I suppose you've also heard all about the magic curse-removing book in the woods, then." The woman stuck her hand out. "Well, welcome to Shadowvale for however long you're here. I'm Emeranth. I'm pretty new, too."

"Emeranth." Andi shook the woman's hand. "Are you Amelia's niece?"

"Yes, I am. And call me Em. All my friends do."

"Em, got it. Con and I went to see your aunt this morning. She helped us with my curse a little. I'm Andromeda, by the way, but I go by Andi."

"Nice to meet you, Andi." She went back to work on the coffees.

Andi rewound what Emeranth had said. "What did you mean about a curse-removing book in the woods?"

Em answered while she made coffee. "There's a book in the enchanted forest that, if you can find it and write your name in it, will remove whatever curse is upon you. Constantin hasn't mentioned it?"

"No. But then, we've been busy."

Em operated the beautiful chrome coffee machine like it wasn't the most intimidating piece of equipment Andi had ever seen. "Truth is, a lot of people think the book is just a myth." She leaned toward Andi and whispered, "It's not. It's real. Just saying."

"Wow. Cool." So all Andi would have to do was find the book in an enchanted forest and—what was she thinking? The odds of that were pretty slim. To begin with, she didn't even know where the enchanted forest was.

"This whole town is amazing." Em set Con's coffee on the counter.

"I'm discovering that."

"You think you'd ever move here?"

The question was so blunt, it took Andi a second to process it. "I, uh, I don't know. I've never really lived anywhere for very long."

"Yeah, me either. That was one of the reasons I was so happy to finally put some roots down." She added the whipped cream to Andi's coffee, then set it beside Con's. "There you go."

Andi felt a little dazed, but managed to remember the cake. "I need a pineapple upside-down cake to go, too."

"Sure thing. Give me a minute, and I'll box one

up." Em came back shortly with the cake boxed and in a shopping bag, ready to travel. "There you go."

"How much do I owe you?"

"Two bucks."

Andi blinked at her. "I meant for all of it."

"Two bucks. Bakery goods are all free."

"For real?" Then she remembered the crazy-low prices at the Bargain Bin and how Con said the gem mines made a lot of money for the town. Was that the explanation? She'd have to ask.

"Yep. Didn't Constantin tell you that?"

"No. Seems like there are a lot of things he left out." Andi handed Em two dollars, then hooked the shopping bag handles over her wrist and grabbed a coffee in each hand. "Thanks for the information, Em. Nice to meet you."

Em leaned on the counter. "You, too, Andi. Come back again."

"I will," Andi said as she backed through the door. But first, she was going to see what else she could find out about this town.

CHAPTER SIXTEEN

She went straight back to the Gilded Page. The gentle chimes above the door announced her arrival as she pushed through with her hip. "Hey."

Con looked up from a ledger he had open on the counter. "Need help?"

"No, I've got it."

"I see you got the coffees and the cake."

"I did. Spent almost all the money you gave me, too."

He frowned. "What? The cake should have been free and the coffees a dollar apiece."

"They were." Grinning, she stuck her tongue out at him. "You could have told me."

He smirked. "I thought it would be more fun for you to be surprised."

She set the coffees down, then put the shopping bag beside them. "It was quite a surprise. How is that possible? The gem mines?"

"Not in Nasha's case."

"Who's Nasha?"

"Nasha Black is the woman who owns the bakery.

Her father is one of the Four Horsemen of the Apocalypse. He happens to represent famine. Let's just say the bakery is Nasha's way of balancing things out, since she's spending his money to make it possible."

"And he doesn't stop her?"

"She's his only child. He indulges her."

"That gives daddy issues a whole new twist." Andi came around to the side of the counter where he was, grabbed her coffee, and settled in on the stool. "I met Amelia's niece, Emeranth, at the bakery. She's the barista, apparently."

He nodded as he took the top off his to-go cup. "Yes, that's right. She works there."

"She's very nice."

"She is. She's fairly new in town, too." He sipped the hot coffee and gave a nod of approval.

Andi hadn't tasted hers yet, but she would just as soon as she dropped the interesting little bomb she'd gotten from Em. "She mentioned that. She also told me about a very special book in the enchanted forest. One that removes curses if you can find it and write your name in it."

He turned to look at Andi, the steam rising out of his cup. "It's a great story, but it's not true."

She drank her coffee carefully so as not to burn her tongue, but the mocha was the perfect temperature and very delicious. Chocolate really did improve everything. "That's not what she said."

"Well, it's in her best interests to keep that legend going, being that she's Amelia's niece. A lot of people's hopes are kept alive in Shadowvale because of that book. Many search for it on a regular basis. I don't think anyone has found it, though. Not lately anyway. Doesn't stop them from looking, of course."

"Where's the enchanted forest?"

He narrowed his gaze. "It's not a safe place to go wandering."

"I'm a sprite. I can take care of myself. Especially in a forest."

"You're a sprite without wings. That puts you at a disadvantage."

She sighed, because he was right. And it sucked. But his reminder also underlined the fact that getting her wings back and being made whole again was very important. "Have you ever looked?"

"No. I don't have a curse." He went back to his ledger.

"Some might think being a vampire is a curse." She held her cup with both hands, savoring the warmth coming through the thick paper.

"I don't. Not living here." He looked at her again. "Please don't go into that forest. It's not safe. There are creatures in there that will do you harm. Ways to get lost that you can't imagine. Not to mention the more troubled citizens that live out that way."

Her ears perked up. "Like who?"

He sighed. "How about if I promise to take you for a drive through there tomorrow? But no getting out of the car."

That was all she needed, just an idea of where the

forest was. Then, if she wanted to look at some point, she could. She nodded. "Okay, deal."

But he was still watching her. "You really want to go look, don't you?"

"Can you blame me?"

His brow furrowed. "If you go out there and get snatched by a griffin or toasted by a drox or stung by a lightning bug, then yes, I can blame you all day long."

She knew what lightning bugs and griffins were, but a drox? Whatever it was, it was obviously dangerous, which raised another question. "Would you miss me if something did happen to me?"

A contemplative smile curved one side of his mouth. "I think I would miss you very much. Does that surprise you?"

"Yes." She took another sip of coffee. Maybe he really did like her after all. Maybe she was getting closer to those three magical words than she'd realized. Prompted by hope, she hopped off the stool, set her drink on the counter, and hugged him.

He tensed as his hands lifted. "What's this all about?"

"Just because you've been so kind and wonderful to me. Thank you."

He relaxed, and his arms settled around her. "You're welcome, Andromeda. Having you around has been kind of life-changing for me. Not something I'd expected at all."

She pulled back. "I'm glad I've been able to do something for you in exchange for all you've done for me."

He studied her, his eyes softly gleaming in that vampire way of his, then he pressed a tender kiss to her forehead. "You're welcome."

She smiled up at him. "I should get that dusting done."

"Doesn't need it. Why don't you go find an outfit for tonight? I'm sure that would be a lot more fun."

"True, it would be. But I want to help you, too."

"Fletcher will be here at noon. He can dust when he's not helping customers. And once he's settled in, you and I will go have lunch somewhere. What do you think about that?"

"I love that idea." She had a feeling he didn't usually leave the store to eat. If ever. But he was going the extra mile to make her happy. She absolutely was going to sit him down and have a big heart-to-heart with him after tonight's dinner. He deserved to know what lay ahead for her. And for them.

He looked at his watch. "Then you have about two hours to get your shopping done."

"Way more time than I need. Just point me toward the Bargain Bin."

After Andi left to do her shopping, Constantin got to work sending emails, checking a few auctions, and making all of his necessary calls. Several customers came in, along with one small delivery, but otherwise the morning was quiet. He'd nearly finished the calls and was about to start an inventory of new releases when the door chimes announced a customer.

He looked up. Not a customer. His youngest sister, Juliette. "Hiya, Con."

"Hello, Juliette. How are you?"

"I'm great." She smiled, showing off her pearly-white fangs. "But apparently, I'm not as good as you."

"Why do you say that?"

She put her elbows on the counter, leaned her head on her hands, and batted her eyelashes at him. "Because I heard someone has a girlfriend."

He sighed, even though he'd known that this was the inevitable result of his lie to Valentino. "Yes, well, let's not get all worked up about it."

She made a rude noise. "Oh, please. Of course we're going to get all worked up about it. You haven't looked sideways at a woman since Miranda, and now all of a sudden you have a girlfriend? This is major news."

He tried to change the subject. "Where's Daniella?"

"Dani's at Mama's helping with the food for this evening, which is where I'll be later, too. In the meantime, where's the mystery woman?"

He sidestepped that question with one of his own. "What's on the menu?"

She frowned at him. "You're dreadful at conversation, you know that?"

"Only when it comes to talking about what you want to talk about."

"Do you love her?"

"*Juliette.*" He might. But he wasn't about to tell his sister that.

"What? It's a valid question."

"Where's Marcus?"

"Where my boyfriend is has no bearing on this. Especially because he's not my boyfriend anymore."

Well, *that* was news. "When did this happen?"

"When he told me that my painting wasn't really going anywhere and that it might be time to think about a different hobby."

"He decided to go full idiot, I see." Constantin barely controlled his surprise. Juliette's painting was a sacred subject. Any man who thought otherwise was in for a world of hurt. But to call it a hobby… Constantin cringed. "Is Marcus still alive or…?"

"Yes," she growled. "Barely."

"Are you okay?"

She sighed. "I'm upset, but I'll get over it. I'm also never dating a centaur again." Then she smiled brightly. "Hey, so I'm talking to the library about doing a mural in the new children's expansion."

"That's great."

"They're supposed to be hiring a new librarian, too." She leaned against the counter with practiced nonchalance. "Does your new girlfriend need a job?"

And there it was. Right back around. "You're like a dog with a bone, you know that?"

She snorted. "Come on, you can tell me something about her. I'm going to meet her tonight anyway. So I can pester you with questions now, or I can lay them all on her this evening. Your choice."

He sighed. "She's a sprite. She's outgoing, smart, witty, and doesn't back down from much. But she's also sweet and kind and lovely."

Juliette grimaced and reared back a little. "But she's got a horseface?"

"*Juliette.*"

"What? You didn't say anything about what she looks like, so I just figured—"

"I said she's lovely."

"But lovely doesn't necessarily refer to looks."

"Well, in this case it does. She's beautiful."

Juliette's nose wrinkled in mock confusion. "And she's with you?"

He gave her a hard stare. "I'm going to finish up these phone calls now. I'll see you this evening."

Juliette grinned. "Wow, you do like her."

He sighed. "Don't you have a mural to paint?"

"I like her, too, especially if she's already bringing out this protective urge in you." She leaned way over the counter to kiss his cheek. She stayed there for a moment, her gaze resting on something behind him. "Is that a pineapple upside-down cake in that Black Horse box?"

"It is."

"Nice. Greasing the skids with Mama. I approve."

"I'm not greasing anything. It was Andi's idea."

"You're right. She is smart." With an exaggerated raising of her brows, Juliette headed for the door, calling over her shoulder, "See you tonight, Con. You and *Andi*."

Then she bounced out of the shop, leaving him to his work.

He stared after her for a moment, thinking about what the night would bring and hoping everything went smoothly. Seemed like Juliette was on his side, but he wanted his entire family to like Andi. Even more so, he wanted Andi to like his family.

He wasn't a fool. He knew that if she had that connection with them, it would go a long way toward her having a favorable view of him and this town.

And that would go a long way toward her staying.

CHAPTER SEVENTEEN

The Bargain Bin was fast becoming Andi's favorite place to shop. As she rifled through the racks, she swore there were new items that hadn't been there the night before.

Della had greeted Andi when she'd come in, but was busy helping another customer.

Andi didn't mind looking around on her own, she just wasn't sure what a good family dinner outfit was. Probably a dress. But something a little more conservative than the slinky velvet number she'd worn to the jazz club.

A few minutes later, Andi had a few things over her arm, but she wasn't sure about any of them.

The other customer left, shopping bags in hand, and Della came over. "How are you doing?"

"Great. Not entirely sure what I'm looking for, but I'll find something."

"I'm Stella, by the way, and I'm happy to help if you give me a few hints."

"Hi, Stella. I'm Andi. I should have realized you

weren't Della. Different-colored hair. Sorry, I'm a little preoccupied."

Stella smiled. "Who isn't in this town?"

"Well, I met your sister last night. She was very helpful. And kind." Andi didn't mention the free jewelry, just in case that wasn't something Stella would approve of. No point in getting Della in trouble.

Stella nodded, a knowing look in her eyes. "Della mentioned you."

"She did?"

"Sure. Constantin Thibodeaux comes in here with a woman? On top of that, a woman who looks like you? That's news worth sharing." She sized Andi up with a head-to-toe glance. "So you're Constantin's new girl. What's the occasion?"

"Family dinner."

"At the parents', right?"

"Right."

"No wonder you're preoccupied. Is there anything more nerve-racking?" She shook her head, but her flaming-red beehive didn't move. "I have just the thing."

"You do?"

She nodded. "Just came in. Give me a sec. Meet me at the dressing rooms."

She disappeared into the back, while Andi went to wait by the changing rooms.

Stella reappeared a few minutes later with a wheeled rack of clothes. She patted the rack. "This is all new stuff, but I've been through it, and there's a couple things that could work on you."

"I was sort of thinking a dress," Andi offered.

"Maybe. But try this outfit first." Stella handed her a pair of pants and a shirt.

Not exactly what Andi had been thinking, but trying something new never hurt anything. She took the outfit from Stella, then Stella took the items Andi had already picked out.

She looked at the clothes and shook her head. "None of these are right. Go on, put those on. You'll see."

"Okay." Andi slipped into one of the dressing rooms, got out of her jeans and T-shirt and into the clothing Stella had chosen. She didn't look at herself in the mirror until she was dressed.

She turned to see the final effect and blinked twice. "Huh. That's amazing."

"Told you," Stella said from the other side of the curtain. "Come out here and let me see how right I was."

Andi walked out to get a second look in the big mirror. "This is really cool."

"It's your style, too."

"It is. Kind of glam, but with a little retro edge." She turned, admiring the slim black cigarette pants with their satin tuxedo stripe down the side of each leg and the crisp lines of the gleaming white shirt.

"Hang on." Stella moved in and adjusted the shirt's collar, popping it a little. "Your hair should be in a high ponytail. Little diamond studs. Maybe a strand of pearls. Choker length."

"What about shoes?"

"Two shakes of a lamb's tail." Stella went off for a moment, returning with a pair of black satin ballet slipper flats.

Andi put them on. "Yep. Those are perfect." She turned again. "Who does this outfit remind me of?"

"Audrey Hepburn. Can't go wrong with a classic like that."

"No, you can't." She looked at Stella. "You don't think this is too casual?"

"Not with the accessories I mentioned and a red lip. How do you feel in it?"

"Like an undercover rock star." Andi smiled. "You're really good at this."

"We all have our calling." She turned and started toward the counter. "Take your time. I'll be up front. I'll have those accessories for you, too."

"Thank you." Andi glanced at her reflection again. She did look very put together, but in an easy, elegant kind of way. Somehow, even though she was very covered up, she also felt sexy. Maybe it was the glamorousness of the look. Whatever the reason, she felt confident that Con would like it, too.

She changed back into her street clothes, then took everything to the counter to pay. The total was again ridiculously low, but Andi was starting to realize things worked differently here. Not just in this shop, but in this town.

She could get used to a place like this.

Stella handed Andi her shopping bag full of purchases, including a pearl choker and some imitation-diamond stud earrings. "Here you go. I hope you have a great time tonight, honey. And don't sweat it. The Thibodeauxes are good people."

"I'm sure they are. Thanks again for your help." Andi paused. "Where can I get a nice red lipstick?"

"Couple blocks down there's a little shop that does custom cosmetics, handmade soaps, all kinds of good-smelling bath stuff, and the best hair dyes you can buy." She patted the side of her bouffant hairdo. "Bombshell's Bath & Beauty. If she doesn't have the right color, she'll make it up for you. Tell her Stella sent you."

"I will, thanks." Bag in hand, Andi left the Bargain Bin behind and went in search of the perfect red lip.

Bombshell's Bath & Beauty was a couple of blocks down and on the other side of the street. Andi could tell even before she crossed that it was the kind of place she could spend oodles of time just browsing.

She walked in and was greeted by all kinds of wonderful scents. The place was packed with everything Stella had described and more. Andi stood there in a slight daze for a moment, taking in the sights and smells and wondering where to start.

"Hi there. Can I help you find something?"

She turned to see a gorgeous woman with lavender hair. Here and there, her skin seemed to shimmer. Down her throat, at her wrists, at her hairline. A second later, Andi realized that was because the woman had iridescent scales in all those places.

Holy fish out of water, the woman was a

mermaid. There was no other explanation. "I, uh, I'm looking for something."

The woman laughed, a light bubbly sound. "Isn't everybody? Anything specific? Maybe I can point you in the right direction."

"Um, red lipstick." Andi, never one to beat around the bush, dived in. "Are you a mermaid? I'm sorry to be blunt, but I have to know."

The woman smiled and nodded. "Guilty as charged." She waved one hand, showing off webbed fingers. "I'm Sirena, and this is my shop."

"Hi, Sirena. Nice to meet you. Your shop is amazing."

"Thank you. So you're looking for red lipstick?"

"Yes. Stella hooked me up with a great outfit, then sent me here to find a great red lipstick."

"Love Stella." Sirena nodded. "And I've got just the color for you."

By the time Andi left the shop, she had a great red lipstick, a killer black eyeliner, and a face powder guaranteed to make her skin look perfect all night. The bill was about what she'd have paid normally for ordinary drugstore makeup, which was fine. There was no way every place in town could have free goods or crazy-low prices.

As she strolled back to the Gilded Page, she practiced the conversation she was going to have with Con after the dinner.

She'd have to start with what had actually gone on between her and Cassi, and what Cassi thought had happened, because without the whole truth,

Andi came off pretty badly. But she also had to be able to explain why Cassi had reacted with the curse the way she had.

Then she'd tell Con that going back to see her sister was the only way forward. And probably the only way to get her wings back. And that there was no telling how long that would take. No telling what hoops Cassi would make her jump through for them, but Andi had no doubt there would be hoops.

And that she would do the jumping. Because without her wings, she had no ability to fly, no magic dust to help her through life. Her powers, such as they were, would continue to diminish until…

She stopped walking. Would she die? Was she already dying?

It did happen. Sprites who were physically stripped of their wings rarely lived out the year. But her wings hadn't been cut off. They'd been removed with magic.

Hadn't they?

Honestly, she'd just assumed that was why they were gone. She'd been so preoccupied with getting Con to fall in love with her that she hadn't thought that much about how they'd been removed, only that they had been and how much she wanted them back. But she needed to know. And she needed to know now.

With a soft whimper, she ran the rest of the way to Con's shop, hoping her time wasn't running out for a wholly different reason.

CHAPTER EIGHTEEN

"Con, Con, Con—"

At the sound of Andi repeating his name with such urgency, Constantin looked up, a small frisson of panic running through him. "What is it? What's wrong? Are you hurt?"

She shook her head, tears in her eyes. "I don't know. I need you to look at something for me."

"Okay, sure. What is it?"

"Not here. In your office."

"Let's go, then." He led the way. Fletcher would be in shortly, but the man didn't need Constantin's guidance to take over the shop floor.

Once in his office, Constantin shut the door. "Tell me what's going on."

"My wings. I need to know if they look like they were removed cleanly with magic, or if they were physically cut off."

"Wouldn't you feel that?"

She shrugged impatiently. "I don't know. Being trapped in that book was like being stuck in a nightmare. I was more worried about surviving than thinking about my wings. I couldn't use them in there anyway."

She dropped her shopping bags, then shucked her jacket and turned her back to Con. With her arms wrapped around her waist, she grabbed the hem of her T-shirt and yanked it up, revealing her bare back.

And a black lace bra.

For a brief moment, Constantin's breath caught in his throat.

"Can you tell anything?" she asked.

He could tell that she was the most beautiful creature he'd ever seen. "I don't know where to look."

"Where my shoulder blades are, a few inches out from my spine. My hair might be in the way."

He brushed her hair aside, his fingers coasting over the warm silk of her skin. He'd forgotten how tantalizing the feel of a woman could be. "I see two small slanted lines. But they look more like birthmarks than any kind of wound."

"Magic, then." She exhaled and slumped forward, rounding her back a little. "Good. Can you touch them and make sure? They should be smooth. If they're bumpy, it could be scar tissue."

"I can do that." His hand paused a half inch above the marks. He'd touched her when he'd moved her hair, but this was intentional. His fingers traced over the marks.

Goose bumps rose on her skin, and she shuddered.

"Sorry," he said quietly. "I know my skin is cold. One of the downfalls of my kind."

"It's not that," she said. "It's…" Her voice hitched oddly. "It's been nearly a year since anyone touched me so intimately."

He nodded, then realized she couldn't see him. "I understand." It had been longer for him. A good deal longer. He focused on what she'd asked him to do. "The marks are flat. No bumps. Not scar tissue. Really, just like birthmarks."

"Thank you. That's what my skin should look like when my wings aren't on me." She pulled her shirt down and turned to face him. "That buys me more time."

"More time for what?"

She was about to answer when a knock on his office door interrupted her.

"Mr. Thibodeaux? It's Fletcher. Just wanted to let you know I'm here."

Constantin frowned. "So you have."

"I'll be at the counter if you need me."

"Good." Constantin looked at Andi, lost in her lilac gaze. What had they been talking about? He couldn't remember. But staying in the shop wasn't going to help. "Should we go eat lunch?"

She nodded as she pulled her jacket back on. "I'm ready."

"What are you in the mood for?"

"I don't know. What's your favorite place for lunch?"

Here. In his office. And lunch usually came from the small fridge next to his desk, which held the only sustenance vampires truly required. "I…"

She laughed softly. "You don't usually go out for lunch, do you?"

"Not often. No. But I don't usually have such a lovely guest to feed either. Come on, what's your favorite thing to eat?"

"Sweets. But that's not really lunch. How about something simple like a burger? I think I saw a diner. They probably have burgers."

"They do, but they also have UV bulbs in their overhead lighting. Hence the name Sunshine Diner. It's a great place for people to get a sunlight fix, but not *my* people."

"Oh. Ouch. Okay, new plan."

"How do you feel about sushi?"

"You realize that's kind of the opposite of a burger, right?" She grinned. "But I'm in. Haven't had it in ages. Well, obviously."

"They have other things besides sushi, but that's all I get there." He grabbed his wallet off the desk. "Let's go. We can walk, if you don't mind."

"Nope. Walking is great. I get to see the town better that way."

As they passed by the counter on the way to the door, he spoke to Fletcher. "Going out to lunch. Back in an hour."

Fletcher's face lit up. "You got it, boss."

Constantin narrowed his eyes. "Don't break anything."

Fletcher nodded vigorously. "No, sir."

Constantin constrained the urge to smile, going ahead of Andi to open the door for her. "Head right."

She did, and he kept stride beside her, shortening his steps a little so she didn't have to jog.

Two blocks down, they took another right onto Warlock Avenue. A few more blocks and they'd arrived.

Andi shook her head. "Once again, the name gives me pause, but if you say it's good, I'm willing to believe."

He glanced at the sign. Maybe Finding Nemo was a little tongue in cheek, but the food here was excellent. He leaned in closer. "The man who owns this place is named Nemo. And he's a merman."

Andi's eyes widened. "Is he related to Sirena who owns Bombshell's? She's a mermaid."

"I don't know. You can ask him if we see him." Constantin held the door for her.

The restaurant was small, about ten tables and another dozen seats at the sushi bar that traversed most of the back wall, and because it was lunchtime, seats were at a premium.

Constantin pointed to one of only two tables available. "Let's go there."

Once they got settled, Andi leaned toward him. "It has to be good with this kind of crowd. Or aren't there that many places to eat in town?"

"There are a good number. But only one sushi restaurant."

She glanced around. "We need a menu."

"Right here." He picked up the little notepad and pencil stuck between the soy sauce, the napkin dispenser, and the chopstick holder. "Just put a checkmark by what you want."

"Cool." She studied the menu in earnest for a moment before looking up at him. "What do you recommend?"

"I've never had anything here I didn't like. The dragon roll is good. So is the volcano roll. And the lava lava roll."

She snickered. "You do like your hot stuff, don't you?"

"Especially the one across from me." The words slipped out before he could stop them.

She grinned. "You're cute. I'm glad you're the one who opened that book and not some boring, crusty old academic."

He snorted. "There are some who might say that label applies to me."

She lifted one shoulder. "Well, you are old. And academic. But not boring."

"Good to know." He picked up the pencil. "Start marking, or we'll never get anything to eat."

She took his words to heart and got busy. A server came by to pick up their order and get them drinks, returning a minute later with the waters they'd both asked for.

When they were alone again, Andi folded her hands on the tabletop. "What's on the menu tonight?"

"Hard to say. Could be some kind of roast. Could be seafood. Jambalaya. Possibly gumbo and corn bread. My mother's even been known to make fried chicken with all the traditional sides. Whatever moves her in the moment."

"Wow, I'm hungry all over again."

"Good. A healthy appetite is very much appreciated at the family dinner."

"And your brother and sisters will be there?"

"They will. And my cousin Isabelle, although she's having a flare of laryngitis and can't speak."

"How does a vampire get laryngitis?"

"It's her curse, actually. Placed upon her by a jealous rival. Another singer who wanted Isabelle's job."

Andi clucked her tongue. "What? That's awful."

"It is, but it'll pass."

Andi sipped her water. "Do you guys do the dinner every week?"

He nodded. "Every week."

Her expression was wistful. "It sounds really nice."

"Does your family have any traditions like that?"

She shook her head slowly. "Cassi and I were raised by our grandmother. Sprites don't make the best parents. We're a pretty flighty lot, no wing pun intended. It's kind of fifty-fifty if you're going to get any maternal instincts at all. Cassi takes after our gran."

"Who do you take after?"

Andi exhaled a long, unhappy sigh. "Our mother."

"You don't seem pleased about that, but I'm guessing that if your grandmother raised you, then it was because your mother wasn't around."

She twirled the little pencil on the table. "She was

in and out of our lives. More out, really. Always busy with some new guy. Kind of the way…the way I've been with Cassi."

She looked like she might cry.

He didn't like her feeling bad. "But you're young. And that's what young people do. You certainly don't owe your sister all of your time. She can't expect that either."

"She doesn't. But…I need to be a better sister. I was actually trying, but things don't always go the way you hope, you know?"

He nodded, wishing he knew a way to comfort her. "Trying is better than not trying."

She shrugged, sniffing hard.

His heart ached for her. He had to say something to make her feel better. "I'm not a very good brother."

She looked up. "I doubt that."

"I could be better."

Her mouth bent in disbelief. "Thank you for trying to cheer me up, but I need to make changes in my life."

"So do I. More than the ones I've made since you showed up." And he realized as he said the words how true they were. "I don't want to be a stick in the mud."

"Who called you that?"

"Who hasn't?"

The server returned with two of their rolls, which he put in the center of the table, and two small plates and tiny soy sauce bowls, which he set in front of them. "Lava lava roll and blue sky roll."

"Thank you," Constantin said.

The server nodded. "I'll be right back with the rest."

Constantin helped himself to a pair of chopsticks.

Andi did the same, slipping them out of their paper sleeve and snapping the two wooden sticks apart. She nestled them in her fingers and clicked them together like a duck's beak. "I'm starving."

He smiled. "Dig in. I'm about to."

She did, and he had a feeling they were both happy for the change of subject. That didn't mean he wasn't wondering what Andi felt so bad about.

After all, she had yet to tell him what she'd done to her sister that had caused Cassi to curse Andi into a book.

And that was a question Constantin was really starting to want the answer to.

CHAPTER NINETEEN

Andi kept herself busy the rest of the afternoon by helping Fletcher, who was a very nice young vampire, with inventory and straightening and changing out the window display. They discussed in detail the lack of a romance section, and Fletcher confessed, in a hushed voice, to loving books by Nora Roberts.

It was one of the best afternoons she'd had in a long time.

She'd never really had a job that she cared about, but she cared about her work here. It was Con's business after all, and she wanted him to be pleased with everything she did. That mission made the time fly, and she was surprised at how satisfying it was to get things done when you cared.

A life of apathetic leisure didn't really give you the fulfillment of accomplishing anything.

Con stayed in his office, for the most part, coming out now and then to do something at the counter or add a book to the shelves. But every time he was on the shop floor, he seemed to make a point of catching her eye and smiling at her.

It was sweet. Sweeter than she deserved, because she couldn't stop thinking about Cassi. If she were here, Andi had no doubt her sister would warn Con away, telling him what a nightmare he was in for if he let himself care about Andi.

The saddest thing was, Cassi wouldn't have been wrong. Not about the Andi of the past.

But Andi didn't want to be that person anymore. Not even a little bit. She'd already begun the change—or at least she had before Cassi had spelled her into the book. But if completing that change meant settling down in a town like this with a guy like Con, then Andi was absolutely positively in.

In fact, she was ready for it. The very thought erased most of the cloud that had been following her since lunch. She started to wonder if maybe she had inherited a little of her gran's nurturing goodness. And why couldn't Andi be a nurturer? If she didn't want to turn out like her mother, she didn't have to. She was in charge of her own destiny.

Or would be as soon as the curse was broken and she had her wings back.

Then she'd tell Con exactly how she was feeling and that she wanted to try life with him as his real girlfriend. No pretending.

Con was a very independent guy, but even the most independent of men liked to be looked after by the right woman.

And she wanted to be that right woman for Con. With all of her heart.

Scary, that. Like, involuntary shivers right down

to her toes scary. But being afraid of change, this kind of good change, wouldn't move her forward in life. She had to face the fear and get over it.

Around five o'clock, she and Con left Fletcher at the shop to work the evening shift, and Con drove them back to his place to get ready for dinner.

She was a little nervous about her outfit, but when she came out to meet him in the living room, he nodded appreciatively. She'd put her hair up in a ponytail and donned the accessories and red lip that Stella had suggested.

"You look very glamorous," he said. "Like a Hollywood actress from the Golden Age. It really looks like something that came from Parks & Main."

"Nope. The Bargain Bin."

"Really? Impressive. You should shop there all the time."

"I know, right? But speaking of impressive, you look very handsome." He did, too, in charcoal trousers and a navy sweater that fit him beautifully and showed off what a nicely muscled physique he had.

"Thank you." His smile was a little odd.

"What?"

"I haven't been told that in a while. But my ego appreciates it."

"Well, it's true. You're a very handsome man. Especially when you're not scowling about something."

He sighed. "I suppose I do that a lot."

"Not as much as when I first met you and thought I was doomed."

He laughed. "I hope you don't feel that way now."

"I don't. At all." She looked around. "Where's the cake?"

"I left it in the car. Ready?"

She took a deep breath. "As I'll ever be."

"Nervous?"

She nodded. "A little."

He took both of her hands in his. "Don't be. I'm sure they'll love you once they get to know you. And I'll be right there at your side. If anything goes awry, just let me know and we'll leave."

"But they're your family."

"I don't care. I don't want you to feel uncomfortable. And with Valentino, you just never know. In fact, we should have a signal."

She laughed. "Like what?"

"How about you rub your nose? If you do that, I'll know you want to leave and we'll go, no questions asked."

"Okay. But it won't happen." She lifted her chin. "I can handle a family dinner."

She hoped.

Constantin had no doubt that his nerves were worse than Andi's. In fact, he wasn't sure she really understood how...complicated his family could be. And not just because they were vampires.

Valentino was an established quantity, so Andi knew what she was in for there. And Juliette would most likely be fine. If anything, she seemed overly eager to welcome a new woman into Constantin's life.

But Daniella was much like their mother, and Josephine could be stunningly brutal. Not that he thought his mother would be that way toward Andi. At least not at first. But she had high standards for her children.

Fortunately, their father, William, was adept at tempering Josephine's occasionally mercurial moods.

He pulled into his parents' driveway and turned off the engine. Valentino hadn't arrived yet, but that was no surprise. Daniella and Juliette had probably been here for an hour.

Andi leaned forward and looked at the house through the windshield. "Beautiful place."

"It is." The house was on stilts, like most bayou homes. The wraparound porches made it feel very welcoming, a feeling that was aided this evening by the amount of light pouring from the windows. "My father designed it. He's always had a knack for such things. He helped plan and lay out expansions of the town, too."

"Hey, that's pretty cool."

Constantin nodded. "I suppose it is. Ready to go in?"

She took a breath and smiled. "Yep. Can I carry the cake?"

"Sure. It was your idea after all."

Together, they climbed the steps leading to the first floor.

Constantin knocked at the side door that led into the kitchen, then opened the door and called out, "Mama? We're here."

It was a politeness only. His parents had the same unnaturally attuned hearing that he did and had no doubt heard the car when they'd turned into the driveway. If not sooner.

His mother walked into the kitchen, smiling thinly. That was how she greeted most strangers. It was a look that said judgment would be reserved until she knew you better. "Hello, Constantin."

He kissed her cheek. "Hello, Mama. This is my friend, Andromeda."

She looked at Andi, a slow, appraising gaze that went from head to foot and back up without any attempt at subtlety. "Welcome to our home, Andromeda."

"Thank you. It's very nice to be here." Andi held out the cake box. "We brought you a pineapple upside-down cake."

Josephine's smile widened so slightly that Constantin wasn't sure Andi would even notice. But it was a good sign.

She took the box from Andi. "That was very thoughtful of you. Please come into the sitting room and have a drink." Her next glance was at Constantin. "I apologize that my son brought you in through the kitchen instead of the front door like a proper guest, but perhaps his mind is elsewhere these days."

Before Constantin could reply, Andi spoke. "But your kitchen is so beautiful and warm. My gran always said the kitchen is the heart of the home. Coming in that way feels like a privilege. Not to mention, it smells wonderful in here."

Josephine tipped her head, lips pursed in amusement. Her eyes narrowed for a second, then her smile broadened considerably, and she nodded. "I like you, Andromeda. You're quick on your feet. That makes you a good match for this one."

She looked at Constantin. "This is the kind of woman you need. Not like the other one."

She put the cake box on the counter. "Go on into the sitting room and have a glass of wine. Dinner will be served shortly."

Andi smiled back. "I can't wait."

Constantin was too gobsmacked to speak. So he took Andi's hand and led her out of the room. She'd won over his mother. Miranda hadn't been able to do that. Not for all the showboating and kowtowing in the world. And Miranda had been a vampire, a partner choice he'd come to think his mother preferred for him.

Unbelievable.

They joined his father and two sisters in the sitting room. Constantin found his voice. "Father, Daniella, Juliette. This is Andromeda Merriweather. My girlfriend."

All eyes turned to them, but Juliette also let out a soft squeal as she got to her feet. "Oooh, it's so nice to finally meet you. Val says you're something else."

Andi held her smile with great poise. "I hope that's a compliment."

Juliette laughed. "Honestly, with Val you never really know. But you made it past the empress, and you're not in tears, so I'd say you have nothing to worry about." She glanced back at the kitchen. "Speaking of, I'd better go see if she needs any help. Nice to meet you finally."

"You, too."

Constantin put his hands in his pockets. "I expected Valentino to be late, but not Isabelle."

His father shook his head. "Isabelle texted to say that she's not up to dinner with how she's feeling. I expect she didn't want to meet Andromeda while unable to speak."

"That's too bad. I thought she and Andi would enjoy each other's company." Constantin looked at Andi and shrugged. "Sorry."

"It's okay," Andi answered. "I can understand not wanting to be out when you're not feeling your best."

"Very kind of you, Andromeda." His father, who'd also stood at their entrance, gestured to Juliette's now empty spot on the couch. "Have a seat. Would you like a glass of wine?"

She glanced at Constantin. He nodded. "I'm having one."

She relaxed a little more. "That would be lovely, thank you."

William went to pour them both a glass.

Daniella was perched on a club chair at the end of the conversation area. Her gaze was just this side of haughty, setting Constantin's teeth on edge. "What do you do, Andromeda?"

Andi's smile faltered a little. "I've been thinking about going back to school, actually. I wasted my first attempt. Too immature to realize the opportunity I'd been given. The fallacy of youth, I guess."

Daniella's haughtiness disappeared into surprise. "That's awfully honest. What would you study?"

"Art, maybe? But business definitely, too. Get both sides of my brain working." Andi accepted a glass of wine from William. "Thank you."

"You're welcome." He nodded in approval. "Smart areas of study. Balance is very important in life."

Constantin brought his wine over and sat beside her. Everything was going so well, he was almost afraid he'd do something to jinx it.

Andi was amazing. She wasn't even pretending to be anything but who she was. No wonder his family was reacting so well to her. She wasn't putting on airs or trying to play at a different level. She was just being herself. And that was pretty awesome.

He realized in that moment that it was impossible not to love her.

And he was done trying not to.

Chapter Twenty

A rivulet of sweat that had nothing to do with the room's temperature trickled down Andi's back, right between her shoulder blades. Sweat that was all about nerves. She was racked with them, had been since she and Con had entered the house, but they'd slowly begun to subside.

She'd thought she was going to be fine, but then Con's family turned out to be frighteningly perfect. Vampires usually were, but this bunch was also so reserved and proper. Well, all but Juliette, who'd been warm and welcoming from the start, but she'd disappeared too quickly. Andi couldn't wait for her to come back.

She could see where Con had gotten his uptightness. His mother and Daniella could make ice shiver, although even they didn't seem as bad as they had upon first impression.

That didn't stop Andi from feeling a little like she was on trial. It was such an odd sensation. She'd met parents before. But with that feeling came the realization that she had these nerves only because, unlike in times past, she *cared* what these people thought of her.

She sipped her wine, maybe a little too much of it, but she was hoping it would take some of the edge off. She'd chosen to be as honest and forthright as she could without making a fool of herself. So far that seemed to be working.

But could they tell how nervous she was? They had to. Vampires had the kind of senses that laid a person bare and made it nearly impossible to hide anything but thoughts.

Wait. Could vampires read minds? No, that was some random paranoia kicking in. *Breathe. You've got this.*

She drank a little more wine. Thankfully, it was a very nice one and went down easily.

The front door burst open, and Valentino walked in, a bottle of wine in each hand and an easy smile on his face. "Hello, my darling family."

Before any of them could respond, his gaze arrowed in on Con and Andi. "Well, there's the lovebirds. How are you two doing?"

Con stood up, partially blocking Andi's view. "We're fine. Are you alone?"

Valentino clucked his tongue indignantly and rolled his eyes with great drama. "Yes. I told you I wasn't bringing Miranda. You think she'd come here voluntarily? She knows how Mama feels about her."

As petty as it might be, Andi was pleased that Josephine Thibodeaux had no love for Con's ex. The knowledge made her like Josephine more and helped to further combat some of her nerves.

William got up and took the bottles of wine from his son. He inspected the labels. "These are good years."

"Only the best for my family." Val helped himself to a glass from the bottle that was already open, then sat on the arm of the sofa across from Andi. "Where's my baby sister?"

"Jules is in the kitchen," Daniella answered. "Where I should probably be, or I'll hear about how unhelpful I was." With a wry smile, she got up and started for the back of the house. "Don't have too much fun without me, now."

Andi sat up a little straighter and called after her. "Do you need any help? I can help if you need help." Could she say *help* a few more times? They were going to think she was simple.

Daniella paused and shook her head. "You're a guest. Relax and enjoy yourself."

Sure, Andi thought. *Easy for you to say. Impossible for me to do.*

But left alone with the men, she did relax a little. Men weren't usually as critical of her as women were, and two of the men in this room already liked her. At least she knew Con did and Val claimed to. That was a good start.

William and Con, their wineglasses in hand, joined her on the chairs and couches that made up the elegant sitting room. The room was an interesting mix of bold florals, jewel tones, gold, and black, which was mostly present in the baby grand piano in the corner. The space felt like money. All of the house did. Old money.

But then, that's what the Thibodeauxes were, she imagined.

Con took his seat beside her, William returned to his chair at the head of the grouping, and Val slid off the arm onto the couch and settled into the corner with one knee up on the next cushion like the whole thing was his.

He lifted his glass. "To Con and his new love."

William raised his glass as well, leaving Con and Andi no choice but to join in. They did, but Andi felt like such a phony.

Good thing she had plenty of wine to dull that feeling.

Con seemed to sense her mood and leaned forward to engage his brother in conversation that wasn't about Andi. "Did Miranda leave, then?"

Val's gaze tapered down with curiosity. "Why? You want to come back and see her again?"

William's brows rose, and he shook his head. "Valentino, you shouldn't have had her at your club in the first place, but please tell me, Constantin, that you did not go to Miranda's show."

"I did."

Andi had to chime in. "I went with him." She let a little half smile slip across her face. "It was boring. We left early."

William's eyes widened a little. "Ah, I see." He nodded at Con. "Wanted her to see the new flame, eh? Can't say that I blame you for that. Always nice to regain the upper hand, such as it were."

Val looked miffed. "Con said he was over her. I wouldn't have done it otherwise."

"Right," Con said.

His father and Val looked at him like he'd spit on the floor, and Andi got the sudden impression that his response had been a little out of character. Would the old Con have just sat there and let Val be the victor? Maybe.

It was interesting, for sure, but before the conversation went any further, Juliette bopped back into the room.

"Dinner's ready," she announced. "Mama wants everyone in the dining room *tout de suite.*"

Like obedient soldiers, the men got to their feet. Con offered Andi his hand, which she took, thankful for the support.

They followed his father in. Val lagged behind to collect the wine and bring it along.

The dining room was cranberry red (thankfully not quite the color of blood—a thought that nearly made Andi snort) and ivory with the most interesting crystal chandelier over the table.

It looked like a pirate ship.

"Fascinating," Andi whispered as she stared up at it.

Of course, everyone heard her, and all heads turned in her direction. There was no such thing as whispering in a house full of vampires.

William smiled. "It's an homage to our family

business. We were in the shipping business. It's why we lived in New Orleans. The town was one of this country's great ports many years ago."

Andi nodded, thankful her comment hadn't gone wrong. "Thank you for the explanation. I love the chandelier. Even more now that I know the story behind it."

Con guided her to their seats. She was between him and Juliette, which suited her just fine. That also put her in the middle of the table and directly across from no one, although Val and Daniella were on the other side. She guessed she might have been across from Isabelle, if she'd come.

Josephine didn't strike Andi as the kind of hostess who'd leave an empty seat at her table, though, so Andi really had no way of knowing for sure.

Con's parents had the ends of the table, although Josephine was still bringing in dishes.

When she finally sat, William smiled broadly at her. "Everything looks and smells amazing, my love."

Josephine smiled back. "The girls helped."

Dishes were passed, and food was served. For all her traveling, Andi had never been to New Orleans. Or Louisiana, for that matter. Most of what was in front of her wasn't familiar. The ingredients, yes, but not the exact preparations.

Maybe it was her expression of uncertainty, maybe it was her hesitation, but Con seemed to understand she was trying to figure things out.

He handed her a large bowl. "This is crawfish étouffée."

Everyone else had put theirs over rice, which had come around first. Fortunately, she'd taken a big spoonful of that since it was a known quantity. She helped herself to the stew-like dish, adding it to her rice as well.

The next dish he passed her had some kind of vegetable in it. Green semicircles. "This is mirliton. Although in the Carolinas, they call it chayote. It's a kind of squash."

"I like squash." She added some to her plate, thankful she wasn't a picky eater. There wasn't a bone in her body that wanted to offend Con's mother.

And so it went until her plate was fairly full. Which was good, because she'd had a little too much wine on a mostly empty stomach. She did not want to make a fool of herself in front of these people.

The food was delicious. She took seconds on the oysters Bienville and the biscuits, which were the lightest, fluffiest version she'd ever eaten. She made sure to tell Josephine that, too.

The conversation was nothing serious. Mostly everyone telling stories about their week. Andi was happy just to listen and eat and laugh. It was nice not to be the center of attention, that was for sure. Her nerves were nearly gone, and she felt surprisingly at home.

Until Daniella turned her attention to Andi. "So, Andromeda. I'm dying to know. How did you meet my brother?"

Andi went still, a biscuit halfway to her mouth.

She and Con hadn't talked about what their story was going to be. She took a bite of the biscuit to buy some time and tried to think. She couldn't tell the truth, could she?

Her nerves were back. Big-time.

Con laughed softly and squeezed her knee under the table. "You wouldn't believe it if she told you."

Daniella's smile was steely and didn't reach her eyes. "Try me."

Con's hand stayed on Andi's knee. "She came out of a book."

The truth. She wasn't sure whether to laugh or cry, but it felt like a relief that he was going with what actually happened.

The table was silent. Daniella frowned. "What does that mean? Is this some literary joke I'm not getting?"

"No, no," he answered. "I bought a lot of antique books from an estate sale, and when I opened one of them, Andi appeared."

No one budged, fixated on Con's words.

Juliette raised a finger in thought. "She was *in* a book."

"Cursed into it." Con looked at Andi. "Weren't you, darling?"

Andi swallowed the last of the biscuit crumbs and nodded. "Cursed into it. A practical joke by my sister." Okay, that part wasn't true, but she didn't want to explain Cassi's actual reason to these people.

Juliette snorted. "Wow. That sounds like something Val would do to Con."

Daniella let out a soft laugh. "It does, actually."

Josephine lifted her glass. "Here's to my son's love of literature finally paying off."

Laughter filled the space as everyone joined her in the toast.

Andi relaxed. All was well.

When the wine went around, she held her glass out to be filled. And when dessert was served, she unabashedly had seconds. Mostly because Daniella and Juliette did, too.

She could see herself fitting in here. Being a part of this family. Being friends with these women.

Living in this town. With this man.

She glanced at Con, admiring how handsome and wonderful he was, and for the first time in her life, she understood how one person could want to spend their entire life with another.

CHAPTER TWENTY-ONE

"I can't believe how well that went." Con was amazed in the best possible way.

"Me, too," Andi said.

He was smiling and couldn't stop. He pulled out of his parents' driveway to head home. "You were so good. I mean, you just being you, but that was perfect. They would have seen through anything else."

"I kind of thought that would be the case," Andi said.

He glanced over at her. She was leaning against the car window, eyes half shut, a wine-tired smile on her face. "Sleepy?"

"A little." She sighed contentedly, blinking herself awake. "I haven't eaten that much in a long time. Your mom can cook. And that bread pudding with the whiskey sauce? Wow, I need more of that."

"More?" He laughed softly. "You had two helpings."

"Only because your sisters did. I was trying to be polite. And it was delicious."

He nodded. "I see, I see. Well played, then."

Still smiling, she closed her eyes.

He let her be. She'd done a remarkable thing tonight. She'd charmed his very judgmental family. They'd always been that way. A close family often was, as a way of protecting its members, but his family had learned to protect each other in a way most didn't have to. Being a vampire had that effect.

But since the nightmare of Miranda, his parents had taken their critique of anyone new in his life to the next level.

It was one of the small reasons that he'd given up trying to find a new partner. His reluctance to be so deeply hurt again was another one. The big one.

Finding love was hard. It required a person to put so much of themselves out there. He'd risked it all once before. He glanced at Andi. Was he really ready to do it again?

Shockingly, his head and his heart seemed to agree that he was.

He knew he was being impetuous. That the speed at which his heart was responding to this woman was so out of character for him that it ought to be setting off every alarm in his system.

But that was the old Constantin. The new Constantin was taking the opposite approach. Letting go and being, as Andi would say, less uptight.

It terrified him as much as it thrilled him.

Andi was not his kind of woman at all. Which seemed to indicate exactly why she was so perfect. He didn't need another woman like Miranda, a woman who aspired to perfection in every aspect of her life.

He needed the chaos and impetuousness of Andi. He needed that kind of carefree joy. He'd never experienced it before her, and living in a place like Shadowvale made that a sad thing. He had nothing to fear in this town.

And yet he still lived with the kind of caution he had in the old days.

A bold wave of decision swept through him. Enough was enough. He knew what he wanted. Who he wanted. And waiting wasn't going to change that.

He pulled into his driveway, turned off the car, and looked at the woman who'd captured his heart.

She was deeply asleep. He could tell by her breathing and by the relaxed rhythm of her heartbeat. He smiled. His beloved.

He could wait until morning to tell her. He hoped. There was a very good chance he'd get cold feet. But he didn't want to wake her up either. She'd earned this rest.

Unsure what to do, he got out of the car and went around to her side. He opened her door carefully, catching her as she leaned with it. He scooped her into his arms and carried her into the house.

He bent his head to inhale the fragrance of her hair. Despite her curves, she was birdlike in his arms, delicate and fragile. What would she look like when she got her wings back? he wondered. He couldn't wait to see them. They must be as beautiful as she was.

Nudging the guest bedroom door open with his

foot, he slipped into the darkened space and gently laid her on the bed.

He took her shoes off, then straightened, looking around. There was a throw on the bench at the foot of the bed. He retrieved it and draped it over her, pausing to kiss her forehead.

There was something innocent and compelling about her when she was sleeping. Even if that sleep had been brought on by her overindulgence in wine and rich food. He smiled. He didn't blame her. He would have drunk himself silly meeting his parents for the first time.

"Sleep well, Andromeda." Their talk could wait until the morning. He was not going to chicken out. His feelings weren't so fickle that they'd fade with the morning's light. In fact, he ought to put voice to them now, even if she couldn't hear him.

He cleared his throat softly, intent on keeping his voice soft so he wouldn't wake her. Yes, this was a good way to practice his words. To see what they sounded like.

"Andromeda Merriweather, I am besotted with you. I cannot imagine my life without you in it. I don't want to either. I hope you'll stay. You will, won't you? Because the truth is…I love you."

A small flash of light filled the room, and he glanced at the windows, his ears focusing on any sound of a storm. He heard nothing, not even the slightest rumbling of distant thunder. He went to the windows anyway, closing the curtains so Andi wouldn't be disturbed.

He turned to wish her good night and stopped cold.

The throw he'd covered her with was flat. The bed was empty.

Andi was gone.

*

Andi pushed at the thing that was pushing at her. She was deep in a dream that involved a shirtless Con, bread pudding, and a mine full of jewels.

The thing nudged at her again. A voice followed. "Wake up, you lazy brat."

Andi knew that voice. Her eyes blinked open. "Cassi?"

"Who else did you think it was?" Cassi stared down at her, fists on her hips.

"I..." Andi pushed up to her elbows. "Where am I?"

"On the floor of my living room."

The same spot Andi had been standing when Cassi had trapped her in the book. Except now she was lying down. And wearing the clothes she'd worn to meet Con's family. "Why am I here?"

Cassi rolled her eyes. "Really? You're that clueless?"

Andi sat up and pushed to her feet. Definitely still wearing the black cigarette pants and white shirt, but no shoes. "Yes, really. Why am I here? Where's Con?"

"You're here because obviously you tricked some poor sap into breaking the curse. I only hope you fell for him, too."

A breath-stealing chill went through Andi. "I'm in Paris?"

"That's where I live, so yes, you're in Paris. Wow, being cursed made you dumber."

Andi spun, her bare toes digging into the carpet, desperation taking hold of her. "Con isn't here? Constantin? Where are you?"

"Is that the sucker you tricked?"

Andi whipped back around. "I didn't trick anyone." She'd started out to, but then her heart had gotten involved. "Where is he?"

Cassi folded her arms and shrugged. "Wherever he was when you left."

"He's still in Shadowvale," Andi whispered to herself. She had to get back there. Fast. Or Con was absolutely going to think she'd played him. Or worse. Her heart ached at the thought. "Send me back. You have to send me back."

"You want to go back into the book?"

"No, to Shadowvale. To Constantin."

Cassi just stared at her. "I don't have the magic to do that, you know that. Take yourself back."

"Right, right." Andi felt like she was having a heart attack. But she could do this. "I have to go, Cassi, but I'll come back, and we'll sort this all out, okay? I have a lot to tell you."

"I bet you do." Cassi snorted. "Good luck on your *trip*."

Her words rang with spite. Instantly, Andi understood. She didn't have to look over her shoulder to know her wings were still gone. "Give me back my wings."

"Why should I? After what you did to me?"

Andi shut her mouth for a moment, trying to compose herself. Her urge was to yell, but that wasn't going to get her anywhere. And she understood her sister's pain now in a way she never had before. "Cassi, I am very sorry about Rolph."

Anger filled Cassi's gaze. "Oh, right. Good time to be sorry, too. But yeah, that's not going to fly." Then she laughed. "And neither are you."

"Cassi, listen to me. I know you think I came on to Rolph, but I didn't." She swallowed at the knot in her throat. "He came on to me. I didn't want to tell you because I knew it would hurt you."

Cassi's haughty expression faltered, then she righted herself. "More lies. Just like you to spin one on top of another."

"No, Cassi, it's not a lie. It's the truth I was trying to spare you from. I know we don't always get along, but you're still my sister and I still love you. I thought it would be easier for you to be mad at me than heartbroken because your fiancé wasn't true."

Tears welled in Cassi's eyes. "Why would you make up such a horrible thing? It's not going to change what you did to me. I don't believe you anyway. Rolph is just one more man you ruined. That's it. Now get out of my house."

"Cassi. I swear it on my wings. Wherever they are."

Her sister paled and took a step back. "He wouldn't do that to me."

"I'm so sorry."

"First, you tell me you actually fell in love with a man. Now you're trying to tell me that you were looking after my best interests?" She laughed as tears started to fall. "Gran would be so disappointed in who you've become, Andromeda."

Andi nodded. "I know, but I was already trying to change. Con helped me realize how much more I need to do. And I'm trying. I really am. Being in love with him has made me realize that love isn't the petty emotion I thought it was. I am sorry for everything I've done to you. Every boyfriend of yours I flirted with, every man I seduced away from you. I wish I could take it all back."

She took a breath. "I was wrong to do those terrible things. Not just to you, but to myself. I don't want to be like our mother. I want to be like Gran. And you."

Cassi's lips parted, but no words came out.

"I know you probably don't believe me. I shouldn't expect you to. I haven't given you any reason to, after all. But maybe if you go with me to Shadowvale, and you meet Con, then maybe you'll see I'm telling the truth." She smiled sadly. "I even went to meet his family at their weekly dinner."

Cassi found her voice. "*You* went to meet a man's family?"

Andi nodded. "And I didn't embarrass myself or him. And get this, they're vampires."

Cassi's eyes rounded. "What kind of game are you playing?"

"No game. I'm done with games."

"You had dinner with a family of vampires."

Andi nodded. "And I'm pretty sure I'm in love with one."

Cassi shook her head. "I don't believe you. You can't expect me to."

"I know. That's why I want you to go to Shadowvale with me. And if I'm not telling the truth, you can keep my wings."

Cassi blinked a few times. "This has to be one of your tricks, but for the life of me, I can't figure it out. Fine, I'll go to Shadowvale, but I have to see this man for myself and hear him say that he loves you, or no wings."

"He had to say it to break the curse, right? So I'm sure he'll say it again." Except she wasn't sure. Not if she couldn't get back there in time and explain what had happened. "Deal?"

"Deal. Where is this Shadowvale?"

"Yeah, about that… I'm not really sure."

CHAPTER TWENTY-TWO

Andromeda was gone.

Gone.

Moments ticked by as Constantin stood there, staring at the bed and attempting to process what had happened. He put his hand down where she'd been. Warmth remained. Her scent lingered, too. Proof that she *had* been there. That this whole thing hadn't been a dream.

Or a nightmare.

He slumped into a chair near the windows and tried to think while he stared at the empty place and willed Andi to return. She didn't. Chloe wander through the open door and meowed, reminding him that he hadn't fed her yet.

"Soon," he muttered.

How did a woman just disappear? What kind of magic did that? Her curse? But how? Had he done something wrong? If Andi was hurt or—

"ANDI!"

His voice resounded through the house, causing Chloe to take off running and the sound of cracking glass to come from another room. But that was all. No response from Andi. Nothing. The only other heartbeat in the house belonged to Chloe.

Andromeda had vanished.

And he felt utterly lost. A sudden terror took him, like a clock was counting down toward a very bad thing. He was out of his depth. He needed a witch. Someone who could give him answers. Now.

He needed Amelia.

He got to his feet, dug his phone from his back pocket. His hands shook as he tapped the screen, calling her up.

Three rings…four rings…five—

"Hello?"

"Amelia, it's Constantin. Andromeda's gone. She's just disappeared out of her bed. I saw her. Well, I was in the room, but I thought it was a flash of lightning, but it wasn't, and now she's gone—"

"What happened right before she disappeared?"

"We were at my parents' for family dinner. She had a lot of food and wine and fell asleep in the car on the way home. I didn't want to wake her, so I carried her to the guest room and put her on the bed. That was it."

"That was it? Nothing else?"

He backtracked. "I took her shoes off, put a blanket over her, and kissed her forehead."

"What else?"

"Nothing. That's it. Then there was a flash of light. I thought it was lightning, but when I looked at the bed again, she was gone."

"You did nothing else? Think. Details matter."

"I closed the curtains because I thought a storm was coming. But she was already gone then. I think."

She repeated the question, slower this time. "You're sure you did nothing else?"

"That's everything I did."

"Did you *say* anything?"

"Yes, but I don't see how—"

"What did you say?" Her voice was softer. Almost sympathetic. Like she was pitying him. But for what?

He swallowed. "I told her how I feel about her. I was going to do it in the morning, but she was asleep, so I thought I would practice."

The admission made him feel vulnerable. And foolish. As if he'd done something he should have realized would lead to this. Was that why Amelia sounded like she pitied him? "What did I do?"

"I don't know yet. Can you tell me specifically what you said? The exact words?"

He closed his eyes. "That I was besotted with her. That I couldn't imagine my life without her. That I hoped she'd stay. And that..." He squeezed his eyes tighter. "That I loved her."

Amelia made a small noise that could have meant a thousand different things. "I had a feeling. That's what did it, then."

"That I said I loved her? How?"

"Because those were the words needed to break that curse. You spoke them and meant them, and the curse was broken. That's why she disappeared."

"No, Andi told me it would take three kisses to break the curse. And we'd only had one. At least in the time frame that she said — "

"I'm sorry, Constantin, but that's not how that curse was built. She had to make you fall in love with her to truly break that curse. Getting you to kiss her was just a means to that end."

He sat down again, on the bed this time. Andi's lingering warmth was gone. "Are you sure?"

"Yes. Not only because I'm a witch, but I confronted Andi about it, and she told me the truth herself."

"She lied to me." The words were a whisper, spoken to his own shattered heart, raked out of his tightened throat.

"I don't think she knew any other way to fulfill the curse."

Amelia's words didn't really register. The pain of knowing the truth was too much.

He'd been devastated by Andi's disappearance because he'd been worried something terrible had happened to her. Now he realized that she'd gotten what she'd wanted. The end to her curse.

The terrible thing had happened to him. Again.

He'd been left by another woman. Another woman he'd fallen for. How stupid was he? Did women just look at him and see what an easy mark he was? But for all his hurt, he had to know one thing. "She could have told me the truth. She knew I was falling for her."

Amelia sighed. "It could have been handled better, I agree."

Cold comfort, that. "Where did she go?"

"Most likely back to wherever she was when she was caught up in the curse."

"Back to her life."

"Yes," Amelia said. "Back to whatever life she was living before."

"Thank you. Good night."

"Good night, Constantin. Don't be too—"

He hung up. He was tired of talking. Tired of listening. Tired of trying to be a new and improved version of himself.

His old self had wanted nothing to do with Andromeda when she'd suddenly appeared in his shop. His old self had been smart. Why on earth had he decided he needed to change to be liked? Who cared about being liked?

The muscles in his jaw tightened. The only change he was interested in now was going back to being the man he'd been before. The man with walls up. The man everyone called prickly. And uptight.

The man who never let anyone in.

And never would again.

The trip back to the southern part of the United States had taken nearly three days. Mostly because Cassi was enjoying Andi's misery. Andi understood that her sister was making her suffer, and on one level, she was okay with it. She'd certainly put Cassi through a lot over the years.

But now wasn't the time. Not when Con was probably upside down with emotion. What emotion, Andi wasn't sure.

He might be torn apart with worry. Or livid with anger. Or numb from being left again.

Maybe all three. She didn't know and couldn't predict. But she needed to get back to him to explain just as soon as she possibly could.

So all of Cassi's faffing around and deliberate delaying were about to result in Andi losing her cool, big-time.

"Any car, Cass." Andi leaned in to interrupt her sister's conversation with the rental car agent. "*Any* car."

Cassi's brows lifted. "Cass, huh? You must really be perturbed to call me that." She smiled at the agent. "We'll take the sedan, thank you."

"You're stalling just to wind me up. I know you are. And look, I get it. If I was in your shoes, I might be doing the same thing. But this really isn't the time. Constantin is probably going nuts not knowing what happened to me. Or worse, he's convinced himself that I abandoned him just like the last woman he was involved with."

Cassi sighed. "This whole thing where you pretend to be in love with him is so odd. I just don't know what to make of it."

Andi quelled the urge to roll her eyes and throttle her sister. "I am not pretending. I love him. And being away from him, with him not knowing where I am, is killing me."

A slight, bitter smile bent Cassi's mouth. "Love is shockingly painful, isn't it?"

"Yes. And I've learned my lesson, so can we just go? Please?"

Cassi accepted the keys from the agent. "Let me ask for directions." She turned back to the man behind the counter. "Do you know where Shadowvale is?"

He frowned and shook his head. "No, I'm sorry. I've never heard of it."

Andi grabbed her phone and did a quick search in her GPS app. The town showed up, but was grayed out. Like it no longer existed. Well, Con had said the place was deliberately hard to find. But with Cassi behind the wheel, they'd never get there. "I got it. Looks to be less than an hour. I'll drive."

An hour later, she was still driving. Still looking. And her GPS wasn't helping, sending her in circles and down dead ends until it stopped talking to her altogether.

Finally, Andi pulled over and leaned her head against the steering wheel. She was exhausted, on the verge of tears and possibly a mental breakdown, and it was nearly ten o'clock. Finding any place in the dark was always harder, but knowing that didn't help anything. "All I want is to get back to him and explain. I don't even care about my wings anymore."

Cassi sucked in a breath. "Are you serious?"

Andi tipped her head to see her sister. "Yes. I don't care. I love him, Cassi. I know he's hurting, and that makes me hurt. Love is terrible like that, I guess."

"It is. Sometimes. And sometimes it's the most incredible thing in the world." Cassi went silent for a long moment, then spoke again in a much quieter voice. "You really do love him, don't you?"

"Yes, I do. Desperately. I want to be with him so badly. I don't know what else to tell you to make you understand." Andi sniffed, then smacked the steering wheel in frustration. "I know this place is supposed to be hard to find, but this is ridiculous. He must think I'm never coming back."

"Please make next legal U-turn."

They both looked at Andi's phone, which was propped on the dashboard.

Cassi shrugged. "Might as well give it one more shot."

Andi turned the car around and followed the app's instructions. "Says we should be there in two minutes."

Cassi leaned forward, peering through the windshield with a skeptical expression. "There's nothing but forest around us. I can't imagine there's actually a town here."

"We're not quite there yet." Andi took the next turn the GPS indicated, and the road beneath the car's tires changed, maybe to gravel or dirt, but it wasn't asphalt anymore. Too rough. Or it was asphalt that needed serious repaving.

"I don't like this," Cassi said. "It's too dark to see beyond the headlights. And everything looks really overgrown and—wow."

Andi slowed the car as a pair of enormous, rusted

metal gates came into view. The word *Shadowvale* was spelled out across them, barely visible beneath the vines curling through the scrollwork. "I think we're here."

"I don't know," Cassi said. "Nothing about this says active, functioning town to me."

"Agreed. Except I was here. Not *here* here, but I was in the town. And it's full of people and businesses and life."

"Maybe…it was all an illusion? A dream you had while you were…otherwise occupied?"

"No," Andi said. "It was real, and I was out of the book. Con opened it, remember? He basically saved my life. That book was awful."

With a little sigh, Cassi shook her head. "I shouldn't have put you in that insane-asylum book. That's my fault. Anything could have happened in there."

"Yeah, about that," Andi said. "We're going to discuss that some more later. But for now, I'm going to see if I can get those gates open."

She hopped out of the car and approached. The metallic clicking of nearby insects faded as she walked toward the gates. They were ten or twelve feet tall, easily, and about as wide. Or wider.

They looked very locked.

"Please let me in," she whispered as she put her hands on the metal. It was warm but gritty with rust. She grabbed hold of one section, squeezing with the same strength as the pain gripping her heart. "Please. I have to get to Constantin. I have to explain."

Pain shot through Andi's hands. She let go of the gate. Tiny little pinpricks covered her palms. Blood welled up. "What on earth?"

She took another look at the gates. They were covered with needlelike barbs. They hadn't been there when she'd first grabbed hold of the metal. An eerie feeling spun through her. Whatever had just happened was not going to be without consequence.

She glared at the gates. "If you're going to take my blood, then you'd better let me in. Because I *will* get to Con. If I have to drive that car through these gates, I will."

The creak of metal scraping pavement sounded as the gates slowly parted.

She backed up, sucking in a breath. The gates were opening. "Thank you."

She wiped her hands on her pants, then ran back to the car and jumped in.

"What did you do?" Cassi asked.

"I begged." Telling her sister about the gate drawing blood would only weird Cassi out and complicate the situation. She'd explain later. When things were back to the way they should be.

Cassi snorted. "You begged?"

"Yes." Andi shifted the car into drive and rolled through the gates inch by inch until they were opened wide enough to let the entire car through.

"Are you sure we should be going in here? It still looks pretty abandoned, if you ask me."

"Well, I didn't ask you, but if you're not

comfortable with this, you can get out." Andi stopped the car.

"Andi! You'd leave me here?"

"You stuck me in a book about insane asylums. I'd say you'd be getting off easy. Now make up your mind. I'm done waiting."

Cassi looked a little taken back, but Andi was fine with that. Her sister had slowed them down enough.

"Point taken. Drive on."

CHAPTER TWENTY-THREE

Past a curve in the road and it wasn't long before the town came into view.

"Main Street," Andi announced. "I've been here. Many times. Con's bookstore is here, too."

Cassi was glued to the window. "What's it called?"

"The Gilded Page. Should still be open. Many of the shops stay open well into the night to accommodate the supernaturals that are more nocturnal."

"Wait," Cassi said. "So...lots of supernaturals live here?"

"Tons. But there are humans, too."

"Humans and supernaturals living together?"

"Yep. And it's all cool. No one has to hide who they are."

"Wow." Cassi's wings unfurled behind her. "Might as well be comfortable, then."

Andi glanced over. "Great. Rub it in."

Cassi shot her a look that said, *Deal with it*. "Tell me more about this town. Why is it so hard to find?"

"On purpose. To protect those who live here.

From what Con's told me, it's a sort of safe haven for those who are troubled by who they are or their circumstances. Or different enough to not be able to live comfortably in the ordinary human world. A lot of the people that live here are cursed in some way or another."

"Cursed? Is this guy Con cursed?"

"Only in the sense that he's a vampire, and vampires are cursed in general by the fatal touch of sunlight. Oh, that's the other thing. The sun never shines here."

Cassi grimaced. "So it's night all the time?"

"No, not night. Just overcast during the day. Honestly, it's sort of odd at first, but then you kind of forget about it." Andi snorted softly. "You know, now that I've said that, I realize I thought it was going to bother me when Con first explained it, but after that I hardly gave it a second thought. But that's what makes it such a safe place for vampires to live."

"No kidding. If I was a vampire, I'd totally move here."

"There." Andi pointed. "The Gilded Page. And the lights are still on."

She pulled the car over into the first available spot and parked. Nerves tripped through her. Excited, happy, scared nerves. She got out and stared at the storefront for a moment. Con wasn't immediately visible, but he had to be in there.

Unless Fletcher was working the evening shift.

Well, whatever. She was going in.

Cassi got out. "You want me to go with you?"

"I think you should since you said I'm not getting my wings back until you confirm my story. Just keep in mind, he might be pretty angry right now. I have no idea what to expect."

Cassi nodded. "Understood."

With that, Andi walked toward the store. Cassi fell into step beside her.

The chimes sounded softly as Andi pushed the door open.

Fletcher popped up from behind the counter. "Andi. I did not expect to see you. Mr. Thibodeaux said you were gone."

"I was. But now I'm back. Is he here?"

"No. He left at five."

"Did he go home?"

"I'm not sure. Probably." Fletcher shrugged as if he wished he could tell her more. "You know Mr. Thibodeaux. Creature of habit."

"Right." Andi sighed. "I guess we'll try there."

"Glad you're back."

"Me, too." Andi rubbed the tensed muscles at the back of her neck. "What kind of mood was he in?"

Fletcher's tortured expression said it all. "Not good. At all."

That was exactly what she was afraid of.

Cassi cleared her throat.

Andi managed a polite smile. "This is my sister, Cassiopeia, by the way."

"Hi. Nice to meet you." Fletcher gave a little wave. "Nice wings."

"Thanks," Cassi said, giving a little half turn to show them off better. "Nice fangs."

He grinned. And blushed. Something Andi had never seen a vampire do before.

She grabbed Cassi's arm. "Okay, we have to run. See you later, Fletcher. Thanks for the info."

"You're welcome. Bye."

Andi yanked her sister back out to the sidewalk. "Seriously? You're flirting with a guy while I'm in the middle of a meltdown?"

"Oh, you're not melting down. You're in love, and you just don't know how to deal. Besides, he's cute. And that's pretty much how you've behaved my entire life, so suck it up, buttercup."

Andi dropped her sister's arm, rolling her eyes. "Okay, I get it. I was a terrible person, but your timing could use a lot of work. Get in the car. We're going out to the bayou."

"The bayou?"

"You'll see."

Andi was quiet on the drive to Con's house. She was too busy trying to figure out the best approach to explaining things to him. Her sister commented on the passing scenery, but the best Andi could do in response was a grunt or a nod.

She pulled into Con's driveway. "His car's not here. Unless it's parked around back."

"I can't believe this exists here. It looks so real."

"It is real. This town was built from magic. It's apparently capable of anything." She wasn't even going to get into the gem mines that Con had told her about.

"I'd love to see more."

"I'm sure you will." She opened her car door.

Cassi gave her an odd look. "You're getting out? If his car isn't here, he probably isn't either."

"I just want to look in the windows and check. I won't be long."

"I'm coming with you." Cassi climbed out. "Hey, are there alligators? Because I think real bayous have them."

"This *is* a real bayou, so yes, there are gators. Including one giant one named Brutus. Try not to get eaten." Although at this point, Andi wouldn't mind if Cassi got bitten a little.

They walked to the house together, but Andi stopped at the stairs that led up to the first floor. "Give me a second."

She went around behind the enclosed center storage area, but there was no sign of Con's SUV there either. She returned to the stairs. "Nothing."

They went up to the big front porch. Andi cupped her hands around her eyes and looked in through the front window. There were no lights on, but a few electronics gave off enough ambient light that her sprite eyes could pick up Chloe sleeping on the couch.

She straightened away from the window and sighed. "I don't think anyone's home but his cat."

Cassi snorted softly. "He has a cat? Isn't he a vampire?"

"Yes, but why shouldn't he have a pet?"

She shrugged. "I don't know. Just seems odd. It's kind of endearing, though, when you think about it."

It was. The fact that prickly, uptight Constantin could save an animal's life, then take that animal in and commit to caring for it told Andi that deep beneath that crusty outer shell beat a heart of kindness and compassion.

She hoped that was still true.

"Where now?" Cassi asked.

"I don't know. I guess I could try his parents' house, but that feels like it could get awkward really fast. I've only met them once. I'm not sure I want our second encounter to be all, 'Hey, I ditched your son accidentally, now I need to apologize,' you know?"

"Right." Cassi leaned against the railing. "What about other family?"

Andi nodded. "As a matter of fact, I know where his brother is. And he might actually help me."

Constantin had never been one to drink excessively. Beyond the glass of wine now and then at the family dinner, he never drank at home.

But now, things were different. There was no fixing the destruction Andromeda had caused to his heart and his psyche, so numbing himself with spirits seemed like the only way forward.

Fortunately, he had a brother willing to oblige him.

Out of the shadowy depths of one of Club 42's booths, Constantin lifted his empty glass into the air.

A server appeared almost instantly, mostly because Valentino had made sure one was assigned to Constantin. Constantin knew that, but it wasn't any kind of special, VIP treatment. Valentino had done it to keep his brother from causing a scene.

The server took the glass. "Yes, sir, can I get you another?"

"Yes. Bring the bottle this time." Constantin sat back and watched the server make haste toward the bar. Valentino wouldn't be far away. Constantin had seen him here and there, checking in on how his jilted sibling was doing.

But Valentino hadn't come to the table again since Constantin had first arrived. Constantin had a pretty good idea why. Valentino was nervous about what Constantin had become.

In a dark, depraved way, that pleased Constantin.

He decided in that moment that he wouldn't return to his old self. He *would* change after all. He would become worse than he'd been before.

He would give way to all the bitterness and anger and self-loathing that had built up inside him. Those things would rule him now. Help him make the kind of decisions that kept the world at bay.

He nodded drunkenly at the wisdom of his decision. Fletcher could run the shop. Or not. Who cared?

As for his family...well, they'd been taken in by Andromeda, too, so whether they remained in his life was up to them. If they sided with him, they could stay.

But the first sister who told him there were more fish in the sea would be given the permanent silent treatment. No more platitudes and banalities about how things would improve if only he'd give someone new a chance.

He'd done that. And failed miserably. Again.

The thought of moving to the Dark Acres suddenly had appeal. He'd build himself a rambling mansion out there and spend the remainder of his days alone in a great house filled with books.

Although a book was what had gotten him into this mess. Andromeda had even tainted the one thing he'd considered safe.

The server returned with a bottle of good brandy and a clean glass. "Is there anything else I can get you, sir?"

"Just go away."

With a stiff nod, the server disappeared.

The band onstage, some bluesy trio whose sad music had suited Constantin rather well, took a break, and breezier tunes spilled from the club's sound system.

Constantin's lip curled as he poured himself a drink. "Light jazz. Terrible." His voice rose. "Elevator music," he snapped.

A few heads turned.

Like magic, Valentino appeared. He was frowning. Poor pretty golden boy was unhappy.

Constantin sat back, lifting his glass to his lips. "Problem?"

"I don't know," Valentino said. "Is there one?"

"Just that you play terrible music between sets." Constantin finished the brandy and poured another. "How *do* you stay in business?"

Valentino leaned in, his gaze just barely lit from within. "You're drunk. And I understand why. But if you want to stay here, you need to keep your mouth shut and act civilly. Do you understand?"

Constantin looked over the rim of his glass. "Or what?"

The spark in Valentino's eyes brightened. "Or I'll throw you out. I'm still your older brother, remember?"

"Hmph." Constantin tossed the brandy back. "Go away. I want to be..." His words failed him as a hallucination appeared over Valentino's shoulder. He glanced at his empty glass. He hadn't had that much, had he?

His gaze returned to the mirage. He couldn't look away, no matter how much he wanted to.

"What is it?" Valentino asked.

Constantin just shook his head, his voice gone, his nerves pinging with the stupidity of hope even as his body tensed in anger.

Valentino turned to see for himself. A second later, Constantin heard him whisper the one name he'd hoped never to hear again.

"Andromeda."

CHAPTER TWENTY-FOUR

"This place is astonishingly cool," Cassi said. "And that's from someone who's lived in Paris for the last few years. I would love to hang out here some evening when I'm dressed for the occasion."

Andi just nodded, busy scanning the crowd for—she stopped scanning. Valentino was staring at her. He didn't look happy to see her, but he didn't look bothered by her presence either. More surprised.

She went toward him. He'd know where Con was. A few yards away, she realized Con was behind him, sitting in the booth farthest from the stage. And from the looks of the bottle of brandy on the table, he was doing his best to obliterate a few brain cells.

She stopped short. The crowd swirled around her, indifferent to the torrent of emotions going on inside her. She shifted her gaze back to Val.

He shook his head like he knew what she wanted and didn't think it was a good idea. Well, he could think whatever he wanted, but she *was* talking to Con.

"I have to speak to him." Her voice was low since

there was no need to shout. Val's vampire hearing was capable of picking up her words. Which meant Con could hear her, too. "Please, Val. I didn't leave because I wanted to. I was snatched away by the curse's magic. I just want a chance to explain."

Valentino frowned, then turned and said something to Con that she couldn't make out. They exchanged a few more words, then Valentino threw his hands up. After one last statement to his brother, he walked toward her.

He shook his head again. "He doesn't want to talk to you."

"He doesn't have to. All he has to do is listen."

"He might do that. He's had enough to drink that I don't think he's in any rush to get out of that booth. But he's angry. Very angry. And I don't know that there's anything you can say that will change that."

Her heart ached at that news. "I'm not leaving until I try."

"Good for you." He smiled weakly. "You're exactly the kind of woman he needs. He'd see that if he could just get out of his own stubborn way."

"Thanks." She glanced at Cassi. "This is my sister, by the way. Cassi, this is Valentino, Con's brother and the owner of this club."

Val took Cassi's hand, lightly kissing the back of it. "Enchanté, mademoiselle."

"Merci, monsieur." Cassi grinned. "Your French is beautiful."

"I grew up speaking it. But yours is lovely also."

"I live in Paris. You pick it up after a few years."
She was clearly captivated, which was no doubt
Val's intention. Then Cassi leaned in toward him.
"Your club is amazing, by the way. I already adore
it, and I've only been here ten minutes."

Val grinned right back. "Then let me show you
around."

As the two left, Andi switched her attention back
to Con. He was slouched in the farthest spot of the
booth, one foot on the seat, knee bent. Several days'
worth of stubble darkened his jaw, a strand of
unkempt hair fell over his forehead, and his heavy-
lidded gaze reminded her of embers in a fireplace,
glowing hot beneath a thick layer of ash.

He looked like a storm that hadn't quite decided
where to make landfall.

This was not a version of Con she'd encountered
before, and as his current condition gave her pause,
she could easily imagine how hurt he'd been by her
disappearance. Time to make that as right as she
could. *If* she could.

She gathered her courage and walked toward
him, stopping at the table's edge. "Mind if I sit?"

He didn't look at her. Instead, he poured brandy
into his empty glass. "You're blocking my view of
the stage."

There was no one on the stage, but she figured
mentioning that wasn't going to get her anywhere,
so she did what she did best—exactly what she
wanted. "I'd better sit, then."

She plopped down on the other side of the booth

in a big, exaggerated way that couldn't be ignored. He still wasn't looking at her.

A server showed up. "Can I bring you something, ma'am?"

"A glass of water. Thank you."

With a nod, the server left.

Con drank half the liquid in his glass, his gaze still somewhere off in the distance, but his eyes glowing with emotion.

That was unsettling. She had to make this fast.

She took a breath and started. "I'm very sorry I disappeared the way I did. It wasn't on purpose. I didn't even know it would happen. In fact, when I woke up, I had no idea where I was. I was in Paris, by the way. At my sister's. That's part of why it took me so long to get back here. That, and Cassi has made every step of this trip take as long as possible to punish me."

No response.

She kept going. "I'm also sorry I fell asleep after that wonderful dinner at your parents'. I had too much to drink because my nerves were through the roof. That wasn't my intention—to fall asleep, I mean. I had planned to have a nice long talk with you after we got back to your house. To explain some things and—"

"Like how you were just using me to break the curse? Like how you lied to me about what the curse actually required?" The anger in his eyes matched the bitterness in his voice, and he was definitely paying attention to her now.

She understood his response, but that didn't stop her from getting a little angry herself. "First of all, you opened the book, so there was no one else that *could* break the curse. Secondly, would it have been better if I had told you that falling in love with me was the only way for me to be free? Personal experience has taught me that the fastest way to lose a guy is with that kind of direct approach. And you didn't exactly like me to begin with, so that full-blown honesty felt like a really bad way to go."

He grunted something and finished his brandy.

"Does that help?" she asked. "Drinking yourself unconscious?"

He ignored her question to pour himself another.

He might have been paying attention. Or he might have tuned her out. Hard to tell.

She kept going anyway. "There's something else I was going to tell you that night when we got home." She paused, but there was no change in his level of interest. "How I was falling for you. How I wanted to give us a shot. If you were willing. I wasn't sure you would be. You're a hard man to read sometimes, you know that?"

More grunting that she couldn't interpret, which pretty much proved her point.

"I was going to explain that how after I went back to see my sister and worked everything out with her and got my wings back, I was going to return to Shadowvale and you. To focus on us."

His head lifted slightly, but his attention still wasn't on her.

She sighed and stared at the table. She was getting nowhere. Maybe there was nowhere to get. Maybe he really was done with her.

"You saw your sister."

Finally, a response from him. She picked her head up. He hadn't really asked a question, but she answered him anyway in the hopes of starting an actual conversation. "I did."

"Then where are your wings?"

"She didn't believe my story about what happened here. She wanted to see you for herself. And hear you say again the words that set me free."

He stared at her, unblinking, for a moment. Then his lip curled, and his eyes narrowed. "Not going to happen."

"So in three days' time, you don't love me anymore? I know what you said, and I know you meant it. The curse wouldn't have broken otherwise. Those words that you spoke to me when I was sleeping are what sent me back to Cassi. How can you not feel that way anymore?"

"Because you used me. And you lied to me. And you left me."

"But I explained all that."

"Good for you. Feel better now?"

His words cut. But again, she forgave him because of his past. And because she loved him. "Con, please. I know you're hurt, but I'm telling you—"

"I'm not hurt. I'm done. With love. With women. With you." His mouth twisted into a sneer. "Now you can go, satisfied you've had your say."

"Having my say isn't why I came back."

"Right. You mentioned that. It was so you could convince your sister to return your wings. I hope that works out for you. Or not. I don't really care."

She stood, her eyes hot with impending tears. "I expected you to be angry. I didn't expect you to be a jerk. I guess the upside to that is it'll be easier to stop being in love with you."

She stormed off before he could send another verbal jab at her, going blindly into the crowd in search of her sister.

She found Cassi at the bar, drinking champagne with Val. "I need to leave now."

Cassi made a face. "But we were just—"

"Fine. Enjoy. I'm going." Andi turned on her heels and made for the door. She honestly didn't care if Cassi followed or not, but she had to get out of here. And she had to find someone who could help her make things right.

Only one person in this town might possibly be capable of a thing like that. The same person who'd helped her before.

The witch named Amelia.

She strode out of the club, her heart hurting, but her head full of purpose and determination. Magic had gotten her into this mess, magic could get her out.

She fumbled in her purse for her keys, fishing them out only to drop them. She grabbed them off the sidewalk and pushed the button on the key fob to unlock the car as she walked around to the driver's side.

"Andi, wait." Cassi came spilling out of the club, Val on her heels.

Andi opened the car door, but didn't get in. "If you're coming, hurry up."

Val made it to the car ahead of Cassi. "I know he's mad and he's being awful, but please don't give up on him."

"I'm not."

Val pulled back just as Cassi joined them. "You're not? Then why are you leaving?"

"Because I'm going to see Amelia. Con told me she's the most powerful witch in town, and she managed to break the curse's tether when we first went to her, so I'm hoping she can do something to help me fix the mess I'm in now."

He nodded like that seemed logical. "I can go with you."

"I'd appreciate that, but—wait. You act like you already know about the curse."

"Your sister filled me in. You were saying?"

"Just that maybe you should stay here and make sure he doesn't do anything dumber than he already has. In fact, Cassi, why don't you stay here, too? Val might need help keeping an eye on his brother."

For the first time, Cassi looked genuinely concerned. "Okay, I can do that. I'm happy to help."

Now that was shocking. "You are?"

With a sympathetic smile, she looked at Val. "Valentino told me about you two being here on a date and how you stood up to Constantin's ex and how well you got on with his family at the dinner.

That's when I told him about the curse and how I was the one that did it." She sighed in a hopeful way. "I've never known you like this, Andi, but it's so nice, and I just want to see this work out."

"Thank you. That means a lot. I'll be back as soon as I have an answer one way or the other."

Val tapped the hood of the car. "Call if you need anything. You know where we'll be."

"Will do. Keep him safe."

Val put his arm around Cassi's shoulders, something she didn't seem to mind a bit. "We will."

Andi jumped into the car and took off, going on sheer memory to guide her to Amelia's. It wasn't hard. A house like that stuck in a person's memory.

She arrived after only one wrong turn, parking beneath the porte cochere and going straight up to the front door.

She raised her hand to knock, and the door opened.

Beckett stood waiting. He shrugged one shoulder. "She knew you were coming."

"Am I about to get a big helping of I-told-you-so?"

"Probably. But that doesn't mean she won't help you." He moved out of the way to let her in.

"Good. Because I have never needed so much help in my life."

CHAPTER TWENTY-FIVE

Andi waited for almost twenty minutes before Amelia showed up. Clearly, the witch was making a point. Or punishing her, like Cassi had with her relentless foot-dragging on the way to Shadowvale.

Either way, Andi did her best to stay calm. Upsetting the woman whose help she needed wouldn't get her very far. And without Amelia, Andi was at a loss for what to do next. She knew there were other witches in town, but if Amelia wouldn't help her, why would any of them?

She certainly couldn't pay them.

At last, Amelia walked in, her caftan of emerald silk billowing out behind her. Amethysts sparkled at her ears, throat, and fingers. Products of the mines? Andi wondered. The witch eyed Andi with a look of disappointment, her mouth bent in matching disapproval. "I warned you, sprite."

"You did. And I took it to heart. I planned to tell him as much as I could after we got home from dinner at his parents'. But I fell asleep. A lot of food and too much wine to calm my nerves." She smiled sadly. If only she could go back and change that. "And I never expected him to tell me he loved me. I didn't even know he did it until I woke up in Paris at my sister's."

"I see." Amelia remained standing. "What is it you want from me, then?"

"Help." Andi inched forward on the seat. "A way to fix this. A way to make him forgive me. Or something. Anything to straighten out this mess."

"Why? You got what you wanted. You're free of the curse now, aren't you?"

"Yes, but…" Her breath stuck in her throat, snagging on the emotion welling up inside her. "I love him. I didn't expect that, but it happened. I can't just walk away from him. Not now. Not knowing he feels, or felt, the same way about me."

"Funny thing, love." Amelia finally sat, taking the same chair she had before near the fireplace. She waved her hand at the logs, setting them ablaze.

The heat was instant and comforting, but it was going to take more than a cozy fire to right everything wrong in Andi's world. "Is there anything you can do magically?"

Amelia stared at the fire. "With magic, there is always something that can be done. But there's never a guarantee the result will be what you desire."

Great. Mysterious witch talk. Andi held on to her calm as best she could. "Can you explain that? What can you do?"

Amelia looked at her. "I can make him forget you entirely."

"That seems the opposite of what I'm trying to accomplish here."

"A love spell on a man who already loves you can go sideways very easily and turn into obsession. Or worse. And we're talking about a vampire here, not a human. Magic doesn't always work on other supernaturals with the same intensity or accuracy as it does humans. Sometimes, it's more. Sometimes, it's less. Sometimes, it's something completely different. What you need is to start from scratch."

"So...you make him forget me, and then what?"

"You move to Shadowvale and meet him all over again. Let things take their course."

That filled Andi with several levels of dread. "What if he doesn't like me? He didn't like me the first time."

"But you won't be meeting under those same conditions. You'll have to take things slower, certainly, but there's a good chance the seed of his true feelings will remain. Deeply buried, but there's no reason that seed cannot grow again."

"And if it doesn't?"

"At worst, there will be nothing between you. At best, he will fall in love with you again. But it's also possible that all you will achieve is a middle ground. That you will be nothing more than a friend to him. And if he does fall in love with you again, there's no telling how long that will take."

Andi sat quietly, thinking things through. "I won't forget him. But he'll forget me."

"Correct."

"And what about his family? What about Fletcher, who works at the store? What about the few other people I met in town?"

"Their memories will all be intact."

"So they'll all have to be in on this, as it were." She shook her head. "I don't like that. It feels like lying to him all over again. And making everyone else lie, too."

Amelia nodded thoughtfully. "It would be, in a way."

"And what if someone slips up and says something that throws him off?"

"I cannot control that."

"Then…" Andi thought hard. "Can you cast a bigger spell? Make the whole town forget me instead? Then I could truly have a fresh start."

Amelia sat back, folding her hands in her lap. "I can. But a spell of such magnitude would require a greater sacrifice on your part."

Andi took a breath, afraid of the answer, but she asked her question anyway. "What kind of greater sacrifice?"

"Something dear and personal. Your wings, for example."

She sat quietly, taking that information in. "I'd have to get them back from my sister first." She took a breath. "They'd have to be removed the same way she took them. With magic. Or the loss of them would kill me."

Amelia nodded. "I understand, but you can remove them yourself voluntarily, can you not?"

"Yes." This was so much more than Andi had been counting on, but she'd spent almost a week without her wings now, and it was enough for her to imagine life without them, versus life without Con.

It wasn't a hard decision. "How soon can you cast the spell?"

"Tomorrow evening should be plenty of time. By seven. Will you have your wings back by then?"

"I'm going to work on that as soon as I get back to my sister. Can I have her with me when you cast the spell?"

Amelia nodded. "Of course."

Andi stood. "Thank you for agreeing to help me."

Amelia rose as well. "The hard part is going to fall on you. You love him enough to do this?"

"I do."

"You've only known him a few days."

Andi smiled. "I know. But that's been plenty of time for me to realize that he's the one I want in my life. I feel like a better person around him. Like I'm more than I thought I could be. I can't walk away from all that. It's the most real thing I've ever experienced. Sacrificing my wings seems like a small price to pay for a lifetime of happiness. Does any of that make sense? Have you ever been in love like that?"

Amelia sighed, the sound sad and filled with longing. "I have. And I made a sacrifice of my own."

"Oh, right. The vampire you built the town for. Con's uncle. He told me about that. I'm sorry. I didn't mean to bring that up."

Amelia's smile was weak, but held some warmth. "Living in this town brings it up every day."

"With all of that history and how things didn't work out for you, why would you still want to do this for me?"

"Because I am a foolish old woman who still believes in love? Because I hope that Constantin does fall for you again? Because joy is a better choice than regret? I don't know for sure. But I do want this to work for you."

"Thank you." Andi paused. "If it doesn't work... what then?"

"Then he doesn't love you."

"Will that be my only chance at love?"

"No, I don't think so."

Andi bit her bottom lip. "If he rejects me, will I be able to stay in Shadowvale?"

"I'm sure that would be fine. But if you choose to leave, you may not be allowed back in."

"Why is that?"

Amelia was slow to respond. "The gates often have a mind of their own."

Andi glanced at her palms. "Yeah, I found that out trying to get in."

"Why?" Amelia's brow furrowed. "What happened?"

"I couldn't get the gates open. I grabbed hold of them and shook them, and little thorns sprang out of them. Stuck me pretty good." She held her hands up for Amelia to see all the tiny little pinpoint wounds that remained. "If I had my wings, these would be gone by now, but…" She shrugged.

Amelia's gaze darkened. She took one of Andi's hands and examined it. "The gate took your blood."

Andi had been trying not to think that way. "Are you sure? I mean, maybe it was just a defensive measure to—"

"The gate took your blood." Amelia looked at her. "Your sister, too?"

"No, just me."

Amelia released Andi's hand. "The gates protect those who live here. They knew that you hurt Constantin. The one took your blood so that they will always recognize you. Your sister should be free to go, but you might not ever be allowed to pass through those gates again."

Constantin woke to the smell of coffee and lilies. For a moment, he thought he'd died and was in the funeral parlor.

Then the pounding brandy headache kicked in, and he realized he wasn't that lucky. Next, he recognized the scent of Valentino's cologne. And a vaguely familiar woman's perfume. He was not in his own home for some reason.

With a hand on his head and his eyes closed, he sat up. "What the devil happened?"

Valentino answered him. "You got plastered, and I brought you up here to make sure you didn't go on some drunken murderous vampire feeding binge through town. That would bring a lot of shame to the family, and you know how Mama feels about that."

"I do not get plastered."

"Right. Well, you'd better explain that to the pair of bottles you drained last night."

The clink of ceramic on wood opened Constantin's eyes. Valentino had set a mug of coffee on the table in front of the couch. "And thanks to me, that's all you drained. Drink that, then I'll get you some plasma out of the fridge."

Constantin's lip curled as his stomach knotted in rebellion. "The very thought of cold plasma makes me want to be sick."

Valentino rolled his eyes. "Then I'll warm it up."

"Thank you. For...this." They weren't at his brother's home. They were in the apartment over the jazz club. Valentino often housed visiting musicians here, which explained the lingering odor of Miranda's perfume.

"You're welcome." Valentino was back in the kitchen, pouring a mug of coffee for himself. "You'd do the same for me. I think."

Constantin sighed. "Why did I drink so much?"

Valentino came out, mug in hand. "Do you really not remember?"

Constantin thought, but that made his head hurt worse. He tried to stop, but it was too late. His memories, most of them, came flooding back. "Andi," he snarled.

"Uh-huh. And settle down. I can't handle all that crankiness this early."

With the memories of her, came the pain and regret and betrayal. As the muscles in his jaw tightened, he bent his head so Valentino couldn't see his eyes. "Is she still in town?"

"Yes."

"Someone should tell her to leave." Constantin picked up the mug. "There's no point in her staying."

"She loves you. She just wanted to talk to you last night and explain what happened."

"Doesn't matter, because it did happen."

Valentino sighed. "I know you're in a bad place because of what Miranda did to you, and I know I'm to blame for that being fresh in your mind, but Andi is a very different woman, and this situation is nothing like *that* situation."

"Live your own life, and I'll live mine." Nothing had changed. Constantin still wasn't interested in anyone trying to tell him how he should act or what he should accept or forgive. Done was done.

"What if she can prove how much she loves you?"

Constantin snorted. "Yeah, right."

"I'm serious. What would it take?"

"There isn't anything she can do." He stared at his brother over the edge of the mug. "And don't try to come up with one of your schemes either."

Valentino put on his innocent face. "I'm not up to anything, I promise. But there is something you're going to want to see this evening."

"What? And where?" The words came out in a growl, but Constantin was far too used to his brother's ways to believe he had anything good up his sleeve.

"You'll see," Valentino said. He twisted away, headed back toward the kitchen. "And Indigo House."

"And if I say no?"

"You'll have Amelia to answer to."

Constantin snarled out another word, one his mother would have gasped at.

Valentino snorted. "Regardless, you'd better be there."

"Fine. But until then, I'm going back to sleep." Something was afoot. And whatever it was, he already didn't like it.

CHAPTER TWENTY-SIX

The Sunshine Diner was a lovely place. The inside was cheery, the service was quick, the wait staff all wore smiles, and the breakfasts in front of Andi and her sister looked amazing. Andi was glad they'd come.

For one thing, they'd needed to get out of Valentino's house. He'd been kind enough to offer them a place to stay and had then actually gone somewhere else for the night. Andi hadn't expected him to be so chivalrous.

Secondly, Cassi was insisting that she and Andi spend the day together seeing the town. Whatever that was about.

But all Andi wanted was her wings back. Sure, she now wanted them for a very different reason than she had before, and there was some irony in the fact that once she had them, she was going to lose them again. But at the moment, her life felt like it was on hold. Like she needed to turn the page to the next chapter and couldn't.

And not knowing what that next chapter held scared her.

What if Con didn't fall in love with her again? What if he only liked her?

Even worse, what if he actually disliked her the same way he had the first time they'd met?

She took a breath and tried not to focus on those things, tried to think about the best-possible outcome. Her own personal happily ever after.

Except...could a vampire and a human have a happily ever after? Because without her wings, that was essentially what she'd be. Human.

"You haven't moved in, like, five minutes. Are you okay? Your pancakes are getting cold."

"What?" Andi blinked, focusing on her sister across the table.

"You're thinking about him, aren't you?" Cassi asked. She put her fork down to take a drink of her orange juice.

Andi nodded. "Him and me and us and what's going to happen next. My head's kind of a big mess of what-ifs right now."

"You know, that's why I haven't given you your wings back yet. Why I asked you to spend a day with me away from him and any reminders of him. I want you to think this through. This is a major decision you're making. You're willing to give up your magic and become basically human for this man. And he may not even love you again."

Andi filled her lungs with air, then exhaled, hoping to expel all the doubts with it. "I know the risk. And that it will take some adjustment. But I can't base my decisions on the worst-possible outcome. If people did that, no one would ever take any chances in life. And this is far too important to walk away from."

Cassi gestured with a piece of bacon. "What will you do if things don't work out?"

Andi hadn't told Cassi every detail of her conversation with Amelia. About how the gates were probably not going to open for her again. She put on a happy face. "I'll stay here. It's a great town. It's time I settled down anyway."

Bacon now eaten, Cassi cut a piece of French toast with the edge of her fork. "You're going to stay here? In a town with a man you love but who doesn't love you back? That doesn't sound like you. The Andi I know sees a problem and heads in the other direction ASAP."

"I've changed, Cassi. This whole experience has been eye-opening. It's time for me to live like an adult. Take responsibility for my actions. Get my life together."

"Yeah, so not you."

"Well, it's who I am now. I would think you'd be happy. You've basically been telling me to grow up since we were kids. Isn't that why you cursed me into the book? To learn a lesson?"

Cassi shrugged. "Yes. But I never thought it would happen."

"Thanks for the vote of confidence."

Cassi laughed softly. "Hey, I think it's great. I just...I don't want my baby sister to get hurt. Which, considering our past, probably sounds odd, but just because we've had some problems doesn't mean I stopped loving you or caring what happens to you."

Andi made a face. "Which is why you cursed me so lovingly and caringly into a book about insane asylums."

"Hey, I said I was trying to teach you a lesson. And yes, I acted in anger. But I never thought it would lead to all this."

"I know." Andi took a bite of her pancakes. She was pretty sure they were delicious, but at the moment, nothing had much flavor.

"You would really stay here?"

Andi nodded while she chewed. "I would. It's a great town."

Cassi mulled that over for a moment. "What's so great about it? Sell me."

"Well, it's a safe place for supernaturals to live. And there are humans here, too, but everyone knows about everyone else, and they all live in harmony. People come here to be accepted for who they are, for what makes them different, and it's all okay."

"That sounds good. Kind of weird for humans to know about supernaturals, but it would be nice not to hide that part of yourself."

Andi nodded. "Right?"

"What else?"

Andi leaned in. "This whole town is funded by gem mines. I don't know a lot of the details, but apparently that's what pays for all the great amenities here and keeps prices reasonable. Speaking of reasonable prices, there is some great shopping here.

I'll show you. Oh! And there's a bakery where everything is free, except for the excellent coffee, which is still cheap."

Cassi's brows bent in skepticism. "Free baked goods and cheap coffee?"

"I swear."

"I need to see that."

"We'll go there next."

"Anything else?"

"Well, I haven't been there, but supposedly there's an enchanted forest that has a book in it, and if you can find the book and write your name in it, whatever curse is plaguing you will be taken away."

Cassi's eyes went wide. "Forget the bakery, I want to see *that*. Okay, maybe don't forget the bakery, but this enchanted forest sounds kind of amazing. Let's go there right after the bakery."

"I don't know. Con said it's kind of dangerous."

"You realize that in a matter of hours you're about to do something that's going to change your life forever, and you're worried about a magical forest?"

Andi rubbed her forehead. "True. I don't know exactly how to get there, though."

Cassi called the server over, a nice young man with pointed ears. His name tag said Davey. "Can you tell us how to get to the enchanted forest?"

"Sure." He gave Cassi a funny smile. "You must be new around here. Welcome to Shadowvale."

"Thank you." Cassi looked ridiculously pleased with herself.

Davey whipped out his order pad and pen, tearing off a sheet and flipping it over. "I'll draw you a little map. I'm no good at south and west and all that, but I can show you this way."

"Perfect." Cassi shot Andi a victorious look.

Andi just nodded. At least a trip to the enchanted forest was sure to take her mind off this evening's activities.

Half an hour later, they were back in the rental car with a large box of goodies from Black Horse Bakery to sustain them. In case breakfast hadn't been enough.

Andi drove. Cassi was in the passenger's seat, Davey's hand-drawn map held out in front of her. "Looks like Main Street, past some big park, then onto Fiddler Street—hey, isn't that where Val's club is?"

"Yep. See? You'll have no problem finding your way around when you come to visit me."

Cassi just nodded. She was looking at the houses they were passing. "There must be some money in this town, huh? I mean, besides the gem mines. Look at these places. Gorgeous."

"Wait until you see the house we're going to tonight. But yeah, some of the homes here are beautiful."

They drove on, the houses getting fewer and fewer and the greenery increasing until a sign appeared directing them to the enchanted forest.

"Davey was spot-on with that map." Cassi tucked the slip of paper above the sun visor.

As Andi turned onto the road, she slowed the car and pulled onto the shoulder. "I have no idea where I'm going from here."

"Me either, but just drive, and we'll see if anything looks like a path or a trail. If it does, we'll stop and take it."

Andi frowned. "That's not much of a plan."

"You have a better idea?"

"Not really." Andi got the car moving again, but kept her speed down so they could see the forest better.

What light there was dimmed further, filtered through the overhead canopy so that it seemed tinged in green.

"It's kind of pretty." Cassi's statement sounded more like an attempt to convince herself.

"It is. In a creepy, Venus flytrap kind of way."

"Andi." Cassi frowned. "I'm pretty sure this forest isn't trying to lure us in to eat us. This is a paved road. They wouldn't pave a road through a place like that."

"Con said there are magic meridian lines that run underneath the town, and they leak magic all the time. How do you know the forest didn't create this road on its own? Or that this road is really here? It might be an illusion."

Cassi's frown disappeared in favor of a much more freaked-out expression. "Stop the car."

"What? Why?"

"So I can feel the road."

"Don't be—"

"I'm serious. Stop the car."

Andi pulled over.

Cassi hopped out and ran around the front of the car to bend down and touch the road. Andi put the window down and leaned out. "Well?"

"Feels real. Could that be an illusion, too?"

"I guess, but this is a little beyond my scope."

"Mine, too." Cassi stood.

"You want to go back or—"

Something rustled the bushes across the road. Cassi arrowed in on the sound, her eyes widening. "Do you see that?"

Andi looked. "See what?"

"I just saw a...I don't know what it was. Looked like a purple fox with wings." Cassi put her hand on her head. "I might be losing it."

Andi got out of the car. "I don't know. This is an enchanted forest. Who knows what kind of things live here?"

"Do you think maybe that creature was some kind of sign? Or a messenger? Maybe it can lead us to the book."

Andi smirked at her sister. "Yeah, now you're losing it."

"Um, again, magical enchanted forest."

Andi sighed. She just didn't get why her sister was so fired up about this book and this forest. "Right, but—"

"Okay, whatever, I'm going." Cassi started across the road toward the creature she'd seen.

"Hey, hang on," Andi called after her sister.

"What is going on with you? Why do you care so much about this book? I mean, whose name would you even write in it? You're not cursed, and I'm not cursed anymore, so…what gives?"

When Cassi turned, her face was twisted with frustration. "No, we're not cursed. If anything, you've lived a pretty charmed life."

"I don't know if I'd say it was 'charmed,' exactly."

"Oh, please. You've never had any responsibility. You've flitted around the world, having wild adventures with handsome, wealthy men, and I know, I know, you've changed. And that's great. But going after this book is exactly the kind of thing you would do. So I want to do it. I'm tired of being the responsible one. The safe one." She sniffed. "The boring one."

"Come on, you're not boring."

Cassi put her hands on her hips and cocked her head. "Really? You've never thought that about me? Don't lie."

"I…okay, maybe. But not boring in a bad way."

Cassi rolled her eyes. "Nice try. Listen, I'm happy for you that you've found love and want to settle down and start a life here. But I've done the settling down and having a life thing. It's pretty much all I've done. Just give me this one adventure, and then I'll give you your wings back, and we'll both get on with our lives." She lifted one shoulder, smiling coyly. "Who knows? Maybe I'll even move here now that you're going to be an adult."

"Really? You'd think about leaving Paris?"

Cassi nodded. "I was only there because Gran wanted to see the city before she passed."

Andi nodded. Their gran had died three years ago. "You were a much better granddaughter to her than I was."

"It's not about that, Andi. And you know Gran never felt that way. She loved us both equally. Although she did ask me to hold back a part of your inheritance until I thought you were capable of not blowing it on champagne and shoes."

Andi blinked a few times, trying to process what her sister had just said. "Are you saying... What are you saying?"

"There's a trust fund waiting on you. It's not going to make you a millionaire, but it'll be more than enough to get you started here."

"Wow. That's amazing." Maybe Andi should have been mad at Cassi for holding that info back for so many years, but then, she'd just been doing what Gran had asked her to do. And for that, Andi couldn't fault her. Cassi really was the good one. The responsible one. The one who could be counted on to do the right thing.

"Hang on." Andi grabbed the box from Black Horse, tucked it under her arm, then locked up the car and walked toward her sister. "Come on, let's go look for this book."

Cassi glanced at the box of pastries. "You really think we're going to be gone that long?"

"No. But you're the one who wants to live like me. And this is what I'd do. Traipse through a potentially dangerous enchanted forest with supplies."

Cassi nodded, grinning. "You know, at times, there's a lot to be said for your decision-making."

"I'm glad you approve." Andi just hoped this wasn't a decision she'd come to regret.

CHAPTER TWENTY-SEVEN

Amelia splayed her hands on the gleaming surface of her worktable, the ingredients for the soon-to-be-cast spell sitting out before her. The cool of the basement sanctum, her dedicated space for all things witchcraft, made it possible to have a fire going, something she dearly loved.

Taking advantage of that crackling fire at the far end of the room, Thoreau lounged near the enormous hearth. He didn't spend much time in the house, seeing as how he frightened the staff, except for Beckett, who had no fear of the creature, but then, why would he?

Today, however, the giant cat seemed to crave her company, sitting near her at breakfast while she ate on the patio, then following her inside when she'd finished. She was glad of his nearness. His presence was a comfort.

Maybe he sensed that her thoughts were on Andromeda and all the woman was willing to risk for love. And how such a sacrifice could only remind Amelia of the one she'd made so many years ago.

A sacrifice also made for a vampire.

Amelia sent up a prayer that Andromeda's results would be very different.

But Constantin was Pasqual's kin, and blood was blood. There was every chance her outcome would be much the same as Amelia's had been. Constantin wouldn't leave Shadowvale, but he might very well reject Andromeda.

Rejection was something Amelia knew all about.

A sob caught in her throat. Time had not erased that wound. Eased it, yes. Given her distance and perspective, too. But some days, it all came rushing back. Today was one of those days, mostly due to the task at hand.

She took a breath, tipped her head back, and let the fresh sorrow flow out of her. She couldn't give in to it any more than she already had. There was too much work to be done, and Pasqual was gone. Grieving for him and their failed love wouldn't change that.

After all, if creating a town for him where he could live in safety from the sun's deadly rays hadn't kept him at her side, nothing would have.

A few more moments passed, a few more deep breaths were taken, and she righted herself. "Thoreau, we have work to do. But that work will be for naught if Constantin isn't here."

The big cat lifted his striped head, slow-blinking at her. He whuffed out a sigh, then stretched out again, soaking up the fire's radiating warmth.

She smiled. He was a dear creature. Someday she would figure out his secrets.

But today was not that day. She picked up the house phone and rang for Beckett.

He answered a moment later. "Yes?"

"Get Valentino Thibodeaux for me."

"Right away."

She hung up, waiting for the single ring that would alert her to a waiting call. It took only a few minutes, a good sign that Valentino was taking his responsibilities seriously.

She picked up the phone.

The vampire spoke first. "Good afternoon, Amelia."

"Good afternoon, Valentino. I trust all is well on your end?"

"I wouldn't say Con is well. He's sleeping off the vat of brandy he drank last night, but he was briefly awake this morning, and I made him aware that you require his presence this evening. His head should be clear enough by then."

"Good. You'll make sure he gets here? And stays?"

"I will. I'll even make him shower and get presentable, which he's probably not going to like." Valentino paused. "Do you really think this will work?"

"Which? Our plan or my spell?"

"Either, I suppose."

She took a breath. "I don't know. I'm hoping our plan will do the trick so I don't have to go through with the spell. I'm preparing it nonetheless."

"I hope you don't have to go through with it either. But if you have to, are you sure the potion you gave me will protect me?"

"Yes. You and I will be the only ones who remember everything. And Andromeda, of course."

"Right. I trust you. I hope you know that."

"I do. I'll see you this evening."

"Until then."

She hung up, giving Thoreau a look. There was no putting it off anymore. She had to prepare the spell in case she actually had to cast it. But the beast was sleeping. She sighed. Waking him up was still easier than hunting him down in the garden. "Thoreau, my darling, wake up. I need a whisker. It's for a good cause, I promise."

Twenty minutes into the forest and no book in sight.

Looking was apparently appetite-inducing work, as Andi and Cassi had each partaken in a day-and-night cookie, which seemed to be the bakery's take on a classic black-and-white. It was delicious, but did nothing to quell Andi's concerns that this *adventure* wasn't a good idea.

Had she really grown up that much in the last week? Apparently. She stopped, leaves crunching softly under her feet. She adjusted the bakery box under her arm. "We have no idea where we're going."

Cassi turned, pushing hair out of her eyes. "Not at the moment, but the next sign could be around the next tree."

"There can't be a next sign when there wasn't a first sign. Look, I know you wanted to do this, and we've done it. Can't we just head back to the car and call this adventure over?" She held out the box of goodies. "We could go back to Val's and eat the rest of these."

Cassi stared at her sister. "You just want your wings back."

"I do, of course, but this forest is giving me that prickly feeling on the back of my neck, like we're being watched. Or stalked. And I'm basically human right now, so your supernatural senses must be lighting up like the Fourth of July."

Cassi frowned. "They are, but not in a creeped-out way. Just in that kind of way when there's a heavy presence of magic."

"Do you think you could use that feeling to guide us to the book?"

"Maybe. But we'd probably have a better shot at it if you had your wings and your senses back."

Andi hesitated. "Does that mean…"

Cassi nodded and lifted a slim, silver chain from around her neck. It had been tucked under her shirt, but as she pulled it free, a small glass vial dangled at the end of it. Inside the vial, iridescent colors danced and sparkled.

Andi sucked in a breath. "My wings. In my vial."

Every sprite had a vial in which to store their wings. Some never used their vial, but it was a handy thing to have when it was absolutely necessary to pass as human. A sprite could hide their wings by tucking them against their body, but that wasn't foolproof. Andi often stored hers when she traveled. Nothing worse than falling asleep on a plane and waking up to an entire flight of people staring you down because you'd suddenly sprouted wings.

She'd never do that again. Nor would she ever let her vial fall into anyone else's hands again. But then...that wasn't going to matter after tonight.

Cassi unhooked the vial and handed it over. "Here. They're all yours again. I'm sorry I've been holding them hostage."

"How did you get them into my vial? And how did you get the vial away from me? I don't remember any of it."

"The first part of the witch's spell put you into a hypnotic state. You were very biddable."

Andi shook her head and sighed. "Wow. I have no memory of that."

"Kind of the point." Cassi grimaced. "I'm so sorry about all of that. Do you forgive me for everything I've done to you?"

Andi tucked the bakery box under her arm and took the vial. Sparks of energy lit the container's interior as it touched her hand and the wings recognized her. "Do you forgive me for everything I've done to you?"

"Absolutely. No matter what happens tonight, let's consider this day our new beginning, okay?"

"Even if I end up permanently human?"

"If I can deal with the wild child you used to be, I

can certainly deal with you as a human. Honestly, it doesn't matter. You're my sister. Always."

Andi couldn't help but smile. "Thank you. If I end up being human and alone, I'm going to need you. At least until I get through the heartache of it all."

Cassi's mouth quirked up on one side.

"What?" Andi asked.

"I think that's the first time you've ever said you'd need me. For something other than money or a place to stay or to get you out of a jam."

"Was I really that bad?"

"Sometimes." Cassi shrugged the question away. "But that's all in the past, right? Put your wings back on already, and let's see if two sprites are better than one."

"Thanks, and yes, it's all in the past." Andi opened the vial and spoke the words that would make her complete again. "Wings return."

With the magic imbued in the wings, the gossamer appendages whispered out of the vial in a twist of light and shimmer, coming to rest on Andi's back.

The moment they touched her, she felt whole again. Her senses sharpened, and the forest surrounding her suddenly had a polishing filter applied to it, bringing to life new colors, sounds, and smells. She was fully sprite again.

A small lump formed in her throat. She'd miss this when she gave up her wings. She'd be lying to herself if she thought otherwise. But Con was worth it.

Putting on a happy face, she turned, taking it all in. "Wow. This forest is amazing."

"Does it look that different?" Cassi asked.

"Yes. It looks a lot more magical. I guess I've been without my wings for so long, I forgot how things should look." She stared into the depths of the forest. Fireflies danced through the trees, and clumps of glowing vegetation illuminated the thickets. "I can see now why you want to keep exploring. I wonder if I would have even been able to see that purple fox creature? Or maybe it only reveals itself to the fully supernatural?"

"Hard to say." Cassi twisted back and forth with anticipation. "So you want to keep looking, then?"

Andi nodded. "A little bit more, yes." She glanced back toward the car. Or the direction she thought the car was in. "Are we going to be able to find our way back?"

"Absolutely." Cassi pointed the same way Andi had just been looking. "Right back that way, past that really thick tree with the funny knot on the side."

"Okay." Cassi seemed very sure, and Cassi was almost always right.

"Do you sense anything more now that you've got your wings back?" Cassi asked. "Any idea what direction we should go?"

Andi closed her eyes and listened with her whole self on alert, taking in every sound and smell and strand of enchanted energy. The forest was indeed soaked in magic. She tried to feel where that magic was coming from, where it was the strongest. She opened her eyes and turned a few degrees south. "That way."

Cassi grinned. "Excellent. That matches what I was thinking, too." With a flutter of her wings, she lifted off the ground. "Want to fly? At least until the trees get too thick and we have to walk?"

"Do I ever." She'd never wanted to fly so much in her life, especially with the very real prospect that she might not get to do it again for a very long time. If ever. She stretched her wings, then flicked them into hover mode. Her feet left the ground as she joined her sister in the air. "Let's go."

Sadly, they had been in the air less than five minutes when the forest became too much to maneuver. Branches, hanging moss, thick trunks, sprawling vines...the air space was diminished to the point that they finally settled back on the ground.

"At least we got to fly a little bit," Andi said.

"Right." Cassi grabbed her sister's hand. "I know you're worried about tonight, but it's going to work out, you'll see."

A twig snapped not too far off, and both sisters twisted to look in that direction. Cassi moved in close to Andi. "What was that?"

"I don't know. Do you smell...sulfur?"

Cassi's nose wrinkled. "I smell something. Brimstone, maybe. But why on earth would there be brimstone here?"

"Con said there are some dangerous creatures that live in the darkest depths of this forest."

A long moment of tense silence passed between them, broken only by the caw of a raven.

Cassi's throat moved as she swallowed. "Does it seem a lot darker here than where we took off from?"

Andi nodded. "A lot darker. But the trees are closer, and the canopy overhead is really thick."

A red firefly zipped past.

Cassi's grip on Andi's hand tightened. "What was that?"

"A firefly?" But Andi wasn't sure.

"Fireflies aren't red." Cassi sucked in a breath and pointed to a vine on a tree ahead. "And that's fever nettle. That's poisonous to our kind."

The prickly sensation of being watched hit Andi hard again. "Cassi, I'm sorry, but it's really time to call this adventure over."

"Yeah," Cassi whispered. "I'm good with that. Things have gone downhill surprisingly fast."

"Which way?"

Cassi's exhale had an odd little shudder to it. "I think…that way?"

"You think?" Andi glanced at her sister. "I thought you knew."

"I did. Until we landed and everything closed in. Now I'm not so sure."

Andi rubbed at her temple. "This isn't good."

"How did we get so turned around?" Cassi looked in the opposite direction. "Maybe that way?"

"I don't think so. I think we need to go back there." Andi pointed. "That feels right to me."

Cassi sighed. "I honestly don't know, but I guess we could pick a direction and—hey, what about GPS? On our phones."

"Oh, good thinking." Andi shifted the bakery box to dig her phone out of her pocket, while Cassi did the same thing.

Almost simultaneously, they groaned.

Andi shook her head. "No signal."

"Me either." Cassi took the bakery box from Andi, opened it, and took out another cookie. "We should have done a Hansel and Gretel and left ourselves a trail of crumbs."

"In this place? Those crumbs probably would have gotten eaten. But good thought."

Cassi swallowed the bite of cookie she'd taken. "I got us into this. I'm really sorry. I just wanted to try living life your way for once."

"Which technically means I got us into this."

Cassi laughed softly. "Let's share the blame."

Andi helped herself to a cupcake. "At least we won't starve. Hey, what time is it anyway?"

They both looked at their phones again, then at each other, eyes wide.

Cassi's smile was gone. "How is it possible we've been in here for three hours? That's not right."

Andi tried to put on an optimistic front. "In a magical forest, I imagine it's easy to lose track of time, but we're going to get out of here now, so it's all good."

"How?"

Andi tried to think. Then she tipped her head up.

There was no visible sky. But looking up like that meant she could see the tips of her wings. She smiled. Having her wings back was wonderful. Especially because they were about to save her one last time. "We just have to find a break in the canopy. Then we're going straight up and straight out."

CHAPTER TWENTY-EIGHT

"This is an utter waste of time," Constantin groused. "She's not even coming. That's how much she cares. I told you. All women are the same—"

"Will you shut up?" Valentino glared at him. "She'll be here. She's probably just—"

"She's here," Beckett called up to where Constantin and Valentino were tucked away on the library's second floor.

The rack of books made an excellent hiding place, but with a few volumes carefully spaced, it was also perfect for viewing the spell Amelia was about to perform below. With the second-floor lights off, Constantin and his brother were virtually invisible.

None of that mattered to Constantin, though. He already knew what would happen. Andi would chicken out at the last moment. There was no way she would sacrifice her wings for the chance that he might love her again.

And if she did go through with it, the more fool her. Nothing was going to change his mind. Nothing.

Andi walked in with another young woman

behind her. Both of them sported shimmery, translucent wings. Constantin was surprised by how delicate and beautiful they were. Then he frowned at himself for being distracted by such an insignificant detail.

Valentino leaned in, his voice barely audible. "That's her sister, Cassiopeia."

Constantin cut his eyes at his brother. "Obviously."

Then he went back to watching the woman who'd broken his heart. A sharp pain pierced his chest. The remnants of his hangover, he told himself. That was all. Nothing more. But pain was good. It sharpened his senses. Helped him remember that he was done with love.

Such a stupid, foolish emotion. Almost equal to sorrow, which he no longer chose to feel either.

Andi and her sister looked a bit disheveled. They had leaves in their hair, a few rips in their clothing, and smudges of dirt and streaks of green on their skin. Oddly, none of that did anything to diminish Andromeda's beauty.

He frowned. What the devil had they been doing?

Andi approached Amelia, who was sitting by the fireplace. Every room of her home seemed to have one. "I'm sorry we're late. We got lost in the enchanted forest."

Amelia made a face. "What on earth were you doing there?"

Cassiopeia stepped forward. "It was my fault, ma'am. I wanted to look for the book that takes people's curses away."

Amelia frowned. "Why? Are you cursed?"

"Not particularly." Cassi glanced at her sister. "I just wanted to have an adventure, Andromeda-style."

Amelia's puzzled expression remained. "What does that mean?"

Cassi smiled at her sister. "Of the two of us, Andi has always lived her life wide open. Not necessarily the best thing for every occasion, but her ability to take risks without fear is something I've envied for a long time. I wanted to see what that was like. Oddly enough, she tried to talk me out of going to the forest several times, but I had my mind set on seeing it."

Andi nodded. "Con told me it was dangerous."

Amelia lifted her head. "And you listened to him? Why, if you're such an adventurous sort?"

"Because I knew he had my best interests at heart." Andi shrugged, staring at her hands. "People who care about you don't warn you for no reason. They want to keep you safe." She glanced at her sister. "Cassi's done that for me my whole life, and I never once listened to her. But Con helped me understand that when someone wants to protect you, it's an expression of love. Funny how things work, huh?"

"Yes," Amelia said. "Funny."

"Anyway," Cassi went on, "we're late because of me. I'm very sorry. Please don't punish Andi."

Amelia rose. "No one's getting punished for anything. We're not that fickle. Things happen in Shadowvale. One learns to adapt."

Cassi nodded and stepped back, a quiet, "Thank you," her only other words.

Constantin leaned closer to the rack of books as Amelia walked up to Andi.

The witch stared at the young woman. "Do you still wish to proceed as we discussed?"

Andi straightened and took a breath. Then she clasped her hands solemnly in front of her. "I do."

"You understand that your wings will be required of you as a sacrifice for the spell."

Before Andi could answer, Cassi let out a small sob and shook her head. "Are you *sure* about this?"

Andi's gaze seemed to grow liquid as she looked at her sister. "Yes."

"Think about what you're giving up," Cassi said. "Your wings saved your life today."

Constantin frowned. What exactly had happened in that forest?

Andi raised her chin, a resolute determination shining in her eyes. Her wings expanded slightly, pulsing gently with her breathing. "And for that I'm grateful. I'm really glad I got to fly one last time, too. But I have to do this. I have to give myself this chance." Her voice faltered for a second, then she whispered, "I love him."

The pain in Constantin's chest returned, and he could feel the weight of his brother's stare on him. He glared at Val.

Val frowned and shook his head. "How can you not be moved?"

"Because I know how capricious a woman's heart is. How moods swing and tears dry up. You'll see."

Val's eyes tapered in disbelief. "You're a fool."

"No, I *was* a fool. No longer." Constantin ignored his brother and turned his attention back to the scene below.

Amelia asked again, "Then you still wish to proceed as we discussed?"

Andi nodded. "I do and I'm ready."

"Then let the spell work begin." Amelia removed a scarlet cloth that covered a low table in the middle of the room.

A shallow copper bowl sat in the center of a chalked circle. A few votive candles dotted the chalk, and the bowl held a few items. Herbs or dust or something. He couldn't make out what it was exactly, but it didn't matter, they were just the random elements of the spell.

Witchcraft held little interest for him. Unless it was a book of spells he could turn over for a tidy sum.

He snorted softly. That was who he was now. A buyer and seller of books. They were all he cared to protect, outside of Chloe and his family. He shot a look at his brother. And even some of them were questionable.

Amelia spoke low and soft as she lit the candles, her words indecipherable to Con, but again, he didn't really care.

He yawned, making no attempt to hide his boredom from his brother.

As suspected, the move earned him another look of chastisement.

He rolled his eyes and went back to watching.

All the candles were lit now. Amelia waved her hands over the bowl, and gentle flames erupted. More words were spoken. Latin, he thought. A single curl of pale green smoke rose from the bowl.

Amelia held out her hand to Andi. "I need your wings."

Even Constantin had to concede that Andi's smile was brave. She didn't falter, didn't hesitate, just took something from her pocket—a vial, he could see now—and removed the top.

She took one breath, one glance up, then whispered, "Wings away."

Like a stream of liquid glass, the gossamer pair spun off of Andi's body and funneled into the vial. In a few seconds, they were contained.

Andi replaced the top and held the vial out to Amelia. "Here you are." But then she pulled the vial back toward her body. "I...I'm not sure I can do this."

It was all too much for Constantin. All too precious and pointless. Especially when he'd been right. He vaulted over the top of the bookshelf, over the second-floor balcony railing, and came to land on the first floor, mere feet from where Andi stood. "I knew it."

She and her sister both gasped. Amelia seemed unmoved.

He stared Andi down. "This won't change anything. Nothing will."

"Con," she murmured. "Have you been here this whole time?"

"Yes, not that it matters. None of this matters. It's foolishness. You can't change my heart. What you did is done. There is no going back, no erasing it. Not even with magic. But I want to say again that I knew you would back out when it came time to give up your precious wings."

Andi shook her head slowly. "That's not why I said I couldn't go through with this."

He snorted. "What other reason could there possibly be?"

"Because this spell was going to erase your memories of me and make it possible for us to meet for the first time all over again. And the idea of doing that without your agreement has been bothering me. It seems...unfair, I guess."

He leaned closer, knowing his eyes must be aglow with the storm of emotion inside him. "What a kind, gentle creature you are," he mocked. "Is that really all that's holding you back? My permission?"

Her eyes filled with hurt and sorrow. "Yes, Con. Even if it means I have to learn to live without you, that I have to walk away from a chance at real happiness, I can't bring myself to do this to you without you being a willing party."

He straightened, pulling himself up to his full height. "That is terribly convenient, isn't it? And so very noble of you to put my best interests first, even if the result is you get to keep your precious wings."

The hurt and sorrow in her eyes vanished, replaced by angry sparks of indignation. "You have really let your past get the best of you, you know that? I don't care what you think, but my decision has nothing to do with my wings. But keep talking." A tear slipped down her cheek, and more tears thickened her voice. "Every word out of your mouth makes it easier for me to walk away."

He sneered in utter disgust at the display most likely meant to soften his heart. "You know what? You have my permission." He waved a hand at Amelia. "Go ahead and cast your spell, witch. I give my full consent. In fact, I'd be happy to have every thought of this sprite wiped from my memory."

Andi's expression went blank for a moment, then she was overcome with determination. She held out the vial to Amelia again. "Take it. Now. Cast the spell before he changes his mind."

Amelia took the vial. "As you wish."

She held it over the smoldering flames in the copper bowl. "With this sacrifice, complete this spell. Erase all memory. Turn back all thought. Wipe clean the heart's slate."

She dropped the vial into the bowl. Fire and sparks erupted.

Then everything went black.

CHAPTER TWENTY-NINE

Constantin had only opened the shop fifteen minutes ago, and yet his brother was already here. Constantin paused on his way to the history section to cast a skeptical gaze toward Valentino, who was sitting in one of the reading areas of the Gilded Page, poring over a book on jazz in the 1940s.

At least he'd had the forethought to bring coffee.

Valentino glanced up. "Why are you looking at me like that?"

Constantin's brow wrinkled, and he tucked the books in his hand under one arm. "For one thing, you're up remarkably early."

"I actually haven't been to bed yet."

"That makes more sense."

Valentino offered him a curious expression. "Was there a second thing?"

"Yes. Don't you already know everything there is to know about jazz? Why did you need that book immediately? What kind of jazz emergency could there be?"

Valentino frowned. "There's a singer I'm trying to

get for the club. Her influences are some of the lesser-known artists, and I wanted to brush up on my facts before I talk to her. I want to make a good impression."

Constantin shrugged. "One of these days, you're going to bring in someone who causes a problem, and Amelia's going to regret the special privileges you've been granted when it comes to the gate."

He braced himself for his brother's argument.

Valentino paused as if he was thinking. "I believe the gate would keep that person from entering in the first place, but I do worry about that myself."

The shock of his brother's admission almost knocked Constantin over. "You do?"

"Sure, every time I invite a new artist. It's why I only bring in the supernatural ones, but even then I run the risk of something happening." He sighed. "It's a tough spot. Isabelle's great and has a loyal audience, but if I don't bring in new blood once in a while to keep things interesting, people could lose interest in the club. But I run the risk of having to deal with them if they suddenly decide they want to tell the world about Shadowvale."

Constantin had had no idea his brother had actually thought it through. Or even gave such things consideration. "What would you do?"

"I don't really know." Valentino's mouth bent pensively. "I make them sign a nondisclosure, but people still talk."

"It's true, people will talk if they really want to, but breaking a signed contract would certainly give them a bad reputation. And the Thibodeaux name carries some weight in the supernatural world. I doubt anyone would be dumb enough to break a contract with you, knowing the possible repercussions."

Valentino snorted. "Maybe. I think Amelia's the one they're more afraid of. Which I'm fine with."

"Having a healthy fear of her is only smart."

"That, it is." With a little smirk, Valentino went back to reading.

Constantin slipped into the stacks to shelve a few books, but stood where he could still see Valentino and watched him a moment longer. For someone who claimed to need the information the book was offering, he certainly kept looking at the door a lot.

Whatever his brother was up to was his business. Constantin shelved the books in his hands, then left Fletcher to watch the floor and went back to his office.

On his way, he heard the front door chimes announce a customer, but Con didn't stop. Fletcher could get him if he was needed.

Fletcher's greeting rang out. "Good morning. Welcome to the Gilded Page."

"Thank you," a woman answered. "What a lovely store you have."

The voice zipped through him like an electric current. Constantin stilled, his hand on the doorknob and the door to his office halfway open. His gut tightened, his nerves sparked with anticipation (of what, he didn't know), and he was pinned to the spot. By a voice. How was that possible?

Maybe it was the light, melodious quality of the tone. Almost as if it held the brightness of sunshine. Or the way his spirit had responded in some sort of inexplicable Pavlovian way, as if it knew that voice meant good things. But how could that be? Had he met this woman before? No. He'd remember that, wouldn't he? Then what was it? Why had a few simple words caused him to feel alive again?

What a curious thing for a vampire to feel.

But even as he thought that, he realized he'd turned his head toward the shop floor to hear her better.

Odd to be so fascinated by something that ordinarily would have been ignored. He stood there, vacillating between going into his office and returning to the shop floor. But that indecision lasted only another second before he turned around and walked back toward the register.

He didn't go quite that far, choosing to stay at the end of the hallway. There, he leaned against the far wall to see who Fletcher was talking to. A petite honey-blonde with a smattering of freckles across her nose and smiley lilac eyes. She was human, by the scent of her blood, and therefore, not his type. Even so, she was captivating.

Strange that he should feel this way now when he hadn't felt remotely interested in a woman since his heart had been metaphorically flayed from his chest by his ex.

The female customer and Fletcher were engaged in an animated conversation when another customer, Reston Bellwether, came in.

Reston could talk as long as it took paint to dry.

Driven by a sudden urge to avoid being caught up in another endless conversation that wasn't with the golden-voiced woman, Constantin peeled off the wall and headed for Fletcher. "Take care of Mr. Bellwether, please."

Fletcher looked at him. "I, uh, sure." He went off to greet Mr. Bellwether.

As Constantin stood before the woman, a sudden rush went through him. He couldn't explain it. He only knew he wanted to feel it again. "Sorry to interrupt. I'm Constantin Thibodeaux, owner of the shop. I'd be happy to help you with whatever you need."

She smiled at him. "Hi, Con. I'm sorry, Constantin. Nice to meet you." She stuck out her hand. "I'm Andromeda. But you can call me Andi."

He shook her hand. The touch of her skin against his nearly buckled him, but something, perhaps years of vampire fortitude, kept him upright with the appearance of being unfazed. "Hi, Andi. You can call me Con. What can I help you with?"

As he released her hand, he was struck by a mix of déjà vu and sheer desire. What was going on with him? He couldn't fathom how a human could affect him this way.

Her gaze held him with a warmth that he felt down to his toes. "I'm in need of some reading material, but I'm also new in town, and I thought maybe you might have a map of Shadowvale here? Some kind of visitors guide or something?" She took a breath. Her heart was beating quicker than normal for a human. "I always feel like a bookstore is the soul of a town, you know?"

He nodded. "That's a lovely sentiment. I don't have any visitor guides, I'm afraid. Shadowvale doesn't really get visitors."

"So I've heard, but I'm not really a visitor. I've just moved here."

Behind her, Valentino cleared his throat. "Welcome to Shadowvale."

She turned. "Thank you."

Valentino stood and extended his hand. "I'm Valentino Thibodeaux. Con's brother. And Val to my friends. Nice to meet you."

"Nice to meet you, too." She shook his hand, sending a pang of jealousy through Constantin that he had no right to. What the devil was going on?

Valentino kept up the conversation. "What brings you to Shadowvale?" Then he laughed. "My apologies. No need to answer that. Everyone comes here for their own personal reasons and for the chance to live their life as peaceably as possible despite those reasons."

She seemed happy not to answer. "That's what I'm hoping for."

Valentino nodded. "I promise you, it's true. This town is filled with people fraught with their own burdens, but this place makes them easier to bear."

Constantin stepped in to change the subject.

"What kind of places were you hoping to find on a map? Maybe I can make some suggestions."

She looked at him again, those clear lilac eyes focused on him in the most delightful way. "Well, a good place to get coffee would be a start."

"There are two on Main Street. Black Horse Bakery, which is just a couple blocks south, and Deja Brew, which is a few more blocks north. Both are good, but I prefer Black Horse since they stock a special blend of chicory coffee for my family."

"Louisiana, right?" Andi asked.

"Yes." He nodded. "Have you been?"

"No, but I've heard enough from other locals to know that's added to the coffee there."

He smiled. "Speaking of reading, what kind of books are you looking for?"

"Anything happy or fun. Romance, whodunit where the bad guy gets it at the end, a twisty thriller, even an uplifting autobiography. Just nothing sad or depressing."

He nodded. "No romance, but I have a lot of other books I can recommend."

"That would be great." She glanced toward the street. "Maybe I'll just run up to the bakery and grab a cup of coffee. Would you mind if I brought it into the store?"

"No, not at all."

"Or…" Valentino lifted his empty cup off the table. "Con, you could walk up there with her and bring me back a refill. Then you could tell her a little more about the town on the way."

"Oh," Andi said. "That would be lovely."

A walk with her would be lovely, but he was working. "As nice as that sounds, I shouldn't leave the shop."

"Of course you should," Valentino argued. "Fletcher's here, and so am I. I won't let him burn anything down, promise."

"He's not the one I'm worried about." But Constantin was too intrigued with Andi to debate the issue further. He gestured toward the front door. "After you."

"Thank you." Once they were on the sidewalk, she kept the conversation going. "That's nice that you have your brother here in town."

"My whole family lives here, actually. Even a cousin."

She nodded. "That's so nice. My sister's here with me, but I don't think she's staying. I'd like her to. This seems like a great place for supernaturals to live."

"It is. It's probably the best place for—wait, are you implying that your sister is a supernatural?"

Andi nodded. "She's a sprite."

He hadn't been wrong about the scent of her blood. It was human. There was no two ways about it. "But you're human, aren't you?"

"I am. Now. But how did you know that?"

He tapped the side of his nose. "Vampire sense of smell." Then he almost stumbled. "Did I just out myself? Or did you already know I'm a vampire?" Sometimes he forgot vampires were still terrifying to some people. Especially humans.

She laughed. "You, your brother, and your assistant all had your fangs on display. It wasn't hard to figure out."

"In this town, there's no reason for us—or anyone—to hide their identities."

"I think that's really cool. Such a great way to live."

"It is." He paused, wondering if he should ask his next question or not. "How is it that you're human, but your sister is a sprite?"

Her smile wavered, but there was a determination in her eyes that he admired. "I gave up my wings for a greater cause."

"And giving up your wings made you human?"

She nodded, looking straight ahead now. "It did."

The quietness of her voice seemed to underline how big of a decision it had been.

"That's quite a sacrifice. I hope this greater cause was worth it."

She glanced at him, her smile returning. "I don't know yet. But I have hope."

He hoped for her sake it was. He pointed to the other side of the street. "We need to cross here."

The only two cars on the street stopped for them. They went across and into the bakery.

"Smells so good in here," Andi said.

"It does." Constantin leaned in a little bit. "But the really sweet part is that all the baked goods are free. The coffee is very reasonable, too."

"What?" Andi's eyes widened. "Are you serious? Free cake? Free cookies?"

He nodded as Nasha Black came over to help them. "I'll explain later."

Nasha greeted them. "Hi, Constantin. What can I get you today?"

"Morning, Nasha. Coffees, actually," Con answered. "We just haven't made it to that end of the counter yet."

"No problem." Nasha gestured to the end of the counter. "Em, coffee customers."

Constantin and Andi moved to where Emeranth was waiting. "Hi, Constantin. Your usual?"

"Two chicory coffees, please, and whatever kind my new friend would like."

"Make it three," Andi said.

Constantin glanced at her. "Are you sure? They have regular."

She shrugged. "I want to try it."

He liked that. "Okay."

Em got the coffees right up. They fixed them how they liked them and started the walk back.

"So..." Andi started. "When you said you'd tell me why everything was free later, is that later now or later as in...later?" She laughed. "How's that for a clear sentence?"

He smiled, still utterly taken with her. "How about I explain over dinner tonight?"

"Really?" The light in her eyes was something to behold. She sipped her coffee, then nodded to indicate she liked it.

"Really. There's a great little café down on Fiddler Street. The Table. We could go down there, and I could show you around town a little. We could even see the club my brother owns. If you want."

She nodded. "I would love that." Her grin practically ran from ear to ear. "It's a date."

CHAPTER THIRTY

"I can't believe it's really happening. It's fast, yes, but that doesn't surprise me since it happened fast the first time." Andi gave her outfit a good once-over in the full-length mirror on the closet door.

She and Cassi had gotten a room at the Amethyst Inn, a beautiful Victorian bed-and-breakfast near the park. It was, appropriately, painted in various shades of purple.

Rooms were good size, nicely decorated (not all in purple), and the price was right, although Cassi was paying. She'd insisted as a way of making up for cursing Andi into that horrible book.

There were only two other guests at the inn, along with three permanent residents. But two of the three permanent residents were ghosts—sisters who could turn into owls who weren't ghosts, which was…interesting. But Andi wasn't sure if they, being ghosts, could really be considered permanent or not. Sometimes the supernatural got a little confusing.

Cassi lounged on the bed, looking at the local paper. "I can't believe it either. I'm glad it is happening, don't get me wrong. Giving up your wings for this guy was a major deal, and if it wasn't working, I'd be heartbroken for you. But don't get too eager, or he could think you're squirrely."

"Right. And good point. Heaven knows I've deliberately ditched guys with the overeager act." Andi smoothed the skirt of the borrowed simple black dress she was wearing for her date with Con. Thankfully, Cassi had had the foresight to pack a broader selection of clothes.

Andi, on the other hand, still had very little to her name, although she'd been able to retrieve her purse from her sister's. One of the first things she'd done there was to get her phone turned back on, but that was it. She'd worry about replacing things once she found a job here in Shadowvale. She didn't want to dig into the money her gran had left her unless she really needed to.

She turned around and held her hands out. "How do I look?"

"Nice. Pretty. Not like you're trying too hard. Like you're trying the right amount."

"Good." Andi blew out a breath that lifted the hair around her face. "I can't believe how nervous I am." She closed and opened her hands. "My palms are actually sweating."

"I think that's a good sign."

"Yeah, maybe." Andi started to wipe her hands on the dress, then stopped, remembering it was borrowed from her sister.

She went into the adjoining bathroom to use a

towel instead and give her makeup and hair one more inspection. She was also wearing a pair of her sister's earrings. "What are you going to do while I'm out?"

"I'm going to Club 42."

Andi leaned back to look out the door. "You are not."

"I am. And..." Cassi got up, went to her suitcase, dug in, and pulled out a pair of black leather leggings. "I'm really glad I brought these."

Andi's eyes almost bugged out of her head. "Firstly, I didn't know you even owned anything like that. Secondly, are you trolling for a certain vampire?"

"I'm not trolling." Cassi blushed. "I can't help it. I think he's hot. And this is my chance to make a brand-new impression."

Amused, Andi went back to the mirror. "I think you made a pretty good impression the first time."

"Well, I want to make a better one. A sexier one."

"Don't go overboard. He liked you the first time just as you were." Andi took a breath. There was only so much fixing a person could do before they started looking like they'd gone face first into a bad Snapchat filter. "Okay, I'm as ready as I'm going to be."

"He's picking you up? In his car?" Cassi planted her hands on her hips. "I know you know him, but he doesn't know that. Aren't you afraid he'll think you're...I don't know, reckless?"

"Settle down, *Gran*. I'm meeting him at the

restaurant. It's on Fiddler Street. Only a couple blocks from Val's club, I think."

"Okay. That's good." Cassi smiled. "Have fun."

"I'm going to try."

Cassi fluttered her wings. "If I'm not home when you get back, you know where I am."

"Well, behave yourself. I'd say don't do anything I wouldn't do, but that wouldn't leave much. Don't do anything you normally wouldn't do. How's that?"

She dipped her chin, smirking. "We'll see."

Andi rolled her eyes as she slipped the strap of her small bag over her shoulder and headed out.

The walk was nice. The air was cool and scented with night-blooming flowers and the greenery that seemed to be everywhere in this town. A few fireflies blinked off and on in the distance.

Fiddler Street was busy, mostly filled with smartly dressed couples. She smiled. No matter what happened, she could make a good life for herself here. A happy life. Maybe not at first, if things with Con didn't go as she hoped, but eventually. This town was safe. Not something she'd ever thought she'd want, but she was ready for that now. Ready for roots and responsibility.

But mostly ready for the incredible man waiting for her.

Con was standing outside the restaurant as she approached. He was holding a single red rose. He presented it to her as she joined him. "For you. You look lovely."

"Thank you. You look very nice, too." He was

devastatingly handsome in a simple gray suit and white shirt with the top button undone.

"Thank you. Are you hungry?"

She nodded, but it was kind of a lie. The butterflies in her stomach left no room for an appetite. But she'd manage something.

He held the door for her, and they went in. The Table was as cool and chic as Fiddler Street was funky and artsy. Lots of Edison bulbs, copper piping, dark wood, and polished concrete. White linen draped the tables, and black-and-white photos lined the walls.

He gave his name to the hostess, and they were led back to a table in a secluded spot that offered a nice view of the rest of the restaurant. He held her chair for her, then took his own seat. The hostess handed them menus before leaving them alone.

A glass bowl in the center of the table held what looked like the same glowing moss Andi had seen in the enchanted forest, but she realized that wasn't something she should know about.

Still, she wasn't entirely sure that was what it was. She figured she'd let Con tell her. "How do they do that?"

Con looked away from his menu. "Do what?"

She nodded at the bowl. "Get that moss to glow? It's a very cool trick."

"It's no trick. It's sprite moss."

"For real? That's what it's called? And it glows? I can't wait to tell my sister there's a fungus named after her."

He laughed. "It's naturally phosphorescent. And it really is a moss, not a fungus. But I understand having a moss named after your kind isn't quite the same effect. The only place it grows is in the enchanted forest here in Shadowvale. The glow lasts about a week if kept in water, I understand."

"The enchanted forest? I think I saw a sign for that."

His smile thinned. "Dangerous place. Or it can be. Don't ever go alone."

"Thanks for the warning. I'll remember that." She looked at her menu. She had no intention of going back there. "What do you recommend?"

"All of it, really. But the asparagus and crab risotto is especially nice. And the butternut squash ravioli with sage is supposed to be very good. That's what my sisters tell me. I'm more of a meat-eater myself."

"I can imagine."

He snorted. "Yes, I suppose that's obvious." He put his menu down. "Thank you for coming out with me this evening."

She smiled. "I don't think I've ever been thanked for agreeing to a date before."

His smile was sly and pleased. "Then you've obviously been dating the wrong men."

She let out a breathy little sigh. "Isn't that the truth."

The server came, and she ordered the risotto while he ordered a medium-rare ribeye. She stuck to water when the server asked what she was drinking, but Con requested a bottle of fancy sparkling water for the table.

She was glad he wasn't drinking brandy like he had been the last night at the club. She hoped to never see him like that again, actually.

The server took the menus and left. Con leaned in. "What are you going to do for work in Shadowvale? Or are you one of the many independently wealthy?"

"Hah, I wish." She fixed her napkin on her lap. "I have a little money, thanks to a small trust fund, but I'll get a job somewhere. I don't care what it is, really. I'd be happy bagging groceries. I just want to pay my bills and live my life."

He nodded. "I admire that. I could ask around for you, see who's hiring. I'm not quite as connected as my brother, but I know a few people."

"Thanks, that would be great. But I should warn you. I don't have a lot of skills." She sighed. "I've spent most of my life living off the kindness of strangers. Coming to Shadowvale is part of me turning over a new leaf, as it were."

He shrugged. "You told me you gave up your wings for a good cause. That doesn't sound to me like someone who needs to turn over a new leaf."

"The leaf was already turning when that happened."

"I see. Well, regardless of your skill level, I'm sure there's something you can do."

The server returned with the sparkling water, poured them each a glass, then disappeared again.

A few more minutes of small talk, and the server

came back again, this time with their food.

It was delicious, and Andi managed to find her appetite. It helped that things were going so well.

Con swallowed a bite of steak. "There's a great theater in town. First-run movies, but they mix in some classics, too. Would you like to see what's playing tomorrow night? I'm sure we could find something."

"That would be great." It was all going to be great. She'd never taken such a risk in her life, but it was paying off. She was glad, too, that Con had been present during the spell and had agreed to it.

Otherwise, she would feel bad about all this. Like she was pulling one over on him. But this was better. This was mutual.

As the server came to clear their plates, he dropped off a dessert menu. Andi was drawn to every single item on it, but the deconstructed chocolate-covered cherry called to her.

She raised her brows as she looked at Con. "Are you getting dessert?"

"I don't have much of a sweet tooth, but if you don't get something, I'll be disappointed."

"You really are the perfect man."

He laughed, and when the server returned, Andi ordered the deconstructed chocolate-covered cherry with a scoop of vanilla ice cream and two spoons so they could share.

They were left alone again then.

Andi took the opportunity to ask a question. "What's the best part about living here for you?"

He smiled. "That's easy. Two things. Being safe from the sun and being in the same town with my family."

She nodded. "I hope my sister stays. It would be great to have her here."

"Do you think she will?"

Andi looked down at her lap for a moment, laughing softly.

"What is it?" Con asked.

"It's your brother." She glanced at him again. "My sister has a little crush, you might say."

Con groaned. "On Valentino? The poor woman. He's a playboy, I'm sorry to say. Most people know that, seeing as how word gets out in this community, but that doesn't stop a lot of women from going back for seconds or thirds."

"Yikes."

"Yes, exactly. I mean, if your sister is just looking for a little fun, she's headed in the right direction. If she expects more than that, she's going to have her heart broken."

"Well," Andi started, "I think she might be looking for fun at the moment. But then again, I'm not sure. Cassi's suddenly found her wild side, so who knows?"

They both went silent for a moment.

Then Con spoke. "Have you ever had your heartbroken?"

Yes, she wanted to tell him. *By you*. Instead, she smiled wistfully. "I have. But I don't blame him. There were circumstances beyond our control. And we're already moving on with our lives, so it's all good. What about you?"

He sipped his water, the distance in his gaze a telling sign that he wasn't focused on the present but the past. "Yes, I have had my heart broken. Very badly, actually."

His focus shifted to a random spot on the table. "She put me off women and love for a very long time. In fact, you're the first woman I've been interested in since her."

"I'm flattered," Andi said. "Can I ask why she hurt you so much? Did you love her that much?"

"I did. I thought we'd be married. But at the last moment, she changed her mind." His jaw tightened. "I don't like talking about her."

"Sorry." Andi sat back, crossing her hands in front of her like she was cutting the conversation off. "No more Miranda."

"No, no more of—" Con's eyes narrowed. "How do you know her name?"

Oh boy. Big mistake. "You must have mentioned it."

"I'm sure I didn't."

"Maybe someone else—"

"No one else did either." The telltale glow of emotion shone in his gaze. "Her name is never to be mentioned in my presence."

"I'm sorry, I won't—"

"And how would your sister have a crush on my brother when you've only just come to town?"

"She, uh…" A pit opened up in Andi's stomach. She'd slipped up, and she knew it.

"Andromeda." The glow in his eyes brightened. "The book. You were…in a book. That I opened." A growl rumbled out of his throat. "You left me."

"Oh boy." She grimaced. So much for things going well. If only she could sprinkle a little sprite dust on him.

Then everything went black. Again.

CHAPTER THIRTY-ONE

When the inky darkness cleared, Andi was looking up at a very fancy ceiling, the tops of bookshelves, and what appeared to be a rather perturbed witch.

Namely, Amelia Marchand.

Her arms were crossed. "I told you there was a high probability it wouldn't work."

Andi pushed up to her elbows. Her head was swimming, and the edge of her vision was a little blurry. She blinked, trying to clear it. "What's going on—how am I still in your library?"

"You all are." Amelia walked away. "Because I arranged it that way."

That wasn't really an answer, but Andi looked around in hopes of learning more. Cassi was sprawled on a couch nearby and just coming to. Val was leaning against some shelves, shaking his head slowly.

And Con was still comatose a few feet away. Scratch that. He groaned and reached a hand up to rub his face.

Andi blinked a few more times. "What happened?"

Amelia was picking up items from the coffee table where she'd performed the spell. "I cast a different spell than what you asked. A spell that would show you the most likely outcome of the one you wanted. And it went exactly how I thought it would. Badly."

"So...that was just...what? A dream?"

Amelia snorted. "Something like that. Although 'nightmare' might be more apt."

Andi sat all the way up, then got to her feet, wobbling slightly. She felt a little hungover. An effect of the spell, no doubt. "Why would you do that?"

"To spare you, sprite."

Anger wormed through Andi's spine. "I didn't ask to be spared. I asked for a second chance to make Con fall in love with me."

His grunt broke the silence behind her. She turned to see him sitting up.

He scowled. "I told you it wouldn't work, and it didn't, did it?"

"Because it wasn't the spell I asked for," Andi countered.

Amelia clucked her tongue. "No, but it was an excellent simulation spell. You should be thanking me. Now you know the outcome without having to give up your wings."

Andi spun around, which did her head no favors. The air was thick in her lungs, and she was on the verge of having a full-on meltdown complete with an ugly cry. "I don't care about my wings. It's not what I asked for."

Amelia glanced at her, but said nothing. Cassi was coming around now, sitting up and rubbing her temples.

"I'm leaving." Con spat the words like he was as frustrated as Andi felt.

She twisted to face him. "Wait."

He stopped. "Why?"

"Because I want to talk to you. I want to work things out."

His cool expression remained unchanged. "There is nothing to talk about and nothing to work out. I am not interested in you or any other woman. I'm not interested in love, or trying to make things work, or being a new me. I am done. With you. With love. With the whole idea of a romantic partner. I have learned my lesson. Enough is enough."

He twisted around and left.

Val called after him, "Where are you going?"

"Home. Don't follow me. I won't invite you in." He disappeared through the library door, and a few moments later, the slam of another door followed.

Beckett appeared then. "Anything I can do to help, Amelia?"

"Not at the moment, thank you."

He nodded and left them alone.

Andi clenched her fists and tried not to cry out of sheer frustration.

Val came to her side. "I'm sorry, Andi. But I think Amelia did you a favor. My brother is too hurt to see what a fool he's being. At least this way you still have your wings."

"I would rather have him. At least the old him. Not the one who currently despises me."

Amelia joined them, the vial containing Andi's wings in her outstretched palm. "I know you're upset with me, but in time, I think you'll see things differently."

Andi took the vial, twisted off the top, and muttered, "Wings return."

She tried to breathe away her anger and disappointment as her wings reattached to her body. She didn't want to snap at Amelia. Andi understood the woman had been trying to help, but Andi couldn't feel anything at the moment but the distress of utter failure.

Cassi stood and walked over to the three of them. "Can someone explain what just happened? Andi, why do you have your wings back?

Andi shook her head. "The spell wasn't performed. Not the one I wanted anyway."

Val frowned. "Why don't we get out of Amelia's way? We can go to my club, if you don't want to go back to the B&B."

Andi nodded, too numb to come up with a better plan. "Fine."

Val put his arm around her and directed her toward the door. "Thank you, Amelia."

"You're welcome."

Val drove their rental car since Con had taken his, but Andi wouldn't have noticed if they'd gone by horse and buggy. She slumped in the back seat, mired in a swamp of regret and pain.

How did you get over loving someone who was never going to love you back? Had all the men she'd broken up with felt like this? Because this was awful. And if they had, then on some level, she deserved this.

But that didn't make suffering through the pain any easier.

She closed her eyes, only to see Con's angry face. She sniffed. Her entire body hurt with the pain of losing him.

And in that moment, she understood why he was done with love. She might be done with it herself.

Maybe she'd spend the rest of her life as a spinster. That sounded pretty good. She'd get a cat and—no wonder Con had a cat. Sure, he'd found Chloe in the back alley, but he'd kept her instead of turning her over to a rescue for adoption. Andi got it. She really did. Animals offered unconditional love. He wasn't going to come home one day and find Chloe packed up and waiting at the door with a Dear John letter for him.

Maybe she'd get a whole houseful of cats and just commit to being a crazy cat lady. That should keep the men away from her.

"Andi, we're here."

"Hmm?" Andi's feline thoughts faded away, allowing her to see that her sister had opened the rear car door and was now standing there, staring at her.

"We're at the club. Let's go in and get something

to drink. What do you say? Val explained everything to me on the way over, so we don't have to talk about anything unless you want to."

She didn't want to. "Fine."

Val smiled gamely. "I'll even order a pizza or something, if you want."

Andi shrugged. "I'm not hungry."

Cassi frowned. "We were out for a couple hours. And it's well after dinnertime. You should eat something."

"Not hungry," Andi repeated. She knew her sister meant well, but not eating wasn't going to hurt anything.

They went inside, and Val settled them into a secluded booth. A piano player was onstage, and his tunes were easy and light, but not overly happy. Andi could deal with that. She also liked that the crowd wasn't too thick yet. But then, it must be early for a club like this.

Whatever. She slumped down in the booth.

Val stayed standing. "What would you like to drink?"

"Champagne?" Cassi asked.

"No problem. How about you, Andi?"

"Water."

"Really? That's all?"

She glared at him. "I'm not interested in getting smashed, if that's what you're asking. That'd only make me feel worse."

He nodded. "I can't disagree with that. How about something to eat?"

"No."

Cassi put her hand on Val's. "Do you have anything sweet? Sugar always helps."

"I can swing that. Be right back."

Andi gave her sister a look. "I know you're trying to make me feel better, but stop. I'm allowed to feel awful. I have every right. And you ought to be happy about it, seeing as how this is all part of the lesson you were trying to teach me."

"I didn't want you to be this wretched. You're hurting in a way that I never anticipated. I love you. I don't want you going through all this. You learned your lesson a while back. This is just extra misery I never saw coming. I'm your sister. I can't help but want to soothe that all away."

Andi sighed. "Well, stop it anyway. Just let me wallow, will you? I'll get through this in my own time."

"I know." Cassi smiled sympathetically. "I'm really sorry things didn't work out. At least now you can go back to Paris with me."

Andi groaned. "About that…"

Val suddenly appeared tableside without drinks or dessert. "I have to go. Con needs me."

"Great." Andi rolled her eyes. "Take his side." She waved a hand at him. "I get it, he's your brother and —"

"No," Val said. "Con just texted the whole family to say he found a screen pushed out of the window he leaves open for Chloe. He's searched the house, and she's nowhere to be found."

Cassi shook her head. "I don't get it."

"Chloe is his cat," Andi answered. "She's a bit of an escape artist, too."

Val nodded. "And we don't live in the safest part of town."

Cassi's eyes rounded. "You live in the enchanted forest?"

"No," Val said. "We live in one of the bayous. And there are gators. And snakes. And birds of prey." He grimaced. "Let's just say it's not the safest place for anyone, let alone a cat, to go walking at night."

CHAPTER THIRTY-TWO

Constantin's gut roiled with worry to the point he thought he was going to be sick. If anything happened to Chloe, he might just drive past the twilight line and sit there until the sun came up. After everything else that these last few days had dumped on him, losing her would be more than he could take.

His heart might not beat any longer, but this would kill him.

"Chloe," he yelled again. He stood a few yards from his rear property line, his voice carrying over the bayou's water. Water amplified sound. That was good and bad. It meant he could be heard for much greater distances, but it also meant that it was much harder to pinpoint where any sounds he picked up on were coming from.

So far, however, he'd yet to hear anything that sounded like his baby Chloe.

"Please don't be hurt," he muttered. "Or worse."

His phone buzzed. He tugged it free from his pocket and looked at the screen. A text from his brother.

Help is on the way.

Good, he texted back. Then he shoved the phone into his pocket and went back to searching.

He hadn't bothered with a flashlight because of his keen eyesight, but that seemed like a dumb idea now. He tried the one on his phone, but it barely lit the ground in front of him. He should have grabbed a real one. After all, he'd taken the time to put his boots on.

But reaching for a flashlight just wasn't something he usually did. Berating himself, he ran back to the house before he got any farther away.

There was one under the sink. He went straight to the kitchen without a care for the swamp muck he was tracking in. Nothing mattered now but finding his sweet girl before it was too late.

He grabbed the flashlight and went back out. Using it, he searched the grounds around his house for any signs of paw prints, any suggestion of what direction she might have gone.

A car crunched down his driveway, followed by the sounds of people getting out.

"Con, we're here." Juliette's voice came from well behind him. "Dani's with me. Where do you want us to search?"

"Front of the house," he answered. "Across the street. In case she went that way. Mama and Father are searching along the road." There was no telling with a cat. Chloe could be anywhere. She could have chased an insect or a lizard in any direction.

"Okay, we're on it," Juliette replied.

Moments later, he could hear them calling for Chloe, their singsong voices cajoling her to come home.

He kept moving forward, retracing the steps he'd already taken, but this time searching the ground more closely for any signs that Chloe had traveled this way.

Another minute or two went by, and a second car arrived at his house. Had to be Valentino.

Con tucked the flashlight under his arm and sent his brother a quick text to fill him in. *J and D are searching across the street. Parents on road. I'm in back of house.*

Valentino's reply came promptly. *We'll fan out.*

Fine. Constantin didn't know who *we* included. Help from the club, maybe. He didn't care, so long as they were willing to look, they were welcome.

He went back to his search, slowly sweeping the light across the swamp in front of him. He caught the last two feet of a water moccasin slithering past. He closed his eyes for a moment. Chloe would think a snake like that was a toy, something to be chased.

That could go very badly.

He didn't want to think like that, but the bayou wasn't a kind environment unless you were at the top of the food chain.

Chloe was a ball of white fluff who might think she was queen, but she'd be dethroned very quickly out here.

"Chloe," he called out again. Then he listened, straining his ears to hear every possible sound.

The croak of a bullfrog. The squelch of something moving through the muck. And the distant rhythm of wings beating the air.

That sound set off an alarm inside him. He couldn't tell if it was a hawk or a bat. Or something else. Hard to tell what might fly out of the darkness in Shadowvale. He glanced up as the beating wings came closer, prepared to fight the thing off if it was after Chloe.

He crossed the flashlight beam over the night sky, but the thicket of trees surrounding him made it difficult to get a clear view in any direction.

Then his light caught something iridescent. He swooped back in that direction.

"Do you mind?" Andi hovered a good ten feet above him. She put her hand up to block the light. "You're killing my night vision."

He switched off the light. "What are you doing?"

"The same thing you are." She put her hands on her hips. A halo of moonlight surrounded her, making her look angelic. Or at least as close to an angel as he'd ever see. "Or don't you want my help?"

"No," he said quietly. "I want it." He was wholly surprised but truly grateful she was there. He didn't deserve her help after the unkind things he'd said to her at Amelia's, but it was absolutely welcome.

"Which way do you think she went?"

"No idea. We're spread in every direction from the house."

Andi nodded. "Okay, I'll circle around again."

"Thank you."

She flew off without another word, leaving him earthbound and humbled. She was mad. That much was plain. And yet she'd come to help him in a desperate hour. She was beautiful inside and out, and he'd turned his back on her attempts to reconcile.

His past had made him a terrible person. But that was an excuse. He knew that. He was as afraid of being hurt again as he was of losing Chloe.

And now here he was, facing down both of those fears.

What a mess his life was.

A tinny, distant, panicky sound turned his head. Then it came a second time. Far away and low to the ground, as best he could tell. His nerves went haywire, tripping at the sudden possibilities. He took one step toward the sound. "Chloe?"

A softer mewling cry answered him.

"*Chloe.* I'm coming." With nothing but the signature of that sound to guide him, he darted forward, marsh and sludge sucking at his boots.

The bayou slowed him. He was still faster than any human could be, but traversing such a piece of ground would slow anyone. Trees and vines were thick in some spots. In others, there was underbrush to contend with. Or swampland that dragged you down. Or a brackish stream that was deeper than it looked. In some places, like the area that lay ahead, the stream became a river.

Another sound reached him from the distance.

The rolling, guttural boom of an alligator looking for a mate.

He wasn't afraid of gators. They might come after him, but he would win. Even against Brutus. Chloe's odds were very different.

He pushed himself to go faster.

A heron screeched as it flew overhead, causing him to lose his tracking. The bird's squawk had almost sounded human. He went still, ankle-deep in muck, gnats swarming. "Chloe? Where are you, baby?"

Another mewl answered him. Not quite as distant now.

Then a voice thin with fear and pain followed. Andi's voice. "Con, I've got her. But you'd better get here fast."

CHAPTER THIRTY-THREE

Andi had been in a lot of tough spots in her life—although ninety-nine percent of them had involved a man. Or his upset girlfriend.

She was really glad that those days were behind her and that this tough spot was a little different. Well, maybe it wasn't that different. It did have something to do with a man. But this time there was also a cat.

And maybe *glad* wasn't the right word either, seeing as how the current fix she was in had a lot to do with one very, *very* large alligator.

That gator was eyeing her and the cat from the water right in front of them. In fact, Andi's toes were a little damp, thanks to her perilous spot on the bank of said water.

"This was not the best place to get a drink, kitty."

Chloe seemed to have gone quiet, but Andi's heart was thumping almost too loud for her to hear anything else.

Thankfully, Chloe seemed to sense that now was not the time to escape again and was staying very still against Andi's chest, where she was being held in a death grip. "Please don't go spastic," Andi whispered.

Because if Chloe clawed her and Andi lost hold of her...

Andi tightened her grip ever so slightly on the cat. "It's okay, baby. Don't panic. We're going to get out of here just fine. You'll see. Your daddy's a big bad vampire, and he's coming for us. Well, he's coming for you."

Andi was pretty sure Con didn't give two licks what happened to her.

Whatever love he'd once felt for her was certainly gone after Amelia's little trick. But at least Andi still had her wings.

Although, without them, she might not be in this mess. Of course, she might be without them again very soon, depending on how this all turned out.

She didn't want to take her eyes off the gator that was inching ever closer, but she had to see how badly her wings were tangled.

She risked a glance up at the thorny vines she'd gotten snared in. "Did I mention you picked a terrible place to get a drink, Queen Chloe?"

Andi hadn't even noticed the thorns when she'd swooped down and wiggled through the underbrush to grab the cat. She'd been too focused on the muddy, but still mostly white, ball of fluff drinking from the stream.

She'd grabbed Chloe, then stood, only to push herself farther into the prickly mess. That's when the pain at her back alerted her to what she'd done.

Trying to free her wings had resulted only in deeper tears in the membranes and more pain. She wasn't sure she could fly with them as tattered as they were, and at this point, ripping herself free would result in the kind of wounded-animal sounds and movements that gators probably loved.

She was up the bayou without a paddle, so to speak.

Her attention shifted back to the gator. Its head looked like a suitcase floating in the water. Except for the beady eyes that shone red in the moonlight. Some seven or eight or three hundred feet back, the dinosaurian ridge of the beast's tail cleared the water.

She shivered. The thing was terrifying.

Death by gator was not how she'd thought she was going to die. She supposed she'd at least make the paper.

Where was Con?

The gator floated a centimeter closer.

Andi was getting angry-scared now. That place where there wasn't much left to lose, so getting crazy didn't seem like a bad idea.

"Get away, you dumb lizard. You are not eating either one of us tonight, you understand me?"

The gator opened its mouth and hissed.

Andi jerked back, meshing herself farther into the brambles and causing Chloe to meow even as a gasp of pain left her own mouth. "Sorry, baby. I didn't know gators could hiss. I thought only your kind did that."

She swallowed, but the knot in her throat went nowhere. A twig snapped nearby. Was there another predator out there? What else lived in this wretched place? "Con, please, if you're on your way, hurry. We might not last much longer."

Like a dream, he appeared out of the mist on the far bank. "I'm here and—" A soft curse slipped from his lips. "Are you stuck?"

"Yeah, pretty bad. I could probably get free, but I'm afraid I won't be fast enough to avoid the gator."

"Gator?" Con's gaze shifted to the water, then he exhaled a curse. "Brutus."

If the gator heard, he didn't care. Nothing took his focus off Andi.

Con jumped off the bank and into the water with a soft splash.

Brutus swished his tail, but stayed put. He was at least ten feet away from Con. Maybe more. And still inching closer to her and Chloe.

"Andi, you have to get ready to fly out of here."

"I don't think I can. My wings are really caught in these brambles. They may not support me if they're too torn up."

He glanced at her, then the brambles and frowned. "But you can at least get free?"

"I'm pretty sure I can." Although it would no doubt cause serious injury to her wings. Not flying wasn't the end of the world, though. She could walk out.

"Good. New plan."

Before she could ask what that plan was, he lunged forward and landed on Brutus's back.

The gator hissed and thrashed, rolling and flexing for all he was worth. Con stayed latched on to him, though.

They pulled away from the bank, moving to the middle of the river. Con and the gator slid under. The water churned in the spot where they'd gone down.

Andi hugged Chloe close. "He's going to be okay, right? It's not like he needs to breathe." But a hard knot was forming in Andi's belly, and her eyes burned with tears. "I should have told him one more time that I love him."

Chloe mewed softly.

"Right. We need to get free while we can."

With Chloe in her arms, Andi started the arduous task of liberating herself from the brambles. Each painful little movement created a new tear in her wings, or deepened an existing one. Seconds ticked by, and she made very little progress. The pain of each slice nearly caused her to blackout, but she held on. For her sake and Chloe's.

There was still no sign of Con either, and the water had nearly stopped moving.

She didn't want to think about what that meant, but she had to save herself and Chloe. "This isn't going to be fun," she muttered.

"Andi, that you?" Cassi's voice rang out.

Andi looked up. "Yes. And I need help."

Cassi hovered overhead. "Coming down."

"Be careful. Everything here is out to get you."

As Cassi descended, Val crashed through the brush on the same side of the river where Con had first come out. "Where's Con?"

"In the water with the gator," Andi answered. "They've been under for at least three or four minutes. Maybe longer. There's no sign of movement anymore."

Eyes aglow, Val ripped off his leather jacket and dived in.

Cassi landed on the bank. "You want me to take the cat?"

"No, I've got her, and I'm afraid we could lose her in the transfer if she gets spooked. But if you could free my wings, then I can get out of here."

Cassi hesitated. "Why don't you store them in your vial?"

"You think they're healthy enough to survive that? Storing damaged wings can kill them."

Cassi glanced at Andi's wings again. "It's too dark to see much, but you might be right. They look pretty torn up."

Andi nodded. "Just get me loose as best you can."

"On it." Cassi stepped up and started gingerly removing the vines and brambles imprisoning Andi.

Daniella and Juliette were next to come through the brush on the other bank. "Where are Con and Val?"

"In the water," Andi answered. "With a very large—"

Just then, Con and Val emerged. But there was no sign of Brutus.

"Where's the gator?" Andi asked.

Con shook his head, looking paler than usual. "Not a problem anymore."

"Gator?" Juliette grimaced. "Wasn't Brutus, was it?"

"I think it was." Val swam for the bank, dragging Con behind him.

That's when Andi realized Con wasn't okay. His shirt was torn and bloody. "You're hurt."

"I'll live," he responded.

Val dragged him onto shore. "Brutus bit through his shoulder. Severed some tendons or something. Anyway, he can't move his arm."

Con shrugged his good shoulder. "I'll heal."

"Yowch." Andi glanced at her sister as pain burned through her back. "You sliced me there, I think."

"Sorry. That was a tough one. I didn't mean to."

"I know. It's okay. Just wasn't expecting that." The pain in her back seemed to be spreading up to her shoulder. Weird. "Keep going. I have to get out of here."

Clouds slipped across the face of the moon, casting them all into new darkness.

Cassi sighed. "I can barely see what I'm doing." She called across the bank, "Could you shine that light over here?"

Juliette held up her flashlight. "I can do better than that." She leaped across the river, landing safely on the bank. "Where do you want the beam?"

"Right here on her wings where the—"

"Cass," Andi whispered. Her knees felt oddly weak, and her vision was getting dim. "I don't feel so hot all of a sudden. Actually, that's not true. I feel really hot. Super hot. Someone should probably take Chloe."

Juliette repositioned the flashlight, and Cassi sucked in a breath. "Oh no. Oh, Andi. This vine. It's fever nettle."

"That would explain…" Andi slumped down as she passed out.

Con propped himself up on his good arm as chaos took over again. Juliette grabbed Chloe as Andi collapsed. A new surge of panic swept over him. "What's going on? What's wrong with Andi?"

Daniella leaped across the river to help as Cassi answered him. "Fever nettle is poisonous to fairy folk, and that includes us sprites. One of the thorns scratched her while I was trying to get her wings free."

"Poisonous?" He got to his feet, pain raking his body where Brutus's teeth had sunk in. "Dani, Jules, get Andi out of there. We have to get her to the hospital. Cassi, back away before you get nicked, too."

Juliette jumped back across the river with Chloe in her arms. "Val, go help. I've got Chloe. I can take her and Con home."

Con stood his ground. "I'm not going anywhere without Andi."

Val joined Dani on the opposite bank. "Do you have her?"

"I do." Dani lifted the limp sprite in her arms. "She feels like a furnace."

"It's the nettles," Cassi said. "They cause a terrible fever, hence the name."

He turned to Cassi. "Are you sure you haven't been affected?"

"So far, I feel fine."

"Then let's go. Back to Con's house where all the vehicles are."

With a nod, Cassi extended her wings to take off. She got a few feet off the ground, then landed again. "Scratch the feeling-fine part." She put a hand to her head. "I don't think I got scratched, but I might have inhaled some of the nettles' pollen. I'm starting to get warm and faint."

Val lifted her. "I've got you."

She wrapped her arms around his neck. "Thank you."

"Hold on." Then he jumped the river and joined Con and his sisters. "Let's move."

As a family, they trekked with as much haste as possible through the bayou to familiar ground. Val carried Cassi, Dani had Andi, and Juliette held the slightly squirmy Chloe.

Con scratched the muddy creature with his able hand. "I'm glad you're safe, baby. We owe Andi a big thanks for this." He glanced at the sprite. "She'd better be okay."

"Dr. Jekyll will know what to do," Dani said.

Con gave her a look. "He won't be in his right mind at this hour, and we can't wait until morning." The doctor was a descendant of the first man to bear the monstrous curse of his family. As a result, he transformed into the demented beast known as Edgar Hyde when the moon rose. He became Jekyll again only when dawn returned.

Juliette ducked to avoid a branch. "Someone at the hospital will be able to help. This is Shadowvale. Nothing is impossible here."

"I hope that's true." Daniella looked at the woman in her arms. "Because not only is she burning up, but her wings are destroyed. When she passed out, they ripped free." She shook her head. "Most of them got left behind in the tree."

Con nodded, more to assure himself than to agree. Andi had to be all right. Because he couldn't lose her.

Not when he'd suddenly realized what a fool he'd been to turn his back on his one true love.

CHAPTER THIRTY-FOUR

Andi was deep in a dream. Or a nightmare. Or a hallucination. She didn't know, couldn't figure it out, and at times, lost herself to the sweltering madness that seemed like it had become her new reality.

Con was there. Sometimes. He shifted from a kind, loving man who was always just out of reach, to a raving, pursuing monster with bright eyes and sharp fangs almost on the verge of catching her. Her sister slipped in and out, too, as did the faces of her gran, Con's family, and Con's cat, Chloe.

The gator was there, too. Brutus the beast. Waiting, jaws open, teeth gleaming. Hissing at her. Spitting out vines with thorns the size of daggers.

The air was thick and damp. Constantly. Even the breeze blew hot.

A barrage of sounds accompanied it all. Water running, branches rustling and cracking, Chloe's distant meow, the gator's hissing. A soft unexplainable beep. But always, the fluttering of wings.

Sometimes she also thought she heard voices

talking to her. Or talking about her. But definitely saying her name.

When she tried to shut out the dream and listen, they went away, and the dream pulled her deeper.

She fought as hard as she could. So hard that she had nothing left. She was exhausted, but there was no way to rest in this delirious world. She couldn't give in, she knew that. There was fighting. Or there was dying.

And yet giving in felt like all she had left.

At last, the haze of pain and heat began to lift. Her grasp on reality grew stronger. She found the strength to fight again. To swim against the murky river trying to drown her.

The sound of beating wings faded, and new noises took their place. The beeping grew louder.

Andi woke to the subtle hum and purr of machines. Then the throbbing in her head started, making those weaker sounds disappear. She moaned softly, glad she'd kept her eyes closed.

"Andromeda?"

That voice. She'd heard it in her dreams. And her nightmares. She shuddered, but the wash of emotion held hope, too. Was she still delirious? Or had she broken free of the madness? "Con?"

"Right here." A hand enveloped hers. Big and strong and *real*.

She opened her eyes. "Con."

He nodded. "How are you feeling?"

"Terrible. But not as bad as before. How long have I been…what have I been?"

"You've been out with a very high fever."

"The nettles, right?"

"Right."

"It's coming back now. The fever explains a lot." Like all of her trippy dreams. She tried to sit up.

"I don't think you should move too much yet. Just rest. At least until the doctor can come in and check on you."

She settled down. As happy as she was to see him, she was sure he hated her. Or had. She might be awake, but things still weren't making sense. "Why are you here?"

He laughed softly and closed the book on his lap. "I was keeping you company. I really should get the doctor now that you're awake." He smiled. "I'm so glad you're awake."

"But why are you—where's my sister? Is she okay? Is Chloe okay? Why are you here?"

"It's okay. Everyone's fine. I'm here because I want to be. Because..." He looked away for a moment before continuing, "Because I have been a fool. And absolutely terrible to you. And I've let my past corrupt my present and possibly ruin my future. I've never been sorrier about anything in my life. And I've lived a long time."

She blinked a few times as she took it all in. He was here because he wanted to be. Then the book in his lap caught her eye. It looked like a romance novel. "What are you reading?"

He let go of her hand to show her the cover. It featured a strong-jawed, shirtless man in breeches and a fiery-haired woman about to lose her very flowy off-the-shoulder dress to the same wind that was whipping her hair back. And they were on a ship. *"The Pirate's Pleasure.* And I wasn't really reading it so much as I was reading it aloud to you. The doctor thought it might be good for you, so..."

He'd admitted he'd been a fool, *and* he'd been reading to her. She fell in love with him all over again, but the need to see exactly how repentant he was remained. "That's a romance novel."

"It is."

Even in her current state, she knew how odd that was. "You don't like romance novels."

"But you do."

"Do you like them now? Maybe a little?"

"I..." He looked at the cover. "I can't lie. I don't love the covers. But I'm starting to see the appeal of the story." He made eye contact with her again. "The whole happily-ever-after thing."

She wasn't about to let him off that easily. "Does that mean you're going to carry them in your shop?"

He sighed without any real conviction behind it as a gleam that seemed almost happy shone in his eyes. "I already have Fletcher setting up a new section for them. You could help me pick out the authors I should stock. If you want. Not now. I mean, when you're feeling better."

Remarkably, she suddenly felt vastly improved. "What's brought all this on?"

He shook his head. "You. I love you. Terribly."

The ache of unbelievable joy almost took her breath away. "All of a sudden you love me again?"

"I never stopped. Not really. I just needed something to snap me out of my self-destructive, poor-me wallowing. And apparently, that was your willingness to sacrifice yourself for Chloe despite everything I did to you and how I acted." He stared at the book in his lap. "You saved my cat. And then you saved me."

She stayed quiet, letting him speak.

"I know you left because of the curse's magic. And I understand why you didn't tell me the whole truth about the curse."

"You do?"

He nodded. "Completely. It could have ruined your chances of being freed of it."

"Go on."

"Well, there's not much more to say except that I'm very sorry. And if you're still willing to give us another try, I would like that very much. But if you're not, I understand that, too. I don't think I deserve a second chance after how awful I was."

Her entire being thrummed with happiness. "I think you deserve a second chance. Actually, I think *we* deserve a second chance."

He looked up, eyes bright. "Me, too. I will endeavor not to be such a fool in the future. And to do everything in my power to show you how good things can be."

She already had an idea about that, but she wasn't going to stand in his way of spoiling her if he wanted to. "Good."

He picked up her hand and kissed the back of it. "Thank you."

She suddenly realized there was a riot of color behind him. Flowers. Enormous bunches of them covering every surface. "Who sent all the flowers?"

"Some are from my family. One's from Amelia. The rest are from me."

That was a lot of flowers. Gardens full. She couldn't help but smile. "I like how you ask for forgiveness."

Relief seemed to sweep over him. "Does that mean I'm forgiven?"

She nodded. "Yes."

He smiled. But his smile faded fast. "I have to get the doctor, but there's something you should know first. I'm afraid it's not great news."

"Oh?"

"Your wings." He grimaced. "They were badly damaged. No one knows if they'll grow back."

She took a few breaths as the news registered. "Wings that sustain a lot of damage often wither and crumble to dust. I'm sure Cassi explained that regrowth is never guaranteed, since you seem to know that already."

"She did."

Andi sighed. "I survived the fever nettle. I have you back in my life. I can manage. But you realize that if my wings crumble away, I'll basically be human. My magic will be gone. Can you handle that?"

He frowned. "You're worried about me? Andi, I'll love you, no matter what. And if that's how things work out, well, I can always turn you."

"Turn me? You mean make me into a vampire?" In a sudden rush of excitement, she sat up. A hard whirl of dizziness spun her head. She reached for it, groaning. "Bad move."

"Lie back. I'll get the doctor." But he bent and kissed her cheek before he left. "And yes, I mean make you into a vampire. But let's not cross that bridge just yet, all right?"

"All right." She stared up at the ceiling, while he went off to find the doctor.

She would miss her wings. But they didn't seem as important to her as they once had. Not with so much else to look forward to in her life.

Love, it seemed, was a great healer. No matter what the hurt.

CHAPTER THIRTY-FIVE

Con rushed out to find Dr. Jekyll and ran into Cassi. "She's awake. Your sister. Andi."

Cassi laughed. "That's great. How is she?"

"Good. She seems like she's getting back to herself again." It had been touch-and-go for the last four days. So much so that Constantin hadn't been sure he'd ever get to talk to his love again.

"I'm so happy to hear that. I guess I showed up at the right time. Has the doctor seen her yet?"

"No, I was just coming to get him. Go in and see her. She asked about you. I'll find Jekyll and bring him in."

"Okay, thanks." Cassi headed toward her sister's room.

Constantin found Dr. Jekyll at the nurses' station. Mercy Hospital wasn't a large facility, given that most of the town's citizens rarely had health issues, but it was a very competent and specialized one.

How many facilities could boast a supernatural blood lab? Probably only this one.

"Dr. Jekyll, Andromeda's awake. I thought you might want to check in on her."

Jekyll turned. "Yes, absolutely. Glad to hear it. I was just considering a course of shifter antibiotics if there wasn't a change today. Happy not to use them, though. Strong stuff." He started for Andromeda's room.

Constantin fell into step beside him. "Have you tried those shifter antibiotics? I mean, personally."

Jekyll snorted. "I've tried everything under the sun."

"Of course." Constantin felt for the man. At least as a vampire, he could control his feral side. Jekyll didn't have that option. Yet. Constantin knew the man would keep trying.

They went into Andi's room. Cassi was explaining how she'd only breathed in a little pollen and hadn't had nearly the rough road to recovery that Andi had.

Andi looked a little nervous as Jekyll approached. "Are you my doctor?"

"I am." He took her electronic chart from the end of the bed, then pulled a stylus from his pocket. "You've been very sick. I'm guessing your fever's broken, but we'll check that in a moment. We'll still need to keep you for another day or two, but you're out of the woods now."

"No pun intended, I presume?" Andi grinned.

"Hmm?" Jekyll looked up. "Yes, right." He scribbled something on the chart, then replaced it at the end of the bed. "How's your appetite?"

Andi put a hand to her stomach. "I'm...wow, I'm starving."

"Then let's get you some food. That will go a long way toward getting your strength back and getting you home."

Constantin stepped in closer. "I'd be happy to get you whatever you like, Andi. Anything. Just name it."

She was quiet a moment. Then her eyes lit up. "I want pizza. Extra cheese. And a big box of sweets from Black Horse."

He laughed. "What kind of sweets do you want in that box?"

"One of everything." She held a hand up. "No. Make that two. Of everything."

"I'm on it." He kissed her cheek, then pulled out his phone and dialed as he left. "Nasha, it's Constantin. I need you to start packing an order for me…"

Andi's head still hurt, and parts of her were aching like she was getting over the flu, but her spirit was light and her heart was happy. She smiled at her sister, then looked back at the doctor. "What else do I need to do before I can be discharged?"

"Some exercise would be good. We want to make sure you're fully ambulatory before you leave. A couple laps through the halls would do just fine. I'll have a nurse come in and set you up with a mobile IV stand after she takes your temp."

"I'll walk with her," Cassi offered.

Dr. Jekyll nodded. "Perfect. I'll head to the nurses station now, then. If all goes well, we might have you out of here as early as tomorrow. Take care."

"Thank you, Doctor." Andi waited until he left to speak to Cassi. "I don't know if I can walk. I tried to sit up earlier, and that little movement almost made me pass out."

"We'll take it slow. No point in doing anything until the nurse comes in anyway."

They didn't have to wait long. In ten minutes, Andi was ready to roll. Or at least her IV was.

Cassi gave her an expectant look when they were alone again. "You want to try standing? I'm right here, so you're not going to fall. And I'll power the bed up higher, so it'll be easier for you to get upright."

"Okay." Andi enjoyed the ride while the bed moved into a better position, then she carefully twisted, bringing her legs off the side.

"How do you feel so far?"

"A little woozy. But if I sit like this for a minute, I think it'll pass."

"Take your time." Cassi grinned. "Looks like things are going to work out for you and Constantin, huh?"

Andi smiled. "It looks that way. We're still really new to this, but after what we've been through, I feel like we already have some extra credit in the bank." Her eyes widened as a new thought occurred to her. "Cassi, speaking of banks, you can't keep paying for that room at the B&B."

"It's all taken care of. Val's going to let us use that apartment over the club until we find a more permanent place. And I'm going to start helping him with booking talent."

Andi's mouth dropped open. "Does that mean you want to be roommates with me? Wait. Does that also mean you're staying in Shadowvale?"

Cassi nodded. "Yes, I'm willing to be roommates with you. At least for a little bit. I'm not committing to forever in Shadowvale, but I like it here." She laughed. "And I like Val. Although that Dr. Jekyll is pretty cute, too."

"Wow, you really are turning into me."

Cassi snorted. "I might be sowing a few wild oats, but I'm never going to get *that* crazy."

"Good." Andi sighed. "I need to get moving. I want to be done with this when Con gets back with the food." She pushed off the side of the bed and got to her feet. Cassi held her hands out. Andi grabbed them, wobbling a little bit. "Don't move."

Cassi shook her head. "I won't. What do you think you'll do for work?"

"I honestly don't know. I don't have much in the way of skills, like you do. But Con did ask me to help him get the romance section going in his bookstore. Of course, that won't take long. But it's something." Andi let go of her sister's hands, grabbed the IV stand, and took a few steps.

"How does it feel?"

"Weird. But okay if I'm holding on to this thing." She got to the end of the bed and turned slightly, bringing the IV stand around. "Is this gown completely open in the back, and do I have any underwear on?"

"No, and I hope so."

"Okay, good. I don't need the whole hospital seeing my backside."

"I'm not that excited about it either." Cassi laughed. "Ready to walk, then?"

"I am. One more question."

"Shoot."

"Honestly now, how bad are my wings?"

Cassi hesitated. "Not good."

"Okay." Andi smiled at her. "It's okay."

Together, they made two slow laps around the hospital.

Con was waiting in Andi's room when she returned from the second go-around. "How are you feeling?"

"Better." She smiled at him. "Really and truly better."

"I'm so happy to hear that." He gestured toward the pizza box and Black Horse bag. "Ready to eat?"

"Definitely."

Cassi gestured toward the door. "I should catch up with Val. He wanted to go over a few things at the club with me."

Andi sat on the end of the bed and gave Con a look. "Your brother's hiring her."

His brows lifted as he faced Cassi. "You're staying? That's great."

Cassi smiled. "Thanks. Paris was getting a little boring."

He laughed. "I doubt that, but Shadowvale can be a very interesting place, too."

"Oh," Cassi said, "it already is." She winked at Andi. "Call me if you get a checkout time. Otherwise, I'll be back to visit in the morning."

"Thanks, sis."

With a nod, she was gone.

Con looked at Andi. "What did she mean by that interesting comment?"

Andi opened the pizza box and inhaled the cheesy goodness. "She's got a little thing for your brother."

He grimaced. "I hope that doesn't end badly, but I feel like that's a book that's already been written."

"I don't know." Andi picked up a slice. "Cassi is the kind of woman that men go all domestic for. You might be surprised."

"I'd love to be, actually." He pulled the visitor's chair closer and sat, pulling her feet up to rest in his lap. "But the woman that tames Valentino might have to be some kind of a saint."

"Time will tell." She took a big bite and let out a little moan of happiness. Pizza had never tasted so good.

"Yes, it will. With us, too, I suppose."

She looked at him as she finished chewing. "What's that mean? Are you having second thoughts?"

"No, I..." His expression went deeply earnest. "I was thinking about our future. I need you in my life, Andromeda. It's probably too early to talk about marriage, but that is where this is headed, isn't it? Because if it's not—"

"Yes." She felt breathless and lightheaded for reasons that had nothing to do with why she was in the hospital. "Are you…is this a proposal?"

He jerked back. "No."

Her heart sank for a moment.

His brows bent. "When I propose, there will be no question what's happening. It's going to be a grand gesture. With a grand ring. And all the things that go into a question like that. It's not going to be while you're half dressed in a hospital gown and still focused on recovering."

"I *am* wearing underwear."

He stared at her for a second, then chuckled. "Okay, so you're a little more than half dressed. But still. I want it to be right."

She put the slice of pizza down and wiped her hands on one of the paper napkins he'd brought in. "I think any situation can be right if those involved are ready."

A moment of silence passed. "Are you saying you don't care about all the pomp and circumstance?"

"I'm saying…" What was she saying? That she was ready to be engaged to this man? She bit her bottom lip, thinking hard. Apparently, that was what she was saying. "Yes. Or no. Whichever answer means I don't care about all that pomp and circumstance. I care about how you feel and what your heart is telling you and what my heart wants and us. That's it. Does that make sense?"

He nodded, a slow smile spreading across his face. "It does."

He reached into his jacket pocket and pulled out a small black velvet box. He cracked it open, revealing a breathtaking diamond ring. "Andromeda Merriweather, will you marry me?"

She didn't know how he already had a ring, but the fact that he did told her how very committed to their future he was. She put a hand to her mouth as happy tears slipped down her cheeks. "I will."

He took her hand and slid the ring onto her finger. "Good. Because from now on, I want everything we do to be about us working on the rest of our lives together. No more questions about will we or won't we, just what comes next."

"Me, too." She glanced at her hand. "I have to know. How did you already have the ring? I mean, this is some ring. It doesn't look like the kind of thing you can just walk into any jewelry store and pick up."

He smiled a little sheepishly. "It's not. I had it made the day after you ended up in here. I was hoping to dazzle you into forgiving me as a last resort."

She tipped her head and looked at him, more overwhelmed with love than she'd ever been in her entire life. "That means...you had no doubts that I was going to recover."

A muscle in his jaw twitched, and he swallowed like he was fighting emotion. "I refused to believe there was any other possibility."

"No one's ever had that much faith in me before."

He leaned in and kissed her, then smiled. "Well, then. I guess I'm the right man for you after all."

Want to be up to date on all books and release dates by Kristen Painter? Sign-up for my newsletter on my website, www.kristenpainter.com. No spam, just news (sales, freebies, releases, you know, all that jazz.)

If you loved the book and want to help the series grow, tell a friend about the book and take time to leave a review!

OTHER BOOKS BY KRISTEN PAINTER

PARANORMAL ROMANCE
Shadowvale series
The Trouble with Witches
The Vampire's Cursed Kiss
The Forgettable Miss French

Nocturne Falls series
The Vampire's Mail Order Bride
The Werewolf Meets His Match
The Gargoyle Gets His Girl
The Professor Woos the Witch
The Witch's Halloween Hero – short story
The Werewolf's Christmas Wish – short story
The Vampire's Fake Fiancée
The Vampire's Valentine Surprise – short story
The Shifter Romances the Writer
The Vampire's True Love Trials – short story
The Dragon Finds Forever
The Vampire's Accidental Wife
The Reaper Rescues the Genie

For more Nocturne Falls
Try the Nocturne Falls Universe Books
New stories, new authors, same Nocturne Falls world!
kristenpainter.com/nocturne-falls-universe/

Sin City Collectors series
Queen of Hearts
Dead Man's Hand
Double or Nothing

STAND-ALONE PARANORMAL ROMANCE
Dark Kiss of the Reaper
Heart of Fire
Recipe for Magic
Miss Bramble and the Leviathan

COZY PARANORMAL MYSTERY
Jayne Frost series
Miss Frost Solves a Cold Case: A Nocturne Falls Mystery
Miss Frost Ices the Imp: A Nocturne Falls Mystery
Miss Frost Saves the Sandman: A Nocturne Falls Mystery
Miss Frost Cracks a Caper: A Nocturne Falls Mystery
When Birdie Babysat Spider: A Jayne Frost Short
Miss Frost Braves the Blizzard – A Nocturne Falls Mystery
Miss Frost Chills the Cheater – A Nocturne Falls Mystery

Happily Everlasting series
Witchful Thinking

URBAN FANTASY
The House of Comarré series:
Forbidden Blood
Blood Rights
Flesh and Blood
Bad Blood
Out For Blood
Last Blood

Crescent City series:
House of the Rising Sun
City of Eternal Night
Garden of Dreams and Desires

Nothing is completed without an amazing team.

Many thanks to:

Cover design: Design & derivative cover art by Janet Holmes using images under license from Shutterstock.com
Interior formatting: Author E.M.S
Editor: Joyce Lamb
Copyedits/proofs: Marlene Engel/Lisa Bateman

ABOUT THE AUTHOR

USA Today Best Selling Author Kristen Painter is a little obsessed with cats, books, chocolate, and shoes. It's a healthy mix. She loves to entertain her readers with interesting twists and unforgettable characters. In addition to Shadowvale, she currently writes the best-selling paranormal romance series, Nocturne Falls, and the cozy mystery spin off series, Jayne Frost. The former college English teacher can often be found all over social media where she loves to interact with readers.

www.kristenpainter.com